Dead On Time

By the same Author

Dead On Time

Glyn Idris Jones

Douglas Foote

ISBN 978-960-99470-9-1

www.dcgmediagroup.com

Chapter One

The admiral, if he but knew it, was going to have one bitch of a day... one of those days that starts badly and gets progressively worse. It wasn't as though he had tumbled out of bed on the wrong side. As far as he was concerned he did that every morning. Though as the years advanced, perhaps tumbled was not quite the right word for it, creaked would be a more apt description, an ancient heart of oak disintegrating in the heavy swell of time passing.

Rear Admiral Sir Harvey Bettinger Ulric D'urban Bart. had been trying for years to persuade his lady wife, who in their halcyon days he used affectionately to refer to as his "shipmate" but who in later years became known out of earshot as "the barnacle," to slip the painter and allow him to drift into his own fitful sea of dreams in his very own dinghy.

Of late he had tried to use the aches and pains in his aging joints and varicose veins as a valid reason for removing his person from the marital bed but Lady D'urban, whose personality could be described as forceful if nothing else, would have none of it. Lying awake listening to her heavy snoring, or half-smothered beneath her leviathan seventeen stone every time she turned over to usurp his half of the bed, he would reflect nostalgically on their early days. What a trim little craft she was then, and such a pretty face, and what a pretty face she had brought to their union in the form of notes, stocks, bonds, property, and works of art, including a magnificent Vlaminck and a couple of Modiglianis all of which the admiral detested; the Vlaminck because of the violence of its wild slashes of colour, enough to give a chap nightmares, and the Modiglianis because of their grotesque perverted silliness, as he put it. Girls didn't look like that and he had never seen one hold her head at such a ridiculous angle. The admiral knew nothing about art but he knew what he liked and Tretchikov was about as far as he would go. The Oriental girl might have an indigo face but at least it was recognisably human and the man was a genius when it came to teardrops. As the paintings, if auctioned at Sotheby's, would probably fetch enough to buy and refurbish his own luxury yacht, he resented them hanging on his South Kensington walls... correction... her South Kensington walls.

No, Lady D'urban insisted, even if bedbatics were no longer the object of the exercise, bodily proximity was still comforting and they were definitely not going to bunk separately. She had had quite enough of sleeping alone in their earlier days when he was gallivanting all over the world and, in between his normal duties of depth-charging U-boats and, later, blasting away at the Japanese, was doing heaven knows what and to whom. Lady D'urban, despite being an avid reader of the gossip columnists, agony aunts, and the more colourful tabloids conveniently left for her in the kitchen on a Monday by the housekeeper, was still one of the world's innocents as far as the true ways of the world are concerned and even her lurid imagination failed to do true justice as to just what her husband, considering he had inherited all the piratical tendencies of his Danish and Norman forbears coupled with a nanny-in-the-nursery upbringing and a public school education, had been up to and with whom.

Anyway, since he was shore-based, and despite the fact they had three grown-up children and a clutch of grandchildren, she vigorously defended her need for the comfort of feeling him next to her. Sir Harvey was tempted to suggest that if it was comfort she wanted why didn't she trot along to Harrods and get herself a dog? But, knowing Lady D'urban's post-menopausal propensities, the selected animal would more than likely be a bloodhound and the thought of facing Una and a bloodhound every morning was more, he thought, than he could bear. So wisely, as is always the case in time of war, he kept his mouth shut and his thoughts to himself.

The toast burned and the toaster exploded filling the kitchen with acrid black smoke. The milk had curdled overnight. His egg was half-cooked and runny, something that always made his gorge rise and he pushed it away in disgust. He broke one of Una's favourite cups; the Royal Doulton, not the Spode, thank God! Breakfast was a washout.

He cut himself shaving, twice. But, smartly uniformed and great coated, with two incongruous tabs of red and white toilet paper glued to his wounded face, and with the evidence of the broken cup safely wrapped in his briefcase to be disposed of later, thus enabling him to claim total ignorance of its mysterious disappearance, he bade his lady wife adieu with a token peck on the forehead and sailed forth to meet the day.

The lift was out of order.

Keeping a firm hold on the brass handrail he descended the stairs with no more mishap than a sharp twinge in the lumbar region as he slipped on the polished surface and hurriedly caught his balance. With no great damage having been done, or so he thought, he emerged from his haven to be met with what felt like a force nine gale and what the Americans would call heavy precipitation. No point in raising the brolly. In this wind it would be inside out in a second and, anyway, it was only a step to the car; but some idiot, evidently squeezing into the parking space behind him, must have nudged the Jaguar forward and out of its space. Jammed up tight against the car in front; his car was fast on the rocks. The admiral glanced angrily at the miscreant's car that had rammed his stern... Froggie of course, he might have known and he felt a sudden hatred for humanity, the section that rode in foreign cars, French ones anyway. They deserved to be flogged through the fleet if not keel-hauled. He turned the full fury of his countenance on the car in front though he knew it to be blameless. It would be a BMW! Damned Krauts! He had once thought of purchasing a BMW or even a Merc but couldn't quite bring himself to do it having not yet forgiven the Germans for World War II, and of course a Japanese car was totally out of the question. He would also have to report the incident to Una. She had a habit of leaving the car in neutral and forgetting to put on the hand brake and she had used the car the previous evening to go to her bridge club. It was at this point in his ruminations that the admiral realised he was getting soaked to the skin and looked around for a cab but, naturally with such a heavy precipitation, there wasn't a taxi in sight. He seriously considered going back to bed and calling in sick, which, in the light of what was to come, would have been the safest course to take, but three things prevented him. Firstly, he had no desire to haul himself up four flights of stairs. By the evening, after he and a hundred other irate residents, especially those with doggies that needed walkies, had registered their complaints in no uncertain terms, with any luck the lift might be repaired. Secondly, he had not yet disposed of the evidence in his briefcase and, thirdly, what if Una should want to snuggle in beside him? Deciding he'd rather brave the elements and whatever else the day might have in store he set his outward-bound course and headed into the teeth of the gale.

His morning at The Admiralty was uneventful. He was a trifle uneasy about the dull ache in his lumbar region but, as today was the day for his session, the session would no doubt take care of that. So he spent most of the morning staring out of the window and daydreaming on lunch at the club: asparagus in lashings of golden butter, and roast beef well done with the fiercest of horseradish sauces, crispy roast potatoes and glutinous brown gravy; and he dreamt of what Mona would get up to during their session. She could get quite carried away could Mona and the thought of it made him distinctly restless. He adjusted himself beneath the desk and glanced at his wristwatch, ran his tongue across his top teeth, nestled the tip of it for a moment in front of the lower incisors, causing his lip to bulge, and decided it was time for lunch.

The gale had moved on eastwards, probably to give the Froggies a damn good drenching, and serve them right after their shenanigans over deliveries of English lamb, and the sky was blue with just a few fleecy scudding clouds. The admiral in rare good mood set off for his club. But his euphoria was short-lived. He turned the last corner to find his way blocked by a police tape strung across the road and signs expressly forbidding his entry. A young police constable stood by, the peak of his helmet almost meeting the tip of his retroussé nose, a pale blue eye on either side glinting with self-importance and boyish enthusiasm. They say you know you are getting old when every policeman looks eighteen. Well this one looked no more than sixteen and, in the admiral's opinion, far too pretty. If he'd had a peaches and cream midshipman like that on board one of his ships he would have had an anxiety attack over the moral incorruptibility of the officers under his command. He wondered if the lad had ever had to give evidence before that lickerish old libertine Mr. Justice Stampley but he pushed the thought out of his mind as quickly as it had entered. It was too horrible to contemplate. He stepped forward. The youth in blue stepped sideways.

'Sorry, sir, but this street is closed,' he said, stating the too patently obvious.

'I can see that,' the admiral snapped. 'But just why is it closed?'

'There's been an explosion, sir. Terrorist bomb we think.' From his tone it was obvious that, in the aforementioned we, it might just have been he who suggested to his superiors the possibility of a terrorist bomb. He glanced down the street to make sure another wasn't about to go off then turned his attention back to the admiral. At least the child's manner was deferential. The admiral wondered if it would have been so had he, the admiral, not been in uniform.

'Bomb? Good, God, sir! Where?' He knew the answer even as he asked the question but braced himself to hear it all the same.

'Neptune Club, sir.'

'Where in the Neptune Club?'

'In the kitchen I believe, sir,' said the infant bobby, pinpointing the exact location of the device by adding, 'under a cooker.'

Bomb? The admiral thought, not bloody likely. That damned Alphonse has been at the brandy again and done something stupid with the gas. Probably flambéed himself in the process, but bomb or no bomb, he had a vision of cracked white tiles spattered with shreds of roast beef and glutinous gravy and he knew his lunch, if nothing else, was a goner.

'Any casualties?'

'Not that we know of, sir.'

'Good, good. That's something to be thankful for at least.'

'Indeed it is, sir.' The cherub in blue saluted smartly as the admiral turned away.

'Damned terrs,' the admiral growled, thoroughly put out by the inconvenience. It would have to be the Garrick for lunch. God, how he hated that place: effete actors, half-cut legal beagles, and literary hacks all slapping each other's backs, and worse. Could never understand why the club's damned waiting list was so long. And all those gloomy portraits of dead poncey actors.

After two hours of solid boredom, no one wishing to discuss the life and death of Lord Nelson, the sinking of the Tirpitz, or the battle of The River Plate, the admiral swayed out of the club on route to his session. He hadn't gone very far however when he suddenly remembered his routine had been badly affected by the terrorist bomb in that, invariably on this particular day after lunching at the club, he would change into mufti, but here he was heading towards the Charing Cross Road in full uniform and that would never do for where he was going. He looked around as though an answer might be forthcoming from somewhere; a signal from providence saying England expects etcetera, but nothing came. His powers of reasoning, never at their brilliant best in the afternoon, contended with the after effects of a good claret and les brumes du cognac that made him slightly dizzy. He could retrace his steps to Moss Bros and hire a suit for the afternoon or he could detour to Simpsons and purchase a new one. But then he hadn't bought a new suit in years and, if he did so now for no apparent reason, Una was bound to ask questions. Tangled weaves and all that. What about a Burberry? That would do the trick. No it wouldn't. He had left his briefcase at the office and in it were his chequebook, bank, and credit cards. A horny admiral was on the horns of a dilemma. There was nothing for it but to forego his pleasure this once.

It took no more than three steps for him to change his mind. Valour was the better part of discretion, damn it, and he was going to go through with it. He removed his cap, buttoned it up inside his greatcoat which made him look somewhat pigeon chested and, turning up the coat collar as far as it would go, hunched into it and marched on to keep his date with ten dexterous fingers and destiny in the vicinity of Berwick Street Market, his newly adopted posture attracting the curious attention of passers-by which was exactly what it wasn't meant to do.

Melvyn, as immaculate as ever though if anything growing oilier by the day, was at his usual place beside the door, seemingly taking no interest in anything but in fact acutely aware of everything, which was what he was paid for, among other things. He gave no indication of having even seen Sir Harvey as the latter passed through the gaudy plastic streamers that separated the interior from the curious glances of passers by.

Dominique, seated behind her kidney-shaped, glass-topped reception desk of split bamboo, was indulging in her second favourite pastime... manicure... her paraphernalia spread out neatly in front of her. Her scarlet talons were a sight to behold and sharp as a shark's teeth, to which a certain indiscreet young hood would testify if he could still see to sign a statement. She looked up and smiled at Sir Harvey as she gently waggled the five lethal weapons of one hand, pursed her pink glossed lips to blow on them and inclined her head to indicate he should go straight on through. He returned her smile and passed on.

He entered his usual cubicle and stopped dead. Mona was not there. Instead he was faced with a total stranger, a small and shapely stranger with what appeared to be slightly Oriental features. Or it could be she had South American Indian blood, Sir Harvey was on uncertain ground with ethnic minorities. What he was sure about was, here he was in uniform, hardly incognito, in a compromising situation with someone he had never seen before, a situation that could cost him dear and he was only too well aware of the fact. He did an abrupt about turn.

'Good afternoon, admiral.' Her voice was low, sultry, and, heaven help us, she knew who he was! He turned back.

'Where is Mona?' He squeaked, his throat having closed up almost as tight as a frog's cloaca.

The girl moved up to him and started to unbutton his greatcoat. His cap fell to the floor. She picked it up and dusted it off managing, in the process, to be subtly intimate with his crotch, which caused his throat to return to normal.

'Oh, poor Mona,' she said, and her voice sent tingles up and down the admiral's spine to say nothing of what it did to his groin. 'Her little boy is sick and she has to stay at home with him. So I take her place. It's all right. I'm very good.'

"I bet you are," Sir Harvey thought. "Good at blackmail too, I shouldn't wonder."

She had hung his cap on one of the hooks provided and was now helping him out of his greatcoat. She was solicitous and reassuring. 'This feels a little damp, Admiral, you shouldn't be wearing it, you'll catch your death. And, anyway, should you be walking around in uniform? People might see you and that wouldn't be good.' She had hung up his greatcoat and was now unbuttoning his jacket.

'What's your name?' He demanded, squinting down at her. She looked up and smiled.

'Paloma.'

'Unusual name.'

'I'm an unusual girl. Would you like to find out just how unusual?'

The admiral surrendered. It might be scuttling the ship but in for a penny in for a hundred pounds. No point in fighting the inevitable.

From the first light touch of her supple fingers to the grand climax, Sir Harvey Bettinger Ulric D'urban Bart. was in seventh heaven. If Mona got carried away, this little vixen got carried away with flair and an expertise, an inventiveness that was little short of miraculous. The admiral would have liked to ask where she came from and had she studied the Karma Sutra in detail but in this place one didn't ask questions. All he knew was that, from now on, it was Paloma for him every time.

'Shit!' Exclaimed the object of his musing. 'I beg your pardon, Admiral.'

The admiral, in the process of knotting his tie, turned around.

'I meant to give this to Mona for her little boy and I forgot.' She was holding a curious object which, at first glance, made the admiral think Mona's little boy must be a very advanced, if somewhat bizarre, little boy until, on closer inspection, he saw it was a model submarine.

'It's for his bath,' Paloma explained. 'Look.' She unscrewed the cap at the vessel's stern and held it towards Sir Harvey. 'Smell,' she said.

He did so. 'Pine,' he said.

'Huh-huh. Not any old pine though, Calabrian pine with the deep scent of the Mediterranean.'

Sir Harvey turned back to the mirror to finish the knot in his tie. They looked at each other's reflections. Paloma was obviously in chatty mood.

'Do you play with toys in the bath, admiral?'

He chuckled and turned away to continue dressing.

'You do, you do!' She laughed gaily. 'Why, admiral, you're blushing, I do declare, and after the games we've just played?'

'I don't have rubber ducks, swimming frogs, hippopotami, things like that. Oh, no. But I do have a couple of model corvettes, a destroyer. Real models, if you know what I mean.' He said it with pride.

Paloma nodded. 'I tell you what then,' she said, 'why don't you add this submarine to your fleet? I know it isn't a real model but have it as a present.'

'But er... what about Mona's little boy?'

'I'll get him another one.' She wrinkled her tiny nose, encouraging him to accept.

'Well, thank you,' he said, 'thank you very much. Most kind.'

'Admiral, didn't your mother ever warn you about accepting presents from strangers?' She was laughing again.

'Well, hardly strangers,' he chortled, his fleshy body undulating like a wave simulator, 'not after the games we've just played,' and the memory of them made him stir again so that he reached hurriedly for his trousers. She watched him for a while as he finished dressing.

'I suppose a man in your position has to be very careful about security.'

It seemed such a casual remark but the admiral was immediately on his guard. His earlier reservations returned with a vengeance and his heart beat a little faster. Was this the first shot across the bows?

'As a matter of fact I am extremely security conscious,' he said icily.

'Not walking around like that you're not.' The tone was still casual but there was no mistaking the admonishment. So he told her about the terrorist bomb at the club followed by a full explanation as to why he was not in civvies. She expressed concern that no one was injured in the blast and, on being reassured that that didn't seem to be the case, the frown disappeared but she went on, 'I suppose you have to be careful with your car, and with packages too.'

'Yes, indeed. Oh, yes. Any suspect letter or parcel addressed to me, or my lady wife, is examined by security before it is passed on. Nothing suspicious gets through I promise you.'

'That's good.' She helped him on with his overcoat. 'It would be too bad if we never saw each other again,' she pouted a la Bardot.

He wondered if he should drop a few hints about potential blackmailers being liquidated but she seemed genuinely concerned for his safety, the pout was most endearing, and his fears were probably unfounded. As he was about to leave she called after him. He turned back. She was holding out a box illustrated with a picture of a submarine ploughing through heavy seas.

'You forgot your present.'

'Oh, yes. Thank you. Thank you very much. And thank you for the... er... yes... well...'

'Till next week?'

He nodded and cleared his throat, sniffed, and, clutching his box, made his exit. Until next week... what a prospect!

The lift had been repaired. He was more than glad of it as his back had started to ache quite badly. Hardly surprising considering the spasms he had recently gone through. There was no sign of the car. Una must have gone off somewhere with her girl friends. Sure enough there was a note beneath the telephone on the hall table reminding him that, despite constant reminders, he had forgotten one of the grandchildren's birthday. He would never hear the end of it. He looked at the box in his hand. No, damn it! It was his. And what would a child want with genuine essence of pine bath oil anyway? And submarines were probably old-hat as far as kids were concerned. Little buggers didn't know which side their bread was buttered. Any present worth less than ten quid or more would only be sniffed at. When he was a child he had been delighted with a new butterfly net or a croquet mallet. Chattering to himself about the modern generation, he let himself into the liquor cabinet, taking out a balloon and the V.S.O.P. Ten minutes later, with a goodly supply of cognac at hand, he was soaking his aching back in a steaming tub. Almost at the point of dozing off he remembered his present. Removing the submarine from its box he placed it in the water. It sank like a stone. Sir Harvey took another swig from the balloon and lay back. Closing his eyes he sighed deeply and floated into semi-oblivion. His thoughts at first were all of Paloma but, after a while, he dreamed he was back on the bridge. An enemy sub showed up on the sonar. The hunt was on. But the skipper of the sub obviously believed attack to be the best method of defence. The admiral started to open his eyes and squinted. Was that a periscope he could see? And what looked suspiciously like a torpedo heading straight for his most vulnerable parts? Dreams, dreams.

The explosion wrecked not only the bathroom but the flat above and the flat below. Fortunately the Vlaminck and the Modiglianis sustained no damage and, with the amount of water about, there was no fire. They managed to scrape together enough of the admiral to be pretty certain that Sir Harvey Bettinger Ulric D'urban Bart. had joined his Viking ancestors in Valhalla.

The next day Lady Una went out and bought herself a blood-hound from Harrods pet store. She named him Harvey and he took up a lot of bed.

Chapter Two

Thornton King, his legs crossed and with elegantly shod feet resting on his desk, leaned back in his swivel chair and twined his fingers behind his head. He gazed up at the cracked, dingy brown ceiling of his tiny office located on the third floor of what had once been a desirable Victorian residence situated in one of the narrower streets, now given over mostly to the sale of second-hand cars and a couple of curry houses, in the Socialist Republic of Camden.

He regarded the much chipped ceiling rose from which hung a single low wattage light bulb on its length of ancient twisted brown flex. The bulb's already dim light was dimmed even further by a dust encrusted plastic shade, disfigured with burn marks where someone had tried to increase the illumination by the use of too high a wattage and he wondered how, with the passing of time, the rose, seemingly so far out of harm's way, had come to be so mutilated.

His gaze moved on to the cornice, presumably egg and dart, but the mouldings so smothered by layers of various types of paint, from lime and whitewash to emulsion and gloss, applied over the years and never removed, that the original design was no longer discernible.

His gaze moved down to the door with its frosted panels and then sideways to where his old oak filing cabinet stood. It had been purchased, as had the rest of his furniture, from a dealer in the Hackney Road who specialised in second-hand office equipment, not necessarily modern, elegant, or in good working order. Thornton judged the cabinet to be circa 1940 from some government department or other. It had four large drawers with a tendency to jam in damp weather and get yanked off their broken runners in dry. There were also two small card-index drawers. All the drawers were empty. On top of the cabinet stood a round pub tray advertising Guinness and on which was a jar of coffee granules, a bottle of Coffee-mate, cups, spoons, and a dented kettle, the whole covered with a sodden tea towel. The nearest cold water supply and sink was in the toilet at the end of an even dingier carpetless corridor. On the far wall, in front of the boarded up fireplace, stood an ancient cast iron radiator. And for this festering rabbit hutch he had mortgaged an arm and a leg and signed a lease in blood. Every square inch of wormy floorboard sent his overdraft soaring as the minutes ticked away. What the hell did he think he was up to? He should have taken his redundancy money and emigrated to some Third World country where one could live on sunshine and two shillings a day. With the ending of the cold war, the break-up of the Soviet Union and the democratisation of the Eastern bloc couldn't be too far away; so how many ex-agents were there in just his situation? He was tempted to call Yuri in Moscow for a commiserating chat but at the rate the post office was making profits, mostly at his expense it would seem judging by the size of his phone bills, he resisted the temptation. Pity he wasn't Jewish. He could have gone off to Israel and joined Mossad. For a moment he considered conversion but decided adult circumcision might be just a mite too painful and dismissed the thought.

He glared at the telephone he was too afraid to use, daring it to do something off its own bat but it obstinately refused.

Thornton sighed and took up *The Times* that he had earlier dropped on his lap. So old Harvey D'urban had bought it and was finally free of the barnacle. Still, he must have been pleased with his way of going. At least he was in his element when he disintegrated and what was left of him would no doubt be ceremoniously buried at sea. Funny, it was only yesterday in *The Garrick*, as the guest of that star of stage and screen, the expatriate Aussie, Walter Latrobe, that he had managed to avoid the boring old fart. Latrobe occasionally invited Thornton to lunch because Thornton, in exchange, was prepared to put up with the man's outrageous ego and tiresome theatrical anecdotes. It was bad enough trying to turn a deaf ear to a boring actor but, had Sir Harvey joined them, two bores would have totally destroyed his appetite. But Wally Latrobe had been only too anxious to avoid any contact with Sir Harvey. In fact he had been avoiding him like the plague for thirty odd years, ever since that awful cocktail party when, in a state of intoxication, in more ways than one, he had made a play for the admiral, and he did not want his closet-queenery to be loudly discussed at the dining table. Sir Harvey had a voice like a foghorn when he chose to use it, usually in *The Garrick Club*.

The laudatory, if somewhat jingoistic newspaper obituary read exactly as was to be expected, and Thornton wondered how different it might have been if the old walrus had been caught in flagrante delicto by expiring of a heart attack during one of his sessions. He turned back to the front page and reread the report. 'Cause of the explosion not yet ascertained... speculation as to whether there was any connection between it and the one earlier in the day at the Neptune Club... Sir Harvey possibly on IRA hit list...'

Thornton wondered if any of the admiral's secret hoard of specialist pornography had been discovered and what the investigation would make of that. He swung his legs off the desk, threw down the paper and got up, transferred his calls to his answering service, collected his hat, coat, and walking stick from the hat stand (circa 1920), emerged from the office, locking the door behind him, purely a gesture, and set off down the dingy corridor.

At the foot of the stairs he stopped by the bank of mailboxes and opened number thirteen. It had been empty when he arrived that morning which, in a way, was something of a relief as all he seemed to get these days were final demands, and letters from Her Majesty's Inspector of Taxes stating that he had earned twenty times more than he actually had and demanding immediate payment or else. But now a single envelope was lying in the box. Presumably the postman had arrived even later than he. With each increase in the cost of postage deliveries seemed to grow more random. He removed the envelope, slipped it into his breast pocket, closed the box, and moved on.

The tavern was packed with the usual lunchtime crowd. Beating his way to the bar through bodies and cigarette smoke and beating his way out again, Thornton found a corner where he could squeeze and wriggle a few inches of anatomy onto the portion of settle available to him. He pushed away the empties left by the previous occupants, the ashtray overflowing with butts, screwed up crisp packets and twisted, dribbling sauce sachets, and placed his cheese and chutney sandwich and half pint of best on the table in the space he had made for them. Some ash fell on his plate. He flicked it away with his paper napkin. His neighbour cast him a withering look and went back to stroking his companion's thigh indiscreetly beneath her skirt as she sipped her Babycham.

Having finished his sandwich, Thornton took the envelope from his pocket, slit it open with a plastic knife found on the table, and took out a card. It was an invitation to lunch at his favourite restaurant, *L'Éminence Grise*, an invitation for two in a couple of day's time. He smiled. The world had not entirely forgotten him.

Now who should his number two be?

****

Thornton stood looking out of the picture window that formed almost one entire wall of the lounge of Holly's Barbican flat and looked across the two cities that, together with numerous boroughs and suburbs, made up that vast, dirty, noisy, overcrowded, over-expensive, overworked, and over-rated phenomenon the world knew as London. He supposed that, if you had to try and escape it, up was as good as out and on a bright, clear, winter's day, such as this, the city did look beautiful from this viewpoint with its sparkling newish skyscrapers of steel and glass added to the older landmarks; the dome of St. Paul's, the Abbey, The Houses of Parliament, Nelson on his column. But that was from up here where the litter-strewn streets were mostly invisible, where traffic fumes did not choke, where muggers and vandals and football hooligans, fanatical demonstrators of numerous persuasions, street people, beggars, violent or pathetic, the hopeless, the help-less and the lost, the vicious, the nasty or the stressed out neurotic did not have to be faced or contended with. Up here it was all air and light and space. A plane, glinting silver in the sun, was coming in to land at Heathrow. If he could have his way he would stamp the city unfit for human habitation no matter what Doctor Johnson might have said. Despite its magnificent galleries and museums, its theatres and concert halls, great parks, palaces and pageantry, restaurants, fine houses and Old Father Thames just rolling along down to the mighty sea, had it ever really been a city worth living in? Or had it always been a most dangerous place? He turned away from the window, glanced at his wristwatch, and called out, 'Holly? How long are you going to be?' There was no answer. 'I'm taking you to lunch, remember? Not tea at *The Savoy* or dinner at *The Ritz.*'

Holly appeared at the bedroom door and raised an eyebrow. He noted she was still in her slip.

'Are we in a hurry?'

'Wouldn't do to be late,' he gently admonished, his eyes glued to what seemed a pert pair of breasts beneath the silk.

'Sauce for the gander,' she replied. 'You, my dear sir, were late arriving.'

'All of three minutes!' He shouted as she turned on her bare heel and disappeared in a flash of undulating buttocks. He started off across the room in the direction of the bedroom door. 'One more minute and this gander's goose is cooked.' He stopped, frowning, somehow that didn't seem to make sense. Then he shrugged and continued, 'I may be late, you may be late, but François is never late.'

'He shouldn't be,' her voice floated from the bedroom, 'he's already there.'

'Well the invitation is for one-thirty and at one-thirty one the soufflé will be ruined.'

Silence.

Thornton fumed for a moment and then noticed the early edition of *The Standard* lying on a table. The headline grabbed him.

AFRICAN DIPLOMAT FOUND ON CENTRAL LINE

He picked up the paper and, for a few moments, was totally absorbed. Then, as though he were continuing what had been their sole topic of conversation, he said, 'That's the third this month.'

'Soufflé?'

'Murder. Murder? Assassination rather.'

Holly reappeared at the bedroom door, almost ready for going out, stunning in a soft woollen chemise of palest green, a large cameo of The Three Graces at one shoulder. 'Why assassination?'

She slipped into her shoes and stood in front of a slender gilt-framed mirror to adjust her coiffure, not that it needed it but there just might have been a hair out of place.

'Because you know as well as I do that if three John Does get knocked off in a row then it's murder, suicide, or accident but when three V.I.P's are knocked off one after the other then I call it assassination. First there was the physicist, Sir Barnaby Wiltshire, then poor old Harvey, and now this African chappie. Did he fall or was he pushed? My guess is he was pushed. What was a high-powered diplomat doing in the underground at that time of night anyway? Diplomats travel by limousine, usually chauffeured.' Holly turned away from the mirror. It was Thornton's turn to raise an eyebrow. He felt the urge to give an appreciative whistle but instead, 'Ready?' He said, 'So glad.' He was about to drop the paper when she took it from him and started to read. He took it back. 'Holly, we don't have time.' He dropped the paper, helped her into her satin raincoat, and they headed for the door. 'What do you make of them?' He asked.

'They're lovely,' Holly replied as they passed a bowl of splendid yellow roses. 'Thank you.'

'The killings.'

'You're not, by any chance, trying to ruin my appetite are you?'

'Perish the thought. No gentleman would dream of doing such a thing. Especially when there is no bill to pay.' They had reached the front door.

'What's the party in aid of anyway?'

'Not a party exactly. François has invented a new recipe. Whenever he does that he invites a few select guests to taste and, hopefully, approve. François is an artist. Only the most discerning palates are invited.'

'You mean we're guinea-pigs?'

'Such lucky little piggies.'

'Gourmets one and all,' she murmured as he opened the door and ushered her out.

'After you, gourmet.'

Holly paused. 'But why should it be of interest to you?'

'Food is always of interest to me.'

'No! The assassinations.'

'They're of no interest to me whatsoever. Now can we go? Please? I'm hungry. And Maitre François is waiting.'

****

L'Éminence Grise was one of those small Soho restaurants that, like so many of its Parisian counterparts, stood on its reputation for haute cuisine and had no need to advertise itself. Most people would pass by a hundred times and not even notice it was there and the cognoscenti kept the secret to themselves. Even in a recession table reservations were like trying to get tickets for a Cup or Wimbledon final, or a hit show.

The interior was as unprepossessing as the exterior. Just inside the street door a small darkly panelled vestibule with a high desk and a number of wooden coat pegs, empty in summer, difficult to squeeze by in winter without knocking a garment or two to the floor, lead into the dining room itself... plain wooden tables beneath white linen cloths covered with paper ones, plain wooden chairs, thirty-two covers in all. On the walls a few faded signed photographs of half-forgotten stars of the French Music Hall and a couple of Degas prints of girls at the ballet, all covered, as was the ceiling, with a thin brown film from years of cigarette smoke. There were sideboards for china, cutlery, and coffee, yellowing net cafe curtains stretched across the window, and a pair of swing doors with small oval windows led into the kitchen. The waiters, in shirtsleeves and black tie, their sleeves kept up with old-fashioned expanding armbands, wore aprons that reached almost to their ankles. The clientele created the ambience at *L'Éminence Grise*.

François, a figure straight out of a Toulouse Lautrec painting, moved among his guests, his face a picture of beaming self-satisfaction. The new dishes had been acclaimed an unqualified success: an entree of slivers of veal sautéed in butter flavoured with Brandy Alexander and served with water chestnuts and a rich sauce hinting at the perfume of lychees; the dessert a sponge concoction flavoured with latte de mandorle and topped with lashings of whipped cream. There seemed to be a spot of cross fertilisation going on between François and his Chinese and Italian neighbours. Gracefully, as he moved from table to table, he accepted the compliments lavished on his culinary skills. The fact that his friends cholesterol levels had suddenly rocketed to unprecedented heights, that diabetes and a possible case of gout were imminent seemed to perturb him not a whit. For François, who had graduated from just about every five star establishment worth mentioning, food was not simply the fuel that kept body and soul together: it was life itself; a ticket to ride, the supreme experience, a passport to paradise.

So what did it matter if the journey led to a premature demise just so long as you relished each gastronomic inch along the way? Which philosophy a certain dignified looking elderly gentleman at a table for two, his companion being an extremely attractive young lady, would seem to have taken too literally as, in most undignified fashion, he suddenly slumped forward. A wine glass toppled over, its contents staining the white tablecloth a blood red. The man's cheek splodged into the creamy remains of his dessert and one fishlike eye glared balefully across the room. A woman screamed; and a waiter, passing her table at that precise moment, out-screamed her on a note that would have done credit to a Wagnerian soprano, dropping his fully laden tray with such a crash of breaking crockery the resulting decibels should have been enough to alert not just Saville Row police station but Whitehall itself at to the possibility of mischief afoot. As it was, after his first involuntary 'Merde Alors!' It was François who streaked for the telephone in the vestibule to dial 999.

Simultaneously, Thornton was on his feet and moving swiftly to the stricken man's table, assuring the assembly as he went that he was a fully qualified medical practitioner. He lifted the man from his chair, laid him on a section of floor uncluttered by shards of broken china, and proceeded to administer, at great personal sacrifice, the kiss of life. It was hopeless. Looking up from the prostrate figure he noticed the young companion was no longer at the table and a quick glance around the restaurant, where everyone seemed frozen into immobility, assured him she was no longer even in the room. By now Holly was at his side. 'Stay right here,' he whispered and headed for the door, wiping a melting dribble of cream from the side of his mouth.

Even as he gained the crowded street he knew his search was in vain. Of the girl there was no sign. Thornton went back inside. François was still in the vestibule, still yelling at the telephonist on the other end of his 999 call. He gave Thornton a despairing look, the kind that only a Gaul is capable of, and Thornton, in turn, gave François a reassuring British pat on the shoulder before passing on.

For a moment he stood surveying the scene he had so recently and momentarily left. Awed, horrified, or fascinated, the patrons remained at their tables; the only signs of life a whispered remark here and there, an occasional glance in the direction of the dead man. The waiters stood in a huddle against one wall not knowing what to do, and the kitchen staff behind the swing doors vied with each other in trying to get a good peek through the oval windows. Of Holly there was no sign. Thornton frowned and started to return to their table when a voice stopped him.

'Mister King.'

He turned towards the sound. How had he previously missed seeing her? He who had been trained to observe, to take in every detail around him? She sat, ramrod straight, one hand curled over the head of a silver-topped cane, a choker of five rows of pearls at her throat, diamond encrusted double headed eagle brooch sparkling on what was once regarded as the most beautiful breast in Europe, the now skeletal but once regal and still commanding figure of the Princess Olga Tatiana Katarina Spitskaya. The fact that the seat she occupied was partly obscured by a pilaster could explain his lack of observation but he was chagrined nonetheless.

'Princess!' He bowed with old world charm over the much bejewelled hand stretched out to him and, gently supporting the knotty fingers, kissed the liver spotted skin as wrinkled as a tortoise's neck. It was no worse an experience than giving an elderly gentleman the kiss of life. He straightened up, smiling. 'How delightful, if it weren't for the distressing circumstances. Poor François, most upsetting.'

'Nonsense,' the princess contradicted. 'From now on it will be totally impossible ever to get a table at this restaurant. He will be booked up, not weeks, but months in advance.' *Rules, The Ivy*, what will they be? Prrrt! She snapped a finger and thumb in dismissal.

Thornton found himself wondering how, after all her years in England, the princess still spoke with a Russian accent spiced with a French pronunciation of the occasional word.

'If you will excuse me for just a moment, Princess,' he said, 'I have some urgent business to attend to.'

Princess Olga smiled, showing two rows of perfect false teeth behind her thin lips. 'You have done your best for the gentleman, Mr. King, and you can be of no further assistance to him, despite all your medical experience.'

Thornton laughed. Then remembered himself and was immediately serious. 'No, no, I wasn't referring to the deceased. I was talking of my companion.'

'Ah, yes, the beautiful Miss Holly Day.' The princess inclined her turbaned head towards the door that led to the ladies toilets. 'I am sure she won't be long and I hope she is not being sick. The sight of a body, I can never understand why, has that effect on some people.'

"Not Holly," Thornton thought, "and I bet the old bag knows it."

But the princess continued, 'Of course I was only a very very tiny child during the revolution, but I have seen many dead bodies, then and since.'

"Tiny child?" Thornton thought, unwittingly raising an eyebrow. "Who does she think she's kidding? A woman might take five or six years off her life but virtually a quarter of a century is really pushing it."

The princess continued unabated. 'Thanks to the stupidity of mankind, or is it the stupidity of nature? Europe has never lacked an abundance of corpses. The geographical scene might now have shifted a little but there is still a healthy crop, or unhealthy, whichever way you care to look at it. Ah, here is François off the telephone and no doubt ready to make a little speech.'

But François was obviously in no mood for speech making. His face was no longer beaming. In fact he looked decidedly green as he headed straight for the kitchen, disappearing through the swing doors and knocking a couple of curious bodies flying in the process.

'Aaaah!' Princess Olga sighed loudly, looking quite disappointed at not getting the expected speech. She patted the empty chair next to her. 'Come, Mister King, as you cannot follow your lady friend to where she has gone, do sit down and keep me company till she returns or until the emergency services arrive.'

Having no excuse not to, Thornton sat down. The princess cleared her throat and, looking straight at Thornton, discreetly touched the side of her mouth. Thornton got the message and, with a clean napkin, wiped away the last of the creamy remains of the kiss of life. She nodded the all clear. 'Do you know who he is?' he asked, dropping the napkin and inclining his head towards the corpse.

'I believe his name is Anton Shoggi. I believe he carried a Lebanese passport, and I believe he dealt in armaments,' the princess told him.

'You're particularly well informed,' he said, turning back to her.

'I know more than you think, Mister King. I am a veritable mine of information. But the reason why I do know all this is simple. I met the gentleman a few times at the odd society soirée.'

'Really? So maybe you know the girl who was with him.'

'She was sitting with her back to me. I did not see her face.'

'I must say she disappeared pretty fast.'

'Which makes you suspicious.'

'Of course.' He regarded her for a moment. 'Aren't you?' He was fiddling with a fork, turning it over and over in his hands, a sure sign that he was desperately trying to fit together pieces of a jigsaw without a corresponding picture on the box. The princess smiled and laid a cold claw on the back of his hand. Maybe his fiddling irritated her, like someone in a bus queue rattling coins in a pocket, or someone tapping the table top, but it was a gesture of which he wasn't too sure he approved. He felt a prickling at the base of his skull and slid his hand from beneath hers under the pretext of putting down the fork.

'Thornton, my dear boy...' Oh, so it was Thornton all of a sudden was it?

'I am a very old lady. I really no longer have any interest in what the human race gets up to. The short time left to me is to be enjoyed in peace and quiet. I have had my share of life's excitements... more than my share. As for the girl, there could be any number of reasons not to stay around. Panic maybe? Another man in her life and she's in the wrong place at the wrong time? Who knows? Now let us talk of you.' There was the sound of approaching sirens but the princess continued. 'It's been such a long time since we last saw each other. Now where was it?'

'East Berlin.'

'Ah, yes, that unhappy divided city. When will it ever be one again I wonder? The Grotowski Affair, as I recollect.'

The sirens had stopped. This time sending a waiter flying in the opposite direction as he barged back through the swing doors, François re-entered the restaurant and exited into the vestibule. Everyone but the princess was looking in that direction. She seemed totally unconcerned as she went on chatting to Thornton.

'Strange, but inevitable I suppose, how events will come full circle. Where will it start I wonder. Hungary perhaps, maybe Poland, yes Poland seems most likely. All revolutions follow the same pattern. We do not learn the lessons of history and it is only stupid men who believe that violence solves anything; and a lot of innocent people must suffer along the way. But that's what innocents are for, is it not, Thornton? Nature is profligate.'

'Who is innocent?' Thornton murmured, eyes fixed on the entrance.

'You lost a number of agents if I remember correctly, in that little fracas, the Grotowski Affair. But not you, Thornton King, you were too clever, you outsmarted everyone. You slithered out of the net like a slippery eel.'

'Nonsense. I was just damned lucky. That's all.'

'No false modesty, please! Don't underestimate yourself, my dear Thornton. You are without doubt the best there is. But are you still working for the government?'

'Afraid not, Princess. As you say, the situation has changed. The world moves on.'

'Are you nostalgic for what has been and can be no longer? Would you like a souvenir to remind you of the past? I tell you what, when the Berlin wall comes down as, inevitably it must, you may have a piece.'

'To hang around my neck? I am redundant. Thrown on the scrap heap. Cast out in my prime.'

'And now you are being melodramatic.'

She turned her head towards the door as two men entered followed by François. In the vestibule other figures lurked, a police constable and a couple of ambulance men.

François, with a trembling hand and a nod of the head, indicated the corpse, his ashen face reflecting the revulsion he felt. He placed a handkerchief over his nose as though the corpse was already decomposing, though it could have been because of a loosening sphincter.

'I do hope François is not going to be sick,' the princess whispered.

The two men, after a quick glance around the crowded room, moved across to the body and started their examination. Those who could bring themselves to do so watched with morbid fascination. Others turned away. Princess Spitskaya, obviously interested in the proceedings, kept on watching as she continued her conversation with Thornton.

'So exactly what are you up to, my dear?'

'Huh?' Now it was "my dear" all of a sudden was it?

'I said, what are you doing now?'

'Oh, trying to turn an honest buck, as the Americans say.'

One of the men had now returned to the vestibule where he whispered to the constable who nodded, turned away, and started a conversation of his own with his walkie talkie.

'Well?' The princess insisted.

'Well what?' Thornton looked puzzled.

'Just what are you doing to turn that honest buck?' The princess blithely continued.

'Oh.' He was trying to keep an eye on the proceedings and wondering what the hell had happened to Holly and the princess rabbiting on was a distraction. 'Started up on my own,' he said sharply and then, immediately regretting his rudeness, smiled ruefully. 'Not with much success so far.' He scratched an itch at the side of his mouth. 'Well, no success at all in fact. Nobody seems to want the services of a private detective any more.' He noticed the man in the vestibule had now turned his attention to the ambulance men. This body was not going to be moved in a hurry.

'That, my dear Thornton, is because you are not and never were a private detective.'

'It's the nearest thing I could think of to my own field.'

Princess Olga took a sip of the coffee still left in her cup and curled a disdainful upper lip. She hated lukewarm coffee. 'You wait, dear boy,' she said. 'Just be patient. All will come right. Mark my words. There are plenty of cases of industrial espionage to investigate. You will get a great reputation and then you will be so much in demand you'll wish you had more time to yourself. The trouble with being a secret agent, my dear Thornton, is that you are still secret. Nobody knows yet that you are available.'

'Why don't you employ me? Head of security, something like that.'

'I have all the security I want thank you,' the princess laughed.

The man still kneeling beside the body suddenly looked up and stared hard at their table as though deeply offended that anyone should carry on a conversation, let alone laugh, considering the circumstances and while he went about his business. Every other head in the place turned as well.

'That gentleman is a doctor,' a voice piped up. 'He tried to revive the er... the...' the voice trailed off.

'Oh, my God!' Thornton groaned inwardly, 'Trouble!' He took a good look at the man coming towards him. The shoulders beneath the raglan coat were narrow and rounded. The face was sallow and grim. The kind of face that reflected a lifetime of one who had seen it all, heard it all, who knew the depths of depravity humankind could descend to. The man arrived at their table. Thornton was metaphorically kicking himself for having poked his nose in. Why did he do it? Reflex reaction? Force of habit?

'Good afternoon, sir. Madam.'

Thornton nodded weakly and suppressed the desire to giggle. He had not expected the voice to be quite so girlish.

'I am Detective-Sergeant Venables of the Metropolitan Police. Are you a doctor?'

'Er... no.'

Venables' eyes narrowed. 'But I have just been informed,' he glanced back at the informant before returning his attention to Thornton, 'that you are a medical man. Now why should I be given that piece of information if you are not?'

Thornton shook his head. The detective waited for an explanation. Thornton thought he'd better give him one.

'There must be some mistake,' he said.

The look on Venables' face indicated he believed Thornton to be the mistake. Thornton tried not to squirm too obviously.

'I have had some experience of emergencies and er... I tried, unsuccessfully as it happens, to revive the gentleman. This might have given the false impression that I was a... er... a doctor.'

'Oh, no!' The voice piped up in contradiction, 'He definitely said he was a doctor. Didn't he?' It queried, seeking confirmation elsewhere. There was a collective murmur of assent.

'And I wanted to nip panic in the bud,' Thornton hurriedly added.

'Panic? What gave you the idea there would be an outbreak of panic?' The girlish voice with a rising cadence now had a slightly cutting edge to it.

'I guess I anticipated it...'

'You guess?'

'When the woman screamed and the waiter dropped his tray. It was sort of... sort of...' He couldn't find the right word.

'In the air, as it were,' Venables prompted helpfully.

'You could say that.'

'Could I?'

By now Venables had been rejoined by his colleague and they both stared at Thornton for a long time. You could hear the proverbial pin drop and Thornton was feeling more than just a little uncomfortable knowing that every eye in the place was on him. If only he were still with the department he would have had some backing. Taking the detectives aside a whisper would have been all that was needed, but if he were to try that now he could be had for impersonation.

No, as things stood, he was merely another citizen, which didn't mean much at the best of times, and right now he was a suspect one which was worse. He smiled sweetly up at the two men who remained singularly unimpressed. The smile froze on Thornton's face. After a while Venables turned and walked away, followed by the other, not without a backward glance of warning which, correctly interpreted, said "I've got your number, mate." Out loud, 'Find the geyser that runs this joint,' Venables ordered, nodding towards the kitchen into which François had once more disappeared, 'I want a word with him.' Then he addressed the gathering. 'Everybody please be patient. I have to ask you to stay where you are, as you will be required to make a statement before you leave. I'm sorry, it might take a bit of time but it can't be helped. If any of you have urgent business that must be attended to you can leave your name and address and make your statement down at the station later.' He marched back to the vestibule to give orders and Princess Olga immediately picked up the conversation where they had left off.

'And talking of availability, Thornton, are you married yet?'

'What?' Thornton's voice sounded almost as girlish as the detective's as he squeaked in surprise at the unexpectedness of the question. This was a time to talk domestic affairs?

'I think it's high time you were married,' the princess continued. 'It would keep you out of mischief.'

'Since when were married men incapable of mischief?' He countered. 'And the last time you tried to marry me off it was to a Siberian tigress, the juvenile delinquent descendent of impoverished émigrés who was, if I may be permitted to say so, of a highly suspect character.'

'Tartar blood, dear boy. Volatile. Unpredictable.'

'Unstable.'

'Exactly. But exciting.'

'Deadly would be a more apt description. And, as you've put the question to me again, I presume you might have someone else in mind. Who is it this time? A Polovtsian maiden? A descendant of Taras Bulba?' He watched as the constable, accompanied by reinforcements in the shape of two late arrivals, no doubt summoned via his walkie-talkie, advanced on separate tables to start taking statements. At the same time Venables covered the body with a sheet procured from the ambulance, which vehicle, together with police cars, was no doubt creating chaos, not only in the narrow street outside, but most of the surrounding ones as well.

'Yes,' the princess said, fiddling with her coffee cup, 'I might very well have someone in mind. I might indeed.'

'Undoubtedly as hazardous to life and limb as the so-called Grand Duchess Irena. Whatever happened to her anyway?'

'The last time I heard from her, let me see, about a year ago as I remember, it was a card from Kathmandu. I think she said she was setting off on a Yeti hunt.'

'Well I hope she finds him. He would make an eminently suitable mate.' Out of the corner of his eye he could see the two detectives and François looking in his direction and obviously discussing him. He didn't like it.

'At least I'll make sure the next one I suggest is a superb cook.' The princess laughed loudly. Once again every head, including policemen with pencils poised, turned in their direction. Thornton wished the floor would open up. Olga was oblivious to the frisson, or pretended to be, and carried on as gaily as ever. 'And how did you enjoy François' new concoctions?' She asked. Thornton kissed his fingers and grunted his appreciation. 'Bon, then I am glad you came. Despite the unfortunate occurrence. I told François I would not come unless he made certain to invite you.'

Thornton's eyes opened wide. Once again he felt that tiny prickle in his neck. She answered his next question without him even having to ask it.

'Because it has been so long,' she said. 'And, suddenly, only the other day, I thought to myself, I wonder what has happened to my old friend, Thornton. I would like to see him again. And here you are.'

'Here I am. Do you know any of the other guests?'

'One or two.' She waved an imperious hand in instant dismissal. 'But they are such boring people. Not like us.' Thornton had a vision of the skull beneath the skin as she smiled. 'Now we must think of a name for François' new entrée. What shall we call it? I know!' She trilled, 'we'll call it "Veaux a la Holly Day".'

How delightful.'

Her shrill delight rippling through the room invoked a further malevolent glare from Venables who was beginning to find her more than just an irritant. The woman must be stark raving mad to behave so outrageously with the body of the poor sod who had just snuffed it lying within spitting distance of her. Well, not quite spitting distance, but close enough. Did she have no respect for death? As for that ponce with her...

The ponce in question smiled at him, which was more than he could bear. He turned away. The ponce turned back to his companion.

'As long as it wasn't the veal that put paid to our friend over there, I agree, how delightful.' He looked at his watch and then at the door of the ladies toilet, which remained firmly shut. 'And as long as it doesn't put paid to Miss Day as well... or anyone else for that matter... where the hell could she have got to?'

'Do you think, dear boy,' the princess asked, 'we could have another cup of coffee while we wait to make our statements?'

****

Members of the public can gain access to the headquarters of *Midas International* by crossing a piazza whose pavement of reconstituted stone glitters with tiny specks of what looks remarkably like the very stuff on which the *Midas International* fortune is based and dotted with jardinières of a jasper-like material. These are planted and maintained by a firm of "city gardeners" whose fees per annum for consultation, design, implementation, upkeep and renewal could reasonably keep the entire city of Westminster a whole lot cleaner than it actually is. These are definitely not your corporation flower beds of mathematically spaced salvia and zonal pelargonium bordered with lobelia and alyssum.

Crossing the piazza one approaches the elegant tower of steel and sun-reflective bronzed glass. Although symmetrical in structure and not exactly the kind of architecture favoured by the Prince of Wales, the building seems to be forever changing shape as the windows reflect the shifting patterns of the sky, light, and passing traffic. Shallow but wide stairs lead up to the main entrance whose automatic doors, framed in brass, are recessed in a portico flanked by two tall obelisks faced in brown marble. Once through these silently sliding doors a member of the public is faced with a four story galleried arboretum in the centre of which is a man-made mountain complete with tropical plants and splashing waterfalls. The surface of the surrounding pool is almost hidden by nymphae stellata with its flowers of a delicate mauve, with giant fern, and the handsome leaves of gunnera. He, or she as the case may be, is also faced with uniformed security guards who will politely but firmly insist he, or she, must have a very good reason for being there.

It is an ideal glossy location for fashion photography and on a chilly but bright afternoon while Thornton twisted forks and drummed his fingers on a tabletop, worried over Holly, and hoped he wasn't going to be asked any more embarrassing questions, that well-known photographer and discoverer of new faces, Adrian Spangle, warmly cocooned in moon boots, padded jacket, and butch leather cap with chains, purchased at a specialist shop near Camden Lock, was valiantly snapping away.

A number of assistants, enough to crew a feature film, stood by with lights, reflectors, umbrellas, and camera boxes as Adrian squawked instructions to his model positioned a few steps above him. It was probably fortunate no member of the animal rights movement were in the neighbourhood or the piazza might have easily and quickly become the scene of violent demonstrations as the girl was modelling a decidedly Russian looking ensemble: red Cossack boots of softest calf, astrakhan hat, pelisse edged with silver fox; a vision in red, black, and silver. In one gloved hand she held the end of a lead, the other end attached to a diamond-studded collar around the neck of a shivering Borzoi named Boris. It wasn't that Boris was feeling the cold. Being of a highly neurotic nature, and a vegetarian due to a skin condition brought on by the eating of meat, he tended to shiver most of the time anyway. In her other hand she held a long cigarette holder complete with Gold Sobranie thus, in one fell swoop, defying the animal rights activists and the anti-smoking lobby, probably women against the exploitation of women as well. Actually the cigarette was a fake though... no one was to know that.

Click went the camera, click click click.

Adrian straightened up, stepped back and rubbed his chilled fingers together. He'd forgotten to bring his favourite mittens. An assistant rushed forward and replaced the camera on the tripod, taking away the first to reload. Adrian returned to take up his position. 'Head higher, Amelia... chin to me... knee forward a little... good.' Satisfied with his model he turned his attention to the dog. 'Look at me, Boris... here... pooch, pooch!' Boris looked up at the sky. 'Cats!' Adrian yelled, exasperated. 'Cats!' Boris didn't know what a cat was but he turned and looked at this screaming madman anyway. 'Thank you,' Adrian said, returning to his viewfinder. He was used to saying please and thank you to his own King Charles spaniel, Tiddly, short for Tiddlywinks or, if in naughty mood, Tiddlywanks. Saying thank you to Boris was merely extending the courtesy through force of habit.

'Slinkier hips, darling... Amelia! Pelvis forward for God's sake!' He forgot to say thank you to Amelia.

Click went the camera, click click click.

An extended limo drew up at the kerb and a uniformed

chauffeur jumped out, scuttled around to the nearside to hold wide the door from which his passenger was already emerging. A tall elegant man bearing a quite remarkable resemblance to Don Ameche, he stood for a moment buttoning up his vicuna overcoat and looking at the building he was about to enter as the chauffeur reached into the car and came out with a handsome briefcase of crocodile skin, definitely Gucci. Handing it over, he closed the car door and saluted as the gentleman started off across the piazza. By the time the man had reached the steps the limo had moved out into the stream of traffic. Seemingly amused by the photographic circus he smiled at Amelia and gently ran a well-manicured finger across his trim grey moustache. Amelia, in turn, rewarded him with a smile so dazzling it almost stopped him in his tracks. But then, remembering the importance of his appointment and his reputation for always being spot on time, he continued on his way, still smiling. Amelia turned her head to watch him go.

'Oh, lovely, darling!' Adrian shrieked, 'Perfectamente!'

Amelia raised the cigarette holder to her lips.

Click went the camera, click click click.

The man was at the portico when he suddenly stopped and clapped his hand to his neck. He took the hand away and looked at it, then looked up and around as though searching for some predatory insect. Then he continued on his way. The doors slid open and the man, stepping across the threshold of Midas House, fell flat on his face.

The doors slid silently closed.

Chapter Three

Thornton, with the Princess Olga on his arm, eventually emerged from *L'Éminence Grise* to find it already growing dark and, worse, it had started to rain, a steady chilling skin-soaking drizzle. They were lucky in that a taxi pulled up almost in front of them to drop off a passenger and Thornton leapt forward and had Olga safely ensconced before anyone else could claim it or the taxi driver object. He who hesitates loses it as far as London cabs are concerned and a couple of would-be fares turned away inwardly cursing and in desperate search of another as Thornton leaned forward to give the cabby directions. The man listened in scowling silence before informing Thornton in turn that he was about to go off for his tea and couldn't possibly drive all the way to Highgate which, his manner implied, was not far south of John O'Groats. It was only after Thornton quietly and smilingly and with great patience, considering the rain that was trickling down his neck, suggested that a court appearance in order to explain to a magistrate why he was reluctant to accept a fare when he was for hire, would mean a certain loss of income, that the cabby bit his lip and surrendered with that good grace and traditional Cockney humour so typical of London cabbies. And Thornton couldn't resist adding, in a whisper accompanied by a conspiratorial wink, that he was sure 'the princess would see him right.' The cabby, like many a good lifelong labour voter who fervently believed the abolition of The House of Lords and the confiscation of all private wealth would usher in the millennium, still retained a loyal affection for The Royal Family, especially the Queen Mother, God bless her, though he wasn't too happy about the younger generation, and was somewhat mollified to discover his fare was a real live princess. He glanced in his rear view mirror and, reassured by the pearl choker, the kind of thing only a princess would wear; he set his meter and right hand indicator preparatory to pulling out. Thornton gave Olga Tatiana Katarina a cheerful wave and watched for a moment as the cab crawled away towards Shaftsbury Avenue. Then he turned and started off through Chinatown towards Charing Cross where, in the lee of St. Martin's In The Fields, he waited for a number 6 bus to take him home.

No fewer than five number 11's arrived and departed, two of them going no further than The Aldwych, one to Liverpool Street. They were interspersed with three 9's. Of the bus he wanted there was no sign. Typical. If he'd wanted a number 11 there wouldn't have been one in sight. He wished he'd bought an evening paper, also that he had taken a pee before leaving the restaurant. The pressure on his bladder was beginning to make him feel decidedly uncomfortable and he wondered if he would make it home, but he knew, as sure as God made little apples, if he deserted his post three number 6's would arrive in convoy and leave in his absence. He decided to squeeze thighs and bear it and was immediately rewarded for his stoicism by the sight of his bus edging its way passed the National Gallery. Two changes of traffic lights later, by which time his thighs were firmly clamped together, the bus stopped and disgorged a stream of passengers who, huddled beneath umbrellas or hunched into turned-up collars, scurried away in the direction of Charing Cross Station to continue their nerve-wracking journey home to the south eastern suburbs and beyond. Thornton, sopping wet, mounted the lower deck and tendered his fare to the West

Indian driver who somehow managed the transaction seemingly without taking his eyes off his windscreen wipers. Deciding to sit up top, Thornton climbed the stairs to find himself on a deck fairly empty from the recent exodus but the air redolent with the smell of warm wet humanity. He started to make his way towards a seat at the back, his shoes squelching all the way, kicking aside an empty soft drinks can and slipping on sodden pieces of paper as he went. A greasy newspaper, holding the remains of fish and chips, squelched underfoot, precipitating him towards a seat occupied by an ancient crone clutching to her bosom a badly cracked and much worn oilskin shopping bag almost as old as herself. Thornton grabbed the rail on the back of the seat in front of her in order to steady himself and, at the same time, she stretched out her own wizened paw and closed her icy fingers with amazing strength around his wrist.

'Jesus Saves!' She shrieked.

Thornton flinched visibly at the sudden hot blast of wino breath and the other passengers immediately disappeared behind their newspapers or stared intently at the nearest window, opaque with condensation. Thornton felt he needed this like a hole in the head. After all he had just been through he had no desire to humour eccentrics: alcoholic, religious, or otherwise. He tried to extricate himself but she maintained her vice like grip. He wasn't sure which eye either side of the bulbous nose was actually looking at him. It could be the one apparently staring at a notice above and behind his head and he found that particularly disconcerting. He hoped she wasn't going to open her mouth again. Apart from the effluvium of second-hand plonk Espagnol the gums were not a pretty sight, but his silent prayer went unanswered.

'Jesus saves!' She shrieked, even louder than before.

'Shut up, you stupid old bitch,' a voice growled.

Still holding fast to her victim, the old girl turned around to face her unknown abuser. Not sure where the voice had come from she focused one rheumy eye on a black youth with dreadlocks and tribal scars on each cheek and wearing a woolly Rastafarian hat. The old girl's other eye seemed fixed on a light bulb.

'Who you calling a bitch, you ignorant bastard?'

The youth, a red brick graduate in sociology, currently studying for his Master's and actually of a somewhat gentle and retiring nature despite his fearsome appearance, turned away, embarrassed. She was having none of that.

'Oi!' She yelled, 'Darkie! Jungle Bunny! I'm talking to you. You gone deaf?'

Thornton had visions of an incipient race riot for which, no doubt, he would be held solely responsible and two brushes with the law in one day, no matter how innocent he might be, were just two too much. He stood up and with his free hand tried to prize the fingers from his wrist. She suddenly released her grip at the exact moment the bus lurched forward and Thornton was sent staggering back to land heavily in the lap of the woman opposite and behind him, at the same time grinding his heel into her favourite corn. Her scream stopped the bus as suddenly as it had started. Everyone jerked forward and Thornton was pitched in the direction of a navvy who certainly wouldn't have screamed but who might have been tempted to land a lethal left. Thornton managed to save himself at the last second by grabbing a safety pole. There was a sudden silence. Then a voice from below broke it by shouting, 'Wha' happenin' up dere?'

Thornton leaned over the stairwell. 'Nothing,' he croaked, 'nothing. It's all right.' He turned back, prepared to apologise to the woman still squirming and grimacing in agony from the crushing of her corn, but the bus lurched forward once more and he found himself heading in her direction faster than he had anticipated. She saw him coming, shot out of her seat, and fled to the back of the bus. There was nothing for it but for Thornton to take a seat as quickly as possible and it might as well be the one just vacated. Turning back he saw to his horror that late arrivals had occupied every seat bar one and he certainly was not going to sit next to HER!

'No standin' up dere!' The voice called up. 'You know dat. No standin' on de top deck. You come on down here, man, or I stop de bus!'

Thornton took a deep breath and, knowing that every pair of eyes were on him, descended the stairs to the lower deck.

'What you done playin' at, man?' The driver asked, glaring into his mirror.

'Don't even ask,' Thornton replied.

'Jesus saves!' Shrieked the voice upstairs.

'There's your answer,' Thornton told the driver who was not impressed.

'Ah got two-way radio on dis bus,' he informed the miscreant. 'Any more trouble from you, man, an' I calls up assistance.' The driver, whose name was Gladstone, originally from Trinidad, shook his head and thought of his little Victorian terraced house in Stoke Newington, of his amply proportioned sweet natured wife, Orángello, of putting his stockinged feet up in front of the telly, of a plate of pickled trotters and sweet potatoes, and wished his shift were at an end. He liked to gently tease his woman about her name. His mother-in-law was a lady deeply impressionable when it came to the packaging on supermarket shelves and she had named her twin daughters Orángello and Lemóngello. The latter, except for when the law required it, went by the name of Lia, but Orángello liked her name. It was unique and, to her, it sounded romantic and vaguely Italian.

Thornton, unaware of what was going through Gladstone's head, only knew that the driver was keeping a wary eye on him via his mirror as he spent the rest of the journey strap hanging, gazing at the ceiling, and crossing his legs. He loathed strangers who smirked at other people's discomfiture, which meant he loathed virtually everyone on the bus, and it felt like it was going to take forever to get to Mare Street.

Thornton's flat was on the third floor of a block that was part of a modern mixed estate of houses and flats built on crown property. This enabled Thornton to tell everyone, quite truthfully, that his landlady was the Queen of England. From the front door a passage, with his bedroom on one side and the bathroom on the other, led to a high studio with a narrow gallery half way up one wall. He really couldn't understand its purpose as it wasn't fit for anything other than storing a few bits and pieces. Part of the studio was a small kitchen, well fitted out and equipped with fridge and storage cupboards, mostly empty as Thornton seldom ate at home. A packet of Lapsang Souchong, a packet of Jasmine, a packet of Earl Grey, Thornton was a great imbiber of tea, a jar of coffee and a well-stocked liquor cabinet was enough to keep him going.

He made it from the bus stop to the lobby to the lift to his own front door to the bathroom in record-breaking time. The phone was ringing as he let himself into the flat but there was no way he was going to answer it until after that long satisfying shiver and final deep sigh of relief. He'd made it in the nick of time. Then, Mother Nature appeased, he quickly stripped off his wet things and wearing bathrobe and slippers he trotted into the studio, flicked on the lights and lifted the still ringing telephone from its cradle.

'Thornton!' She said, a note of exasperation in her voice, 'where the hell have you been? I've been trying to get you for hours.'

'Where have I been? That's great coming from you. Where

the hell have you been, if one may ask?'

'Following the girl. Where else?'

'And?'

'And I lost her.'

'Great.'

'Anyway, I'm not going to talk over the phone so I'll be right up.'

'Right up? Where are you?'

'Downstairs with Sandra. She's been making me comfortable while I was waiting for you. I'm so glad you get on well with your neighbours.' The phone went dead.

Thornton retraced his steps down the passage, opened the front door and, leaving it on the latch, went back to the studio where he poured himself a good stiff bourbon. He was about to recap and put away the bottle when he had second thoughts, found another glass, and poured a second. She liked it on the rocks and it was ready for her when she waltzed in, closing the door behind her.

'Thank you,' she said, taking the glass as he took her coat. She flopped into an easy chair and smiled. 'Cheers!'

Thornton laid her coat on a bar stool and placed himself on another. 'You might have something to cheer about,' he said, 'but I haven't.'

'You weren't worried about me were you?'

'Oh, no! Not in the least. I'm used to my dates disappearing into thin air so why should I be worried? Anyway, I knew where you had gone.' She looked at him over the rim of her glass. 'You'll never guess who was there today,' he went on, 'at the lunch, hiding in a corner.'

'Surprise me.'

'Olga Spitskaya.'

The one raised eyebrow over the top of the glass was joined by its partner.

'Holly, you know perfectly well who she is. Tatty? Do you mean to say you never had dealings with her?'

'Tatty?'

'That's her nickname. Her second name is Tatiana.' He took a sip of his drink. 'She informed me it was she who insisted François invite me today. And guess who else came in, after you left. A certain detective by the name of Venables, and his brother in arms, one Pocock. Don't smile, that is his name, and they would both like to see you down at the station, at your convenience of course but, naturally, as soon as possible.'

'Oh? Why?'

'Oh don't be ridiculous, Holly! Why do you think? To make a statement and to explain your absence.'

'So it wasn't a natural death.'

'Who knows?' He took another sip. 'Of course it wasn't. And you know it wasn't. Though, as far as the police are concerned, let us just say that, at this stage, they're treating it as suspicious.'

'How did they know I was even there in the first place?' Holly asked.

'Oh, that was Tatty's doing, the silly bitch. I sent her off to the loo to look for you and she came breezing back to tell me in a very loud voice, with Venables standing not three feet away, that you had gone. Naturally that led to a lot more awkward questions, the answers to which I managed to sidestep, I think. Though I am sure he would have liked to have arrested me then and there on suspicion of something or other. I don't know why she did it. Of all the people in the world, Tatty is the one who knows when to keep her mouth shut and when to open it. Maybe she's beginning to lose it in her old age. Or maybe she was playing some mischievous little game, though God knows what. She also described to me your escape route into the back alley. The girl must have known that route and been already prepared to take it, which she did, though she must have mistimed it. She should have made her exit before he collapsed, not afterwards. They'd also like to question her of course. That is if they ever find her.'

'I followed her as far as a mews in Belgravia.'

'Some distance. How did she travel?'

'Hopped on a 22 bus. Got off at Sloane Square and walked. I had to keep a fair distance because she must have seen me in the restaurant and if I'd got too close she would have recognised me. Anyway, she turned into the mews and, by the time I got there... disappeared... not a sign. But there is a studio there, owned by a man named Adrian Spangle. Know him?'

Thornton nodded. 'Does a lot of fashion stuff,' he said.

'Yes. That's where she might have gone.'

'Or into any one of the other houses in the mews?'

'Yes.'

'Or in one entrance and out the other side.'

'Maybe.'

'So you really can't say where she went?'

'No. 'Fraid not. Perhaps she did recognise me and led me a merry dance. Only I do like to think I know my job better than that and I have this gut feeling it was into Mr Spangle's studio that she went. She did, after all, look every inch a model. Not that model's have that many inches which makes them models I suppose.'

'I don't know why you had to follow her in the first place. Why couldn't you just sit at the table like a good little girl and mind your own business?'

'Professional curiosity.'

'And you know what curiosity did to the cat.'

'I still have a number of lives.'

Thornton heaved a sigh. The girl was incorrigible. 'Well we all make mistakes.' He shrugged and pulled a consoling face.

'How magnanimous you are, Thornton but, as you say, we can all make mistakes. Like the time you let Petslov slip away from under your nose and out of the country with five rolls of microfilm. And the next thing we know he's knocking back vodka martinis in Dzerzhinsky Square. But we won't remind you of that.'

Thornton swallowed the remains of his drink in one gulp.

'Who was the man?' Holly asked, smiling sweetly.

'Went by the name of Shoggi, according to the princess.'

'Oh! That Tatiana.'

'That Tatiana. She also informed me that he was in the armaments business though who he was buying from and selling to I don't know. After all, it's a worldwide market. He must be on file. Why don't you check him out?'

'You'd like to know.' Holly dipped her finger in her glass and played with what remained of the ice. 'Curiosity?'

'If you can be curious, I can be curious. After all none of this is any concern of mine. I don't have anyone breathing down my neck anymore saying, "King get on with this, find out what's going on, etcetera." But that makes four deaths now and...'

'Five,' Holly said and stopped fiddling with the ice, most of which had melted anyway. Thornton stared at her. She licked a finger and, for no particular reason, examined it closely. 'I saw it on the early news,' she continued, 'downstairs while I was waiting for you. An American by the name of Domenici, supposedly a dealer in diamonds, but I've come across him before. He's actually a banking expert with Colombian connections.'

'In the laundry business you mean.'

Holly nodded. 'That's what made him newsworthy. Shady background. The Home Office were not at all happy about him being here. Died this afternoon, of a heart attack evidently, on his way to a high-powered meeting. Collapsed in the entrance of the Midas building.'

'Maybe it was a heart attack.'

'And maybe my name's Mata Hari.'

'I hope not, considering her sticky end.'

'So, the question now is... who is going to be number six?'

'What makes you think there's going to be a number six?' He tried draining his glass again, remembered he had already done so and, taking hers, placed them both on the bar ready for a refill.

'Five good reasons. The question is, who? And when? Where? How? And why?'

'And that makes five good questions.'

'That makes a riddle,' Holly said, slipping off her shoes and curling her legs up beneath her.

'You've changed!' Thornton said, admiring her in black crushed velvet.

'You've noticed! How observant. You're really slipping badly, Thornton. Out of practice? Anyway, I had to. I got soaked to the skin on that wild goose chase so I stopped off home on the way over here. But back to the riddle... Thank you,' as she accepted the proffered glass. 'What do these five men, a scientist, an admiral, a diplomat, an international arms dealer, and a shady financial wizard, what do they have in common?'

'Nothing, on the face of it.'

'Nothing? Come on, they must have. There has to be a connection somewhere.'

'Yes, they're all dead.'

'Precisely! Well then, there has to be a reason for them being bumped off.' Her voice had an edge to it. It seemed to her that Thornton was being particularly obtuse.

'Whoa! Now wait a bit. Hold on there.' Thornton held up a hand like a policeman holding up the traffic. 'Nobody knows they were bumped off. Nobody has actually said they were bumped off.'

'You did. And, even if you hadn't, I know you, and your radar is working overtime. Right? Right. So... the only thing I can think of... the only thing they might just have in common... is that they were all men...'

Thornton nearly choked on his drink.

'Laugh if you want,' she persisted, 'but what do all men have in common? Well, most men. Well... a lot of men... the majority of men? Oh, come on, Thornton. Stop sniggering and just answer the question.'

'It's been a tough day,' he groaned. 'Do you know what happened to me on the bus coming home this evening?'

'I don't want to know what happened to you on the bus coming home this evening.'

'You're missing one helluva good story.'

'Look!' She was showing signs of exasperation. 'One way or another none of these guys were all that approachable. They moved in regular circles'...

'One foot nailed to the floor you mean.'

'Are you getting tipsy, Thornton?'

'What! On two?' He looked into his glass. 'One and a half? Are you kidding?'

'Usually surrounded by people,' she ploughed on, 'people they knew, or at least, felt, they could trust. Some expressly hired for the purpose of minding their welfare. It's a dangerous old world we live in.'

'This American...'

'Domenici.'

'Domenici. He had a bodyguard?'

'Usually. But evidently not today for some reason. His was not a well-known face this side of the Atlantic and maybe he felt it unnecessary. I don't know. But the killer in each of these cases must have been known to the victim, known and trusted, or someone whose presence would not arouse undue suspicion, or anyway would allay suspicion.'

'A woman.'

'Bingo! You've got it. A woman. Boy, that was like extracting teeth without an anaesthetic. You need a refresher course, Thornton.'

'I need to retire, Holly. I need to go fishing. For real fish.'

'You loathe fishing. You'd be bored to death.'

Thornton sat mournfully regarding her for a while as she ran the rim of the glass across her lower lip and watched him in turn. He looked beyond her at the Hockney print on the wall, signed and numbered, and then at the Lowrie with its chimney stacks and cobbled streets and its matchstick men, both pictures from his grandfather. He looked at the baby grand which was never played but whose lid was useful as a display shelf for family photographs in silver frames, and the bookshelves filled with books that he'd bought because he thought they would prove interesting but which he'd never had time to read. If he could afford to retire maybe he would get around to them. Then he looked back at Holly curled up in his easy chair.

Maybe Tatty was right. Maybe he should get married. But then the thought of a woman taking over his bachelor existence, of possible children (weren't there more than enough human beings cluttering up the planet?) put him right off the idea. Maybe he should get a pet, a dog, man's best friend. No, dogs needed to be taken out, to be walked, and fussed over. A Siamese cat maybe, but then he had heard Siamese cats get bored if left on their own too long and start to rip up the curtains and scratch hell out of the furniture. He let out a long sigh and looked beyond Holly, through the studio window to the lights of the city.

'The Petslov affair,' he said, somewhat petulantly, 'was not my fault,' and drained his second glass.

Chapter Four

There were two things about movie making that the film star, Cord Wainer, detested. The first was being woken up and having to fall out of bed at a most ungodly and unnatural hour in order to be driven to the studios, or location, as the schedule demanded, for that perpetual early morning call. It wasn't so bad in California where at least it was warm and dry, or even Florida to where more and more filmmakers seemed to be migrating. Though in Florida the humidity brought him out in a nasty, if somewhat colourful, rash that defied every medication known to modern science, and the smell of rotting vegetation knocked hell out of his sinuses.

But in England! In winter! Shee-it! It was like getting up in the middle of the goddam night and, as his bodyguard, Max would say as they emerged from the hotel, cold enough to freeze off those proverbial brass balls. Why were studios always located a hundred miles away? Or what seemed like a hundred miles? He didn't mind the suitcase existence from one hotel suite to another. He carried a lot of suitcases and, after all, the hotels were always the best, nothing but the best, and he wasn't responsible for picking up the tab either for hospitality or excess baggage. He had no objection to dining at the most exclusive restaurants, attending premieres, promos, swanning it with his inestimable charm and sex appeal on TV chat shows. He had appeared on the Winifred Godfrey show during which three deranged females had fainted and been carried out of the studio to the resuscitating room where they were eventually brought round. They were now suing the producers and Winifred herself for a billion dollars for emotional disorientation. 'These ladies have suffered,' their attorney growled to a group of eager reporters. 'No amount of money can compensate them for what they are going through. Their lives can never be the same again. They will carry with them for ever these invisible but very real emotional scars.' Cord's value as a hot property in Hollywood rocketed as a result of the publicity. A Los Angeles psychic stated without equivocation that he was the reincarnation of Valentino and *The Enquirer* went so far as to report that, such was the power of his personality, one of the women was actually suffering a false pregnancy.

He had no objection to being mobbed by adoring fans, so long as his minders took the brunt of the mobbing and kept a wary eye open for the odd screwball who had an overwhelming psychotic desire to blow Cord away, and he signed autographs till his wrists ached. In fact he exercised his right hand every day with a little rubber ball just to keep his fingers in trim and could maintain indefinitely a "Hey, I'm really just an ordinary guy despite my enormous talent and fantastic good looks and thank you thank you thank you, you are all so kind and I love you all," kind of boyish grin. It was one that he had diligently practised and perfected in front of his shard of bedroom mirror when, as a teenager in Roanoke, Virginia, he first realised he was destined to be a star.

Maybe never in the Brando class but he wasn't doing too badly and was already getting into some pretty hefty real estate. He had also practised and perfected his acceptance speeches for Tony and Oscar awards which so far, alas, had eluded him. Not even a nomination. But he knew, when the inevitable moment came, that he would not forget, wiping away a tear, to include his parents in his interminable list of thanks, proclaiming to the world how they loved, supported, and encouraged him from infancy and right down the line.

He would also, just to be on the safe side, give thanks to his good ole boy Protestant God for being so generous with his endowments. Truth to tell, his dad, who spent most of his time in *Mooneys Pool Parlour and Pizzeria* down Main Street, had lost all interest in the boy once he had grown too big to thrash without being thrashed back twice as hard and his mom, who spent most of her time looking into a jug of moonshine, never gave a diddlysquat for his thespian pretensions. So, at the ripe old age of seventeen, Cord found himself hustling his butt on 42nd Street. Strictly for the money, you understand, in order to keep body and soul together and attend those necessary acting classes, in his case with an ageing pervert of unprepossessing appearance, heavily into prosthetics, and whose only claim to fame was his expulsion from a famous English dramatic academy.

"No," was evidently never a word in the old charlatan's vocabulary and his lust was insatiable. Not even rejections in harsh terms like "Piss off, you repulsive old fart!" Seemed to dull his persistent ardour. He did have one success with a fellow student at drama school, a lad from a North Country working class family who, like himself, was destined to fail as an actor but who went on to become an internationally acclaimed playwright.

Fired by youthful virginal curiosity, an innate horniness, and stoked up on a copious quantity of Retsina which fortunately did not lead to brewer's droop, the future internationally acclaimed playwright went to it with abandon. But it turned out to be strictly a one night stand. In the cruel cold light of morning, pulling himself together in his dingy bed-sit and feeling distinctly liverish, he had no desire to repeat the experience. He viewed his recent bedmate with such revulsion he couldn't hustle him out fast enough. He sprayed the bed-sit with copious amounts of Lily of the Valley scented air-freshener and never spoke to him again.

It was unkind but that's the way it was.

Nor did this teacher of aspiring young actors, back in his native New York twenty or more years on, have any luck with the beautiful Cord. That young rebel was sore in more ways than one at having to hustle his butt and was too wrapped up in his own ambitions and a beautiful but vicious brat named Brenda O'Brien who he married in haste and repented, not at leisure, but in even more haste. It was a teenage affair destined to hideous failure from the first disastrous attempt at consummation and from which battlefield Cord slunk away, humiliated, angry, and even more determined to make it big.

And Brenda, disillusioned with life, the big city, and the theatre, returned to her hometown of Decatur, Illinois and settled down with a feed merchant. She attended church regularly, produced five myopic children with buck teeth who cost the feed merchant a small fortune in optician's fees and orthodontics, mellowed with the passing years and grew very fat due to an addiction to "Snickers" purchased and consumed in bulk. Cord occasionally received an if only letter sealed with a loving kiss which gave him a sentimental moment or two before he screwed it up and tossed it away.

Neither, despite his exorbitant fees and his word of mouth reputation for being a wonderful teacher, a veritable guru in fact, did the pedagogue have much luck in producing, with the exception of Cord who was a film star rather than an actor, an alumnus of any note. Like many of his fellow tutors of drama, his pseudo-intellectual theories, culled and mishmashed from earlier pseudo-intellectual theories, were so tortuous and his exercises so bizarre that nine out of ten students leaving his studio were totally spaced-out and capable of few activities more demanding than dish-washing and waiting on tables, which is why no matter what restaurant you go into in Manhattan or Los Angeles your waiter is likely to be an aspiring actor. Despite performing their exercises at home with religious fervour and endlessly discussing Stanislavski they failed every audition they attended. The tenth student never got further than community theatre in Arkansas and Theme Parks in the summer where, due to inadequate technical training, he or she invariably lost their voice after the first week.

The second thing Cord hated, after having to get up in the middle of the night, was air travel. As far as he was concerned nothing could be more conducive to a nervous breakdown than having to pass through an air terminal, especially an international one, with all the hassle of customs and immigration. Airports were hideous places even for those, like himself, who received VIP treatment and were not subject to the trials and tribulations of the hoi-polloi; queuing to check-in, queuing for food, queuing to board their aircraft, queuing to take their allocated seat, queuing to take off, queuing to get off. As for the actual experience of flying, it was a complete bore, even for a member of the mile high club. If he never had to board another plane in his life he would be a happy man. He seemed to remember that in the beginning, a few years back, it had been fun when all the stewardesses were beautiful, oozed charm and couldn't do enough for you. But they were no longer called stewardesses and he had noticed that good looks no longer seemed a prerequisite for the job.

A memorandum must have circulated the airline companies ordering them to indulge in a little positive discrimination to-wards the plainer members of the fair sex. Maybe a couple of them, having applied for cabin crew positions and been rejected, threatened to throw around a few lawsuits and the chairmen at board meetings issued orders to go out and recruit staff who didn't look like walking ads for toothpaste or under-arm deodorant. He remembered one hostess when flying down to Tampa, who was so coyote ugly she could have knocked a buzzard off a shit wagon at a hundred paces, and another with a nose that would have sliced raisins at a similar distance.

When God created man in his own image, and that includes the female of the species, did he use a distorting mirror? Or is it just that He really has a lousy sense of humour? Unfortunately the poor girl also had a chewing gum habit and the personality of a dead bunny rabbit and at the end of her safety demonstration was awarded an ironic round of applause accompanied by suppressed giggles. Though understandable, this was also unwise as it led directly to the most appalling service Cord had ever experienced. Maybe this was one of the reasons why that particular airline went out of business shortly thereafter.

Cord was thinking these things as, with the ever-faithful Max beside him, and the chauffeur anxiously consulting his watch, the limo threaded its way along Knightsbridge, heading west. Although still early there was a fair amount of traffic about but, once past Hammersmith, the chauffeur opened up and they were soon speeding merrily along. Cord felt he should be looking at his script but what the hell, he wasn't known as "One-take" Cord for nothing and he'd pick it up during rehearsals. They weren't heavy dialogue scenes anyway. He just wished the goddam movie was over and done with. He felt claustrophobic and yearned for wide-open spaces and his New Mexico ranch, even if it did mean a couple of plane trips to get there. He didn't have to wonder why he accepted this lousy picture. It had nothing to do with the director who was a nerd, nothing to do with the goddam script most of which he had rewritten anyway and over which he was now fighting the nerd for a co-writing credit while the original writer, who expected sole screenplay credit, sat at home and sulked or sat in the bar and drowned his sorrows.

He hated the Brit actress playing opposite him with her prissy English accent and her way of looking at him as though he were a walking erection constantly threatening her chastity and all because, simply out of habit and not at all because he'd fancied her, he'd made a feeble pass the first day of shooting as if it were expected of him. No, he'd accepted this movie because back home he was in deep shit with the IRS and also because divorce settlements and alimony payments don't come cheap. He sighed deeply. Max turned and looked at him.

'Want a game?' He asked. 'Pass the time.'

'Sure.'

Max leaned forward and opened a cabinet in the back of the seat in front of them, took out a backgammon set and laid it on the seat between them. They were still playing and Max had won two thousand dollars when the car turned in at the entrance to the studios and pulled up before the gatehouse. A commissionaire raised his eyes from his copy of *The Sun*, glanced out of his window, raised the barrier, and waved them on. Cord and Max didn't look up from their game and, by the time the car had drawn up outside Studio 2, Max had won another five hundred. The chances of him actually getting the money were pretty remote and he wouldn't push it. You don't kill the goose. But he'd note it down with his previous winnings anyway, just in case.

Silence is a rare phenomenon in a film studio except, of course, when the place is empty, dark, and quiet as the grave. But during working hours silence reigns for only a few seconds at a time between the red light and a voice shouting 'Roll 'em!' to which, after a few moments, a second voice adds, 'Speed,' and then a third, 'Sound.' And, finally, the director with 'Action!' an oft-repeated instruction that may eventually achieve the desired result the producers have bet their shirts on, magic on the silver screen and long lines at the box office. To an outside observer the long periods between takes may seem chaotic, which they are, albeit it is organised chaos. To an outsider all may seem fascinating. To those involved it is mostly a pretty tedious business that can lead to hunger pains and over stimulated appetites due to sheer boredom. With the director's 'Cut!' at the end of a take the organised chaos immediately breaks out again and, all in vain, does the assistant plead, beg, order, demand, scream for quiet. Pleasant–'Keep the noise down please, folks.' Matey - 'Let's have a bit of hush around here, shall we?' Authoritative – 'Green light, this is a rehearsal. Quiet everyone.' Exasperated – 'QUIET!'

But everyone has to go about their respective business which includes a lot of banging, a lot of dragging about, a lot of yelled instructions, some idle chatter, questions about eight letter words beginning with D, ending with R, and fourth letter E. A soupçon of bitch, a touch of temperament, mumbling of lines from actors with heads bent over a page of script, a bit of touching up here and there, in more senses than one, a few hangovers to be nursed, jangled nerves to be soothed, and thumping hearts from those newcomers whose first film acting job this is and who stand by dreading the moment they will be called to the floor and wondering if, after today, they will ever work again.

Though there is always the exception who knows with absolute certainty that the next time he or she is filming in this studio he or she will be the star if only he or she could catch the director's eye. There is also the one who dreams of it but not with such absolute conviction. Such are some of the ingredients of film making.

The nerd, Mel Preston, director of a number of prize winning commercials with astronomical budgets which gave him the luxury of a ratio of about a hundred to one, was already screening in the theatre of his mind a future scenario which involved rave reviews from all the critics, interviews, a Golden Lion and at least eight Oscar nominations, the most important of course being for best direction, a glittering Hollywood career with every studio head going down on his knees to beg his services, an Olympic size swimming pool, and the mega-income of a Howard Hughes.

At the moment he was having a quiet conversation with his lighting - cameraman as to the best way of shooting the upcoming scene. If the truth were to be told, the paucity of his own imagination was such that, subtly he hoped, he was endeavouring to pick the latter's brains. The cameraman, a veteran of countless movies, who already had enough awards to his credit to start his own private museum, was used to incompetent uninspired directors taking credit for his expertise and was on the point of telling him how to line up his establishing shot when a callboy, clipboard in hand, strolled by.

'Where is Mr Wainer?' Preston barked.

'Make-up.'

'How long is he going to be?'

The call-boy shrugged and moved on but Preston, noticing one of the producers lurking behind a flat touching up the continuity girl, yelled after him, 'Well fetch him then! Come on, I want some movement around here! Time is money! Time is money!' He hoped the producer would stop slobbering for a moment to be duly impressed by his concern for the company's interests.

Max lounged against the wall beside the door to make-up and, studying the contours of a nubile young model in what passed for a fashion mag but which was in reality nothing more or less than soft porn, sniffed his disapproval. He preferred his women to have meat in places other than just the boobs. "She's deformed," he thought. "Look at that. The girl's top-heavy. How does she keep her balance? If she didn't have one leg in front of the other she'd fall flat on her face." Tilting his head slightly to one side, he placed his hand on the page, covering the photograph just above the nipples. "If you didn't know it," he went on to himself, unconsciously running his tongue over his upper lip, "that could be the picture of a bum. Hmn..."

There was nothing mastoconcupiscent about Max. He was definitely a bum man; luscious derrieres that jellied under tight skirts, majestic butts that rippled with the slightest movement and sent shock waves straight to the groin. The very thought of running his hand over an expanse of dimpled flesh made his own flesh creep with anticipation and the hand that held the newspaper trembled a little. The callboy who, whistling tunelessly, came waltzing down the corridor interrupted his ruminations. Max lowered his paper and stretched out an arm to place a hand on the boy's chest.

'Cheeky,' the boy said, in what he fondly imagined to be a husky Marlene Dietrich voice.

'And where do you think you're going?' The bodyguard enquired.

'And where do you think I'm going?' The lad retorted. 'Don't you remember me, John?'

'My name is Max,' Max said, falling for it.

'Oh, excuse ME! For a minute there I thought you were John Wayne.' He looked down at the hand on his chest and looked up again. 'Do you mind? I have work to do. I am a callboy...'

'Don't much fancy your chances,' Max said, getting a bit of his own back.

'I call people. I have been instructed, O Billion Dollar Man, to call the great star. The presence of arsehole number two is requested on the set by arsehole number one.'

'Is that so?'

'Don't you remember me, Incredible Hulk? Dost not recollect my fair features? My handsome visage? My unforgettable eek?'

Ernest J. Bloomberg had ambitions towards one day being a director himself, more specifically a writer/director, and he was already hard at work on an original screenplay, the title page of which read

HOUR OF AGONY
WRITTEN AND DIRECTED BY
ERNEST J. BLOOMBERG

Although this opus was far from complete he couldn't resist printing out the title page, a number of times in fact, just to see what it looked like, and pinned the sheets on his bedroom wall for inspiration. He thought of changing his name. He felt his given one made him sound more like an East End tailor than a high-flying whizz-kid, but not wanting to lose his identity completely he was finding it difficult. Ernest was all right, that simply became Ernesto, but there wasn't much he could do with Bloomberg. He toyed for a while with Ernesto Montefiori but decided the connection was too tenuous.

So far in his young life his career had embraced a three months schools tour as a not too proficient assistant stage manager and a quite disastrous appearance as an elf who a number of children referred to as "that poofy gnome:" a crew member, expenses only and duties not clearly defined, on a short film shot in Germany by a film school graduate and sponsored by a manufacturer of rubber goods; and a six months stint as a showman in a West End theatre, most of his time there being spent under the stage playing chess or cribbage with Charlie. Charlie was somewhere into his nineties and nobody in the theatre seemed too sure anymore of exactly what he was meant to be doing there, but as he had been part of the fixtures for so long it was generally accepted he might as well stay until he died, an event constantly expected and looked for.

Anyway, as an aspiring young director and one who had endured his own hour of agony, Ernest J. Bloomberg had developed his own individual style of patter which he was convinced was both sophisticated and witty and made him one of the most regular guys around. He had an overwhelming desire to be popular, suffering acutely as he did from acne, premature ejaculation, and having long since given up measuring the length of his penis in the fond hope that it was still at the growing stage. His constant urge for comparison nearly landed him in a heap of trouble on a number of occasions in public toilets and, had there really been a sure way to achieve it, he would have attempted artificially to increase his proportions. He contemplated sending off for a vacuum pump he had seen advertised in a magazine and which was guaranteed the best invention around, money refunded if not fully satisfied. But the postman always delivered after he left the house and what if it arrived in its plain sealed package while he was out and his mother grew curious? He could always protest that it was a piece of film equipment he had ordered but somehow he didn't think she would buy that. His mother might be pretty dim but nobody could be that thick, not even her. Why, oh, why hadn't he bought one when he was on location in Hamburg? The same time as he had purchased those magazines on the Reeperbahn, which he then didn't have the courage to bring home.

On second thoughts he was glad he hadn't. What if a custom's officer had discovered them, made sneaky remarks and waved them around for the entire world to see? Oh the embarrassment. His blood ran cold at the thought. A penis enlarger would have been even worse! He could just see the customs officer holding it up and squeezing the rubber bulb while he said something utterly fatuous like, "Well, and wot little gadget 'ave we got here then? Wot might this be do you suppose? Could someone enlighten me as to the purpose of this aforesaid object?" As he held it up to the light, turned it around and around, squinted down the tube, suggestively pressed the bulb. Ernest would have died of shame.

If only he had been built on a par with that Danish chap in one of the mags. That guy might have been the most gruesome looking troll ever to come out of Scandinavia but there was at least one part of his anatomy that was truly awesome–and exploitable.

Or if he were endowed like those German studs in some ancient black and white porno photographs he had found in a drawer of his father's wardrobe which must have been produced sometime in the twenties (why did the participants in that period always keep their socks on?) and which he had since secretly studied on a number of occasions. In fact he had looked at them so often it was beginning to have the most undesirable influence on *Hour Of Agony*, the score for which he had already decided, would be composed by Sir Berrison Flirtwhistle. He had already written to that darling of the more avant-garde music critics, tentatively suggesting he might like to accept the commission but, so far, the great man hadn't bothered to reply. He'd also written to *The Algemene Bank, Netherlands's* for development money, but hadn't heard from them either. As for casting he wondered if Burton and Taylor might be interested if they were available.

Right this minute though, Ernest wasn't thinking about *Hour Of Agony* or of his own Oscar acceptance speech. He was thinking that a Mile End oaf was preventing him from carrying out his duties and he had no intention of standing in the corridor the rest of the morning being obstructed by a brute whose penis he would find, if he ever got the chance to take a look, was probably even smaller than his own.

'Do you mind if I knock?' He asked. 'Or shall I do it by remote control?'

'Stand aside, small boy,' Max sneered.

This was too close for comfort. 'Callboy!' Ernest squeaked, losing his cool. 'Or runner! I'm a runner!'

'You'll be doing a runner in a minute.' Max snarled and rapped on the door with the knuckle of his middle finger.

'My! Aren't we efficient?' It was Ernest's turn to sneer.

'Yes?' Cord snapped from the other side.

'Mr Wainer, you're wanted on the set.'

'Be right there.'

Ernest smiled icily at Max and strutted off down the corridor. Safely out of range of any possible retaliation he turned. 'Tell me,' he said, 'do you warm the seat for him?' and disappeared around the corner.

Cord gently untwined the girl's arms from around his neck and gazed into her eyes in true Hollywood style. 'I suppose we'd better get on with it,' he breathed.

'I thought that's what we were doing,' she breathed right back.

He gave her a peck on the lips. 'Maybe we can pick up later where we left off,' he suggested in his most seductive tone of voice.

'Sure,' she purred, reminding him of his childhood dream girl of the silver screen, her of the mushy eyes and the husky voice, June Allyson, though he didn't tell her that, it might give her ideas above her station. Instead, 'What's your name?' He asked.

'Jasmine.'

'Well, Jasmine, get to it.' He adjusted his crotch, flopped into the chair in front of the mirror and, lighting a Marlborough, gazed with satisfaction at his well-lit reflection. There wasn't a face in the industry to match his. Eat your heart out Rock.

'I'll be as quick as I can,' Jasmine crooned, approaching him with a pale blue nylon make-up gown.

'You take all the time you need, honey,' he said, leaning forward slightly, cupping the cigarette in the palm of his hand, and making his arms available for the sleeves. 'That clown and the whole goddam circus can wait till Cord Wainer is good and ready.'

She fastened the gown behind his neck. He transferred his gaze from his own reflection to hers as she stood behind him. 'They want me, they can wait for me,' he went on. 'That shithead who fancies himself as a second Griffiths come Eisenstein all rolled into one can rehearse with my stand-in. That's what stand-ins are for.'

She smiled at his reflection, 'You must look your best,' she cooed.

'That's what I'm saying.' He ignored the ashtray in front of him and flicked his ash on the floor. 'I always do, no matter what.' Jasmine's smile broadened. 'Then what are we waiting for?' She pressed her hands to his temples and rested her small chin on top of his head. They both smiled into the mirror; a truly delectable couple.

'Where's the girl who made me up yesterday?' Cord asked.

'Looking after your co-star.'

'She'll have her work cut out.'

Jasmine released her hold on Cord's head and picked up a pair of curling tongs from the dressing table. They looked like they'd been part of the studio since J. Arthur Rank was actually into making movies and there really was a British film industry.

'What are you doing?' Cord looked at the instrument anxiously.

'You shouldn't have washed your hair this morning, honey.' There was a slight emphasis on the honey. 'I can't do a thing with it.'

****

Preston was throwing a wobbler and the watching studio, for once shocked into silent attention, was divided into four camps: those who were either disgusted or embarrassed at the exhibition he was making of himself, those who were amused, and those who thought it was no more than was to be expected of the prat anyway. He had thrown wobblers before, usually after he had made a prick of himself, lost face, and didn't know how to cover it up. Cord was not the only one for whom the last day of shooting couldn't come fast enough. Admittedly there was some cause for this latest outburst but that did not excuse it. The fourth camp consisted solely of Ernest J. Bloomberg visibly shrivelling before the entire company in his new role of whipping boy rather than his usual one of callboy.

'So where the hell is he?' Preston screamed.

'I told you. He's in make-up.'

'Didn't you call him?'

'Of course I called him. If he won't come it's not my fault, is it? I can't carry him here on my back, can I?'

Preston closed his eyes, swayed, and lifted a hand to his forehead. Then he turned and glared at his third assistant from whose face the grin immediately disappeared. Maybe this one would carry a bit more clout with that over-rated American gigolo. 'Warren, go and fetch Mr Wainer,' he ordered.

Warren wasn't much more than a year or two older than Ernest but he was more than twice his size... everywhere! Ernest had seen it and been most impressed as well as envious, and he looked as though he could carry Cord on his back. At least he was big enough to defend himself if that ageing one time member of the Brat Pack decided to throw a few ill-tempered punches. Warren swaggered off the set and Preston, throwing himself into his director's chair, picked up his script in its shiny, black, hardback, sprung folder, prominently emblazoned with MEL PRESTON in red and gold, and pretended to do some work on the scene. But he was blind to the page in front of him. Inwardly he was writhing with indignation and wondering, when Cord eventually put in an appearance, just how far he could go with dishing out the withering sarcasm before running the risk of a bloody nose at the hands of the film's one bankable asset.

The studio, which had been so uncannily silent and still but for Preston's tirade, came bustling back to noisy life and Ernest retired to a dark corner to lick his wounded ego and mentally insert a new scene into the script of *Hour Of Agony* in which the chain sawed remains of a shitty film director were discovered in a number of plastic bags in a deep freeze.

The Mile End oaf meanwhile had finally moved on from his girlie magazine and had, for some time, been engrossed in the sports pages of a daily newspaper. He skipped the bit about the sex life of a footballer who cried on the pitch at the slightest provocation but definitely enjoyed his team mates' over-reaction whenever he scored a goal and was trying to decide on a long shot in the 2.30 at Doncaster when Jasmine came out of make-up, closed the door behind her, and shimmied off down the corridor. So absorbed was Max that her bum didn't even appear as a bleep on his peripheral screen. As a punter, Max had a theory he religiously abided by. He never bet on favourites and he never bet on the sticks. Too many things could go wrong with hurdles. But on the flat, if he could find a horse in a field of eight to twelve runners who stood a good chance at odds of about ten to one, he reckoned he had got himself a fair each-way bet. And there was just such a horse in the 2.30, a grey mare by the name of Skippy Sue. Max had a soft spot for grey mares, the horse's form read 0 2 4 3 2 3, the handicapper had been kind, the mare liked the going soft, which it was, and its number was 13, Max's lucky number. It was at this point in his deliberations, having decided that Skippy Sue was a dead cert, that Max looked up from his paper just in time to see Jasmine disappear around the corner at the end of the corridor. He frowned, looked at the door to make-up, looked back up the corridor, looked back at the door and suddenly, thoroughly alarmed, dropped his paper, turned and knocked. 'Mr Wainer?'

He waited.

Silence.

Max put his ear closer to the door. He called again. Still silence. He looked down and tried the handle. The door was locked.

'Mr Wainer!' He shouted, and hammered on the door with his fist. He looked desperately and helplessly up and down the passage, undecided for a second as to what to do next. Then he threw his full weight against the door, again and again until, suddenly, it gave way, precipitating him into the room and almost up to the chair in which Cord was still sitting, with what looked suspiciously like curling tongs clamped firmly to his neck just below the ear, his hands gripping the metal sides of the chair, earthing him well and truly. His cigarette had fallen to the floor where it had burned itself out leaving a line of ash and a deep scar on the linoleum tile. Max's hand flew to his face, thumb and forefinger either side of his nose, not because of what he saw but because the room smelt like a sewer. Cord must have been spared the knowledge of this final indignity and died a happy man. After all, the last thing he saw on earth was the reflection of his beautiful face framed in bright lights. He would never see the last disgusting shots taken of him. These would be strictly for police files and, should a guilty party be found and charged, exhibits in a court of law.

Chapter Five

Holly was in her kitchen studying her Reader's Digest cook-book when the doorbell rang. She was looking for something simple but effective and had almost decided on a tuna and sweet corn bake with scalloped potatoes. That damned tin of tuna had been in the cupboard so long if she didn't use it soon she might as well throw it away. Like a rust proofed car five minutes after its warranty expires the tin appeared to be developing spots. She cursed softly, looked across the wide expanse of lounge towards the front door, and then up at the kitchen wall clock. He was early. Must have had another non-day.

Ah, well, he would have to sit in the kitchen and chat while she cooked. Only she hated that. He could never resist dipping his fingers into everything and it drove her crazy. She set off for the front door, remembered the Pouilly Fuisse on top of the fridge instead of inside it, and returned to the kitchen to set that to rights. The doorbell rang again.

'Patience, patience,' Holly murmured. 'You're the one who's early,' and, having laid the wine in the fridge, set off again before having second thoughts. The wine probably wouldn't chill in time now so she went back, took it out of the fridge, and put it in the freezer. Then she set off for the third time.

'Good evening, Miss Day,' she said brightly and as cute as a button, 'I am Ninette, your Fenella Girl.'

'You are?' Was all the surprised Holly could think to say. She had expected to see a gentleman of above medium height, medium build, medium good looks, in a medium grey suit. What she saw instead was a girl of medium height in a medium grey suit and there all resemblance to her expected guest ended. The chic two-piece was perfectly tailored to the almost perfect figure and set off by what looked suspiciously like an Hermès silk knotted loosely at the throat. The girl was ravishingly beautiful with green cat-like eyes and auburn hair that did not come out of a bottle. Her smile, when she parted her pale glossed lips, revealed two rows of perfect teeth, a credit to her dentist or her genes, or both. She carried a small stylish suitcase.

'May I come in?' She enquired sweetly, showing the perfect teeth.

'When you've told me what my Fenella Girl is, maybe.' Holly sounded really put out which, in fact, she was. Faced with this creature from *Vogue* she suddenly felt like the all time frump, Miss Potato Sack 1969. The sixties might have been swinging but right at this moment as time moved inexorably towards the new decade, still wearing her pinny, Holly felt more like dangling than swinging.

'Surely you must have seen our advertising?' Ninette said in a tone that defied Holly to contradict her. Holly did.

'Obviously I haven't,' was the snappy reply. She hadn't meant to sound quite so bad tempered but for some reason, other than being made to feel a perfect frump, she had taken an instant dislike to this girl and her churlish response was a dead giveaway. Ninette didn't seem in the least put out.

'We sell cosmetics direct to the consumer,' she explained blithely, 'in the comfort of their own homes. So much more convenient don't you think? than trying to barge your way up Oxford Street? I have our range right here.' She gave the suitcase a delicate pat with perfectly manicured fingers.

'For your information I do not barge,' Holly said, 'up Oxford

Street or anywhere else, and some people, I may add, have very uncomfortable homes.' She was going to make this as hard as possible. She eyed the suitcase warily, as one would regard a snake charmer's basket from which a cobra could escape at any moment, and then looked back at the still smiling face of the girl who carried it. Come to think of it, it wasn't so beautiful. There was something disturbing about the eyes and the face was too plastic, like something made up for American television, unreal.

'It's really a very exciting range, Miss Day. Please do let me show it to you. In buying direct from us you make simply enormous savings as well.'

But Holly cut through Ninette's sales pitch. 'How do you know my name?' She asked, still cold, still unfriendly.

'It is on the bell.'

'Ask a silly question.'

'And we do go to a lot of trouble to get to know our customers.'

'I am not a customer.'

'Oh, but I'm sure you soon will be, once you see what we have to offer.' The smile turned into a girlish simper, something Holly hated to see in a grown woman.

'Humph!' She sniffed. She just knew she should close the door on this temptress but she had grown curious as to the lady's wares so, though still a little wary, she shrugged and stepped back from the door, hoping that Thornton would arrive in time to break up the party before her willpower wilted. Just wait till he got an eyeful of this one! He always did have a thing about redheads.

'Thank you.' Ninette stepped into the room and Holly closed the door behind her. 'My!' The Fenella Girl gushed, looking around, 'You do have a lovely apartment.'

"Shit!" Holly thought and then out loud, 'Will you need a table?'

'Oh, no! Why don't we just sit on the couch here where it's

more comfortable?'

'Be my guest.' Holly extended an open hand towards the couch and watched as Ninette sat down, knees together and to the side, opened the case and tilted it forward on the couch beside her for a preliminary inspection. 'See?' She said, and patted the couch on the other side of the case. 'Now do come and sit down, Miss Day. I can't possibly show you anything if you're right at the other end of the room.'

Holly advanced slowly towards the couch and flopped down opposite Ninette. 'I will have to keep my eye on the kitchen, I've just put food in the oven,' she said, hoping Ninette would take the hint and be about her business as quickly as possible. 'And I hope these products are organic, beauty without cruelty, environment friendly, produced under stringent ergonomic approved conditions and packaged in biodegradable containers, otherwise you're wasting your time.' She was still going to make this as difficult as she could. Ninette never lost her smile.

'What do you think you would be most interested in?' Now she sounded like a small girl playing shop. Holly suppressed a threatened scream.

'Shall we start with the lip gloss?' She held up a stick ready to smear on the back of her hand. 'What colours do you like? Do you prefer a dark shade? Or something light? Maybe something totally outré for those uninhibited moments. I see you're not wearing any at the moment.'

'I seldom do,' Holly misinformed her.

'Oh, dear! I see we are going to be difficult to please, aren't we?' She had switched from little shopkeeper to disapproving nanny and was about to put away the stick when Holly stretched out a hand and took it from her. Ninette watched for a moment as Holly examined it. 'What are you looking for?' She asked.

'There's no trade name on it. Isn't that a little unusual?'

'Is it?' Ninette laughed gaily. 'I'm afraid you've got me there. None of my customers have ever thought to ask me that one. All right, let me show you something that does have a brand name. What about a hair spray?' She reached into the case and came out with a brightly coloured aerosol, held it up and pointed to it with one long slender finger. 'See?' She said. 'Fenella.'

Holly's only comment was that the design was not in the best of possible taste. The lettering of Fenella made it look suspiciously phallic. The stuff was patently rubbish, the modern version of snake oil.

'I don't use lacquers,' she said, hoping this last rebuff would finally put the Fenella Girl off but the Fenella Girl carried on regardless.

'Oh, this isn't a lacquer,' she purred, 'oh, dear, no. It's much finer than that. Look...' She held the can up to the light and pressed the nozzle, 'Like the finest mist... so soft... so kind... so delicately scented.' The voice had become almost dreamily hypnotic.

'You know something?' Holly said, taking in the classic profile, 'You shouldn't be doing this job at all.' It seemed quite an innocuous remark and Holly was unprepared for the reaction. The profile turned to full face with such speed the auburn hair bounced like a television ad for conditioner. The eyes flashed and the voice was no longer the rustle of silk.

'Oh? And why not?'

Holly tensed. For some reason a scene from the past flashed through her mind, the memory of a visit to a friend's farm. She had driven through the open gate and up to the house where, stepping out of the car, she was enthusiastically greeted by the household pets, a pack of barking, yelping, tail-wagging, excited dogs of various shapes and sizes, all of them obviously delighted to see a visitor, and two or three of them even walking a step or two on their hind legs or leaping up to make her more welcome.

Holly had never been afraid of animals and she made as much fuss of the dogs as they did of her, though she could have done without the muddy paw marks and the hand licking from the more excitable of her new acquaintances. She knocked on the door and waited, thinking how surprised Fran would be to see her after a fairly lengthy separation. The animals sat around watching her, one of them scratching himself with such enthusiasm that he lost his balance and fell over, making her laugh. She knocked again. There being no answer and, deciding her friend was not at home and wouldn't be surprised after all, she started back for her car. And then the strangest thing happened. The dogs that had so vociferously and rapturously welcomed her only a few moments before, were now ominously quiet as they followed her.

A couple of them raced ahead and got between her and the car. She stopped. There was a low menacing growl, then another, then a baring of fangs. Holly suddenly went very cold. She saw the rising hackles. There was a surge of adrenalin. Her heart pounded. Her legs trembled. She forced herself to move very slowly. She opened the car door, slipped into the driving seat, and slammed the door shut. Immediately all hell broke loose as the animals leapt at the car. But she was safe.

The only danger now was to the paintwork as she drove slowly out of the yard followed by the snarling pack. She glanced in her rear-view mirror to see them standing by the gate and it was a while before she could control her violent trembling. Teach her to visit people unannounced she thought, and she remembered that fear now as she went on, 'No, all I meant was, with your looks, and your figure, you really ought to be a model.'

'Oh, but that's what I want to be!' Ninette trilled. 'But it's not that easy you know. It's terribly hard work, not that I mind that of course, but then your face just has to fit. You can have the most wonderful portfolio in the world but if you're not flavour of the month it will get you absolutely nowhere. And don't you believe all those stories about the casting couch either. I don't mean it doesn't exist but you know what men are like with their promises. And you know what the Germans say, don't you?'

'Deutschland Uber Alles?' Holly ventured.

'No! If you don't mind my being terribly vulgar for a moment, I mean, we are girls together, aren't we? The Germans say, she dropped her voice to a conspiratorial whisper, "A standing prick has no conscience." Only they say it in German of course.'

'Of course,' Holly agreed. That was a bubblehead remark if ever there was one. 'I thought it was supposed to be the Greeks who had a saying for everything,' she went on, 'and I must admit, that one does sound as though it could be Germanic, but I'm afraid it isn't.'

'Isn't it?'

'No, it isn't. It was said by an American novelist, Mister Mailer I think it was.'

'Oh. I stand corrected, pun not intended. But what about you?' She continued, returning to the task in hand, 'You could give it a try.' She tilted her head slightly as she studied Holly's face.

'Oh, don't be silly.' The tension had faded and Holly laughed. 'I'm about as photogenic as a Rorschach test.'

'No, it's a very... interesting face,' Ninette said, suddenly quite serious and regarding Holly intently. 'Though you really should do something with your hair. Perhaps Fenella could help.' She raised the aerosol, aimed it directly at Holly, and pressed the nozzle.

Holly gasped and jerked back as the fine spray hit her full in the face. Her eyes and nostrils burned. She felt as though someone was scraping the back of her throat with a razor blade and her ribs seemed suddenly to have fused together as she choked and gasped for breath. She reeled off the couch, swinging around to the back and clutching at it for support. Ninette moved swiftly in a semi-circle around the other end and, once again, that long slender finger pressed down on the nozzle.

At the same time, a finger pressed on the doorbell.

Still clawing the back of the couch, Holly was on her knees, her head almost to the floor. Ninette glanced towards the door and then, moving in for the coup de grace as it were, as casually as one would spray a fly on the windowpane, she let her victim have another blast for good measure. The doorbell rang again. Ninette's sotto voce language was far from ladylike as she looked around for a way out. She ran into the bedroom, switched on the light, and looked around, crossed over to the windows and, for a moment, contemplated the lights of London. It was a long way down and the escape line that rolled neatly inside her case for use in just such an emergency was of no use from this height. She turned away from the window, heaved the mattress off the bed, opened closets and hauled out clothes, leaving them scattered in untidy heaps on the carpet. She hurried around to the other side of the room and yanked the drawers from the dressing table, scattering their contents. Then, satisfied, she returned to the lounge where she tipped out a few more drawers, replaced the aerosol in the suitcase, snapped it shut and crossed the room to the front door.

She took one look back. Holly's feet and ankles could just be seen protruding from behind the couch. Ninette flicked off the lights and, putting her eye to the door, peeped out through the spy hole through which she could survey virtually the entire landing. It appeared deserted and, directly opposite, she could see the elevator doors and the panel of indicator lights showing the lift was descending and was already half way to the ground floor. Whoever had been ringing the bell, she concluded, must have decided no one was at home and left. After all, she reasoned, Holly had made no mention of expecting a visitor or tried to hustle her unduly so obviously she hadn't been expecting anyone.

Obviously? Ninette opened the door and stepped out.

'Good-evening.'

The voice came from behind her. Ninette's reaction was lightning swift as, with a cry of surprise, she swung around. Thornton never knew what hit him as the sharp hard corner of a small stylish suitcase packed with Fenella cosmetics cracked down on his skull.

****

He looked cute in his shirtsleeves, waistcoat, and floral pinafore, the whole ensemble topped with what looked as though it might be one of Tatty's turbans but which was, in fact, a bandage neatly done. Holding a well-laden tray in both hands he stood by Holly's bed in the still darkened room and looked down at her.

'Good morning,' he said softly.

Holly groaned and stirred. Then lay quite still again.

'Come on,' Thornton urged, 'it's a lovely day, and time for breakfast.'

Holly groaned, a little louder this time, but still she did not move. Her eyes ached, her throat was dry and sore and she had the feeling that someone had attempted to put her through a mangle. She tried to collect her scattered thoughts. Thornton, whose arms were starting to grow tired, coughed.

'Come on, sleepyhead, it's time to wake up.'

'Thornton? Is that you?' She whispered.

'You were expecting someone else?'

'I was expecting...' It hurt too much to talk and she went back to whispering. 'I was expecting you last night, not this morning.' How had he got into the flat she wondered? And what was he doing in her bedroom at this hour of the morning blithely wishing her a good one? Hour of the morning? What hour of the morning?

'Are the sparrows up yet?'

'That's my girl,' Thornton replied, 'never without a quip. If you must know, the sparrows have been up for hours. The bawdy hand is almost on the prick of noon to quote the bard, I think.'

Holly squeezed her eyelids tightly together and then tried to open them. Nothing happened. 'Oh, my God!' She thought in sudden panic, 'I'm blind!' She put a hand up to her face and was somewhat relieved to find herself touching an eye pad. Or was it? Perhaps it was a bandage. The suspicion of blindness still nagged her. Maybe she wasn't at home after all. Maybe she was lying in a hospital somewhere. Panic seized her again. 'Where am I?' She croaked.

'Well that's a silly question,' Thornton said, 'where do you think you are? In your own little bed, my dear. Or, rather, your vast luxurious Gloria Swanson "Sunset Boulevard" type bed.'

'Don't exaggerate.' She heard a noise beside her. It was Thornton placing the tray on the bedside cabinet. His arms ached and he was tired of holding it. The kidneys were getting cold and the toast, slightly burnt hard as a rock. His lovingly prepared breakfast wouldn't be worth eating in a minute. He perched himself on the edge of the bed. 'Here,' he said, 'let me help you.' Gently he tried to take her hand from the pad but she would have none of it and her arm went rigid. 'Come on now, Holly,' he pleaded, 'take it off. You'll be fine I promise. No serious damage.' Her arm went limp and the hand slid on to the coverlet allowing him to remove the pad. 'There you are. Now open your eyes,' he ordered. But the eyes remained firmly closed. 'Oh, come on, Holly! Don't be such a sissy.' Holly let out another groan. If ever she had to live through Orwell's nightmarish vision any threat to her eyes would instantly elicit whatever information, whatever confession, her interrogators required. With Winston it was rats. With some people it's teeth. With Holly it was her eyes.

They would water if she saw someone putting in a contact lens. They would water if someone even mentioned eyes watering. She once sat half blind through an entire movie because it had been preceded by a *Tom and Jerry* cartoon in which Tom, having spent the night on the tiles, was having the greatest difficulty keeping his wildly bloodshot eyes open and, for the next couple of hours, every time she recalled an image from the cartoon, her eyes would stream again. She couldn't even remember what the main feature was. She had once heard of an Oriental torture that consisted of placing spiders in half walnut shells and fixing them to the eyes. The spiders, unable to make their escape through the hard shells, happily nibbled away in the opposite direction. She'd had nightmares for years over this obscenity. Oh, the evil things human beings think up to do to one another! Not that the rest of nature was much better! She'd read about an African parasite that, having entered through the skin, possibly of a bare foot, eventually worked its way up into the eye where it could be seen crossing the eyeball from where it was picked out with a pin. Holly's mind contained a fund of horror eye stories. Murphy's Law. And torturing herself with these thoughts now, she felt an almost irrepressible desire to scream hysterically. She clutched at Thornton's hand and gripped it tightly.

'I can't.' She whimpered, 'I can't open them.'

'Of course you can. Come on now.'

His voice was reassuring and, realising she would have to face her awful fear sooner or later; Holly took a deep breath and opened her eyes. Her worst fears were realised. 'I can't see!' she yelled.

'Yes you can,' Thornton replied, his voice still quiet and re-assuring. Releasing his hand, he got off the bed, went across to the windows and drew back the heavy curtains. Holly flinched and hurriedly covered her eyes with her forearm as light flooded the room. Thornton returned to the bed.

'See?' He said. 'Come on now, breakfast.' He rubbed his hands together and picked up the tray. 'Nothing like a good breakfast to set you up for the day, especially after what you've been through.'

'What have I been through?' Holly asked, still a little on the hazy side. And then, as it all came back to her, 'Oh, yes! My Fenella girl.'

'Your what? Come on Holly do sit up, I can't stand here holding this tray all day.'

Holly pushed against the bed with her knuckles, trying to do as she was bid, groaned again, and fell back on the pillows.

'Now what's the matter?'

'Oh, my God, my head! Somebody's split it down the middle with an axe.'

'No, dear, that was my head.'

Holly opened her eyes again and squinted up at him. She frowned as he came into focus.

'What happened?' She asked.

'If you sit up nicely like a good girl and eat the delicious breakfast I prepared for you so lovingly I'll tell you.'

Holly sat up and Thornton placed the tray on her lap. He rearranged the pillows to give her support.

'There. Comfy?'

Holly stared with distaste at the plate in front of her and wrinkled up her nose. 'What on earth is that?' She asked.

'Devilled kidneys and kedgeree,' Thornton announced with pride. 'Yum yum.' It wasn't every day of the week Holly had breakfast prepared and served to her by a cordon bleu chef. He wasn't to know she was beginning to feel distinctly nauseous.

'The rose is a nice touch,' she said, concentrating with a decided squint on the single wilting yellow bloom in its slender vase. 'Though it might look better on a tombstone.'

'Yes, they didn't last very long, did they?' Thornton agreed. 'Did you crush the stems and put aspirin in the water? You're supposed to give them a really good bashing you know.' Holly looked up at him. 'Oh, dear!' He exclaimed, 'Your eyes really are quite a mess.'

'You should see them from this side,' she retorted and then indicated the tray. 'Take this away please, Thornton. I appreciate the gesture and the trouble you must have taken but only you would think of giving an invalid kidneys and kedgeree for breakfast. I really can't face it. Honestly.' Then on a higher more urgent note as she felt her gorge rise, 'Take it away! Take it away!'

'Well just drink the orange juice then.' He said, holding out the glass.

'All right, if it will make you happy,' and drained it in one go. She didn't drink to please him, despite the pained expression on his face, but because a chronic thirst had taken the place of the nausea. She put down the glass and he removed the tray. Holly flopped back on the pillows. 'So what did happen?' She asked.

'To you? Or to me?' He sat on the edge of the bed.

'I know what happened to me.'

'Tell me about it.'

'You first.'

Thornton leaned back, crossed his legs, and intertwined his fingers over his bent knee. 'I knocked on your door, on the stroke of eight as arranged. I waited. I knocked again.'

'No you didn't.'

'What?'

'You didn't knock on my door. You rang the bell. I heard it just before I passed out.'

'Don't be pedantic. May I continue? Well, after I had rung your doorbell I waited again and, instinct I suppose, I grew a little suspicious that all was not as it should have been. I could see there was a light on in the flat. And then, when it went out, I thought maybe you were playing games.'

'Playing games!'

'My dear Holly, you do have a somewhat bizarre sense of humour at times. But, to continue, when I saw the light go out, I flattened myself against the wall. The door opened. This fantastically good-looking creature came out. A right little raver to use a colloquial expression and...'

'Would you recognise her again?'

'Stop interrupting. No, I doubt I would. She had her back to me.'

'Then how do you know she was a right little raver? Instinct again?'

Thornton decided to ignore this. 'Good evening,' I said, raising my hat in true sexist fashion. That was a mistake. The next thing I knew I was coming round on the landing floor. It must have been only a few seconds and, of course, the bird had flown. You're right, Holly, I really am slipping. Oh, sorry to tell you by the way but the wall and carpet out there are in one helluva mess. I didn't know I had so much blood, so much to lose anyway. It was simply pouring out, like someone had opened a tap. A very pretty shade of red. Though it doesn't quite go with beige. Looks like rust.'

'Quit the gory details, Thornton, just stick to the salient points. A good story needs no embellishment.'

'Jolly good. Well, fortunately your door was still open, so I staggered in and found...'

'Hold it. How come there's no blood on your clothes?'

'I never get blood on my clothes. Other people's walls and floors maybe, but never my clothes. To conclude, I found you... and the mess.'

'Mess? What mess?'

'Looked like the place had been done over, obviously to

give the impression of an attempted burglary. Clothes scattered everywhere, drawers pulled out. Anyway, I gave you the quick once over to make sure there were still signs of life. You had me pretty worried for a while. But this time I had no objection to giving the kiss of life. Then I called Adrian up from downstairs. Lucky he wasn't on duty and lucky you get on with your neighbours, especially handsome young doctors. He came flying up at the double and here we are.'

'That's it?'

'Well at first he wanted to call an ambulance tout de suite and have you rushed off to Bart's but I thought it might be best to keep all this hush-hush for the time being and told him, if he could handle it himself, to do so. He fixed my head too. Five stitches and they didn't half hurt. He looked in again this morning before he went out, just to make sure everything was all right, burbled on about it being his responsibility if anything should happen to you so my instructions are, as soon as you can, you're to go in for a complete check-up. And that includes opthalmics, or whatever the department's called.' Holly went cold at the thought.

'So why did you want to keep it hush-hush?' She asked.

'Well, if you're number seven on the hit list ...'

'Seven?'

'Oh, yes, of course, you haven't seen the morning papers.'

'So who was number six? No, don't tell me now. I have an urgent need to visit the bathroom. And, while I'm there, I'll take a nice long shower.'

'Fine.' Thornton got off the bed and picked up the tray. 'And while you're cleaning up in the bathroom, I'll clean up in the kitchen. Number six can stay a surprise till you feel up to hearing about it. And then you can also tell me your side of the story.' He started for the door, talking as he went. 'Also, if you feel up to it after your shower, I can reheat this for you.'

'Hold it, Thornton,' Holly said. He turned back. 'Who was this number six?'

'Aha! I thought your curiosity would get the better of you.'

'No, Thornton, you thought you could arouse my curiosity and you have, so don't gloat. Just tell.'

'You're in for a big surprise,' he said with a certain lilt in his voice reminiscent of a children's song.

'Don't sing first thing in the morning please. I can't bear it. Just tell me.'

Thornton gazed steadily at her for a few moments.

This was for dramatic effect.

'Cord Wainer.'

'Cord Wainer!'

A montage of images flashed through Holly's mind... a gigantic billboard above a marquee – CORD WAINER in GUNS OF BATASI – a giant Cord, naked to the waist except for crossed cartridge belts, bandanna knotted around his head, blowing away an unseen enemy. Cord arriving for a premiere; crowds, TV cameras, and flashes popping. Cord with this glamorous star, with that glamorous star, shaking hands with Royalty. Cord at The White House, arm in arm with the President. Sitting in a dark cinema gazing at Cord's handsome features on the screen.

'The film star?'

'You know another Cord Wainer?' Thornton turned and disappeared in the direction of the kitchen. Holly threw back the bedclothes.

'Thornton, wait! What happened?' She slipped out of bed and, after a few moments leaning against a closet to steady herself as the room took on the properties of foam rubber, she opened the closet and reached inside for a negligee. None was to be found. Nothing was it its right place. She searched along the row of clothes and then staggered naked to the bathroom where, having impatiently answered the call of nature, she slipped on her favourite "schlep – around – the – house – looking – like – a – slattern" towelling robe, faded and worn and torn under the arms, and tottered to the kitchen, images of Cord still flashing through her mind. But all thoughts of the star disappeared as she reached the kitchen door.

'Oh, my God!' She wailed, 'what hit this place? Don't answer that. Did you have to use every dish, plate, and saucepan I own? And look at my cooker!' The wail turned into a squeal that in turn resolved itself into a hoarse whisper as she pressed her hands to her temples. 'Don't make me do this, Thornton. Oh, my head!' She leaned against the cooker and leapt away as if scalded, setting up another wail. 'My gown! Just look at my gown! What is that stuff? It's never going to come off.' She flew to the sink for a wet cloth and dabbed desperately at the sticky mess which remained obstinately sticky as it soaked into the towelling. 'And, just by the way, where did the kidneys and kedgeree come from?'

'From your cupboards and freezer of course. Oh, and by the way, I found a bottle of Pouilly Fuisse in the freezer. Frozen solid. Tch tch tch, that is no way to treat a good wine.'

Holly glared at him. It was almost Gorgon-like. 'I'm in the bathroom!' She snapped, and fled the scene of desolation.

She studied herself in the bathroom mirror and decided she looked a wreck, which was hardly surprising. Ninette, smiling, looked over one shoulder. Cord, virile, handsome, Cord looked over the other. They both disappeared for a moment as she leaned forward over the basin to make a closer examination of her eyes, trying to keep the lids wide open between forefinger and thumb but their persistent watering made her give it up as a bad job. Maybe a few drops of Broline would stave off that dreaded prospective visit to opthalmics or whatever the department was called. She expunged the vision of opthalmics as quickly as it had appeared and Ninette's reflection was smiling at her again. "If ever she caught up with that bitch," Holly thought, she'd wipe that smile off her face for good. "Flavour of the month?"

She wouldn't stand a cat's chance in a dog show after she was through with her. She saw those classic features so clearly beneath the waves of auburn hair. Funny how the mind could see pictures like that: that the eyes could be looking at the real world while the mind was roving through a landscape all its own; instant playback, forward projection. Even with the eyes closed, seeing lights and patterns around the lid while the brain saw pictures that weren't there. Holly moved away from the basin and turned on the shower reliving, as the water jetted out, that moment Ninette had raised the aerosol. The girl was good, damn it! She'd allayed Holly's suspicions, lulled her into a false sense of security, and then struck. Holly hadn't stood a chance. She stepped into the shower cabinet but could not bring herself to close the curtain. Images of Hitchcock flashed through her mind and she felt suddenly very cold. She shivered violently. Was this delayed shock? Obviously she was still pretty shaken up.

She turned up the hot water until the temperature was almost unbearable. She felt it stinging across her shoulders and in the small of her back. This shower was not just for hygienic reasons. It was a cleansing ritual deeper than skin deep. She poured a measure of herbal body shampoo into her cupped hand and held the hand to her nose for a moment inhaling the delicate fragrance before smoothing the liquid into her arms, her neck, her breasts, luxuriating for a moment in the sensual silkiness of it over the skin but still she could not relax. Her mind raced as she tried to make sense of it all.

Who was Ninette? And who had sent Ninette to kill her? And, above all, why? Who would want her dead? And what connection did she have with any of the previous victims?

She had not known any of them personally nor had dealings with them, directly or indirectly, not that she knew of anyway. Wait a minute. Could it be because of the incident in *L'Éminence Grise*? Because she followed the girl companion? Did someone suspect her of having knowledge she did not have? Knowledge that could be highly dangerous? And what possible connection could the victims have had with one another? Maybe there weren't any. Maybe they were totally unconnected and she and Thornton had jumped to conclusions. There certainly didn't seem to be any pattern to the murders. Were they murders? Even that wasn't clear. But, if they were, could they be random killings? Maybe Ninette was a spaced out screwball, a woman from hell getting her kicks from killing. But no, Ninette was not the girl in the restaurant. Holly groaned and, with her fingers at her temples, pressed her thumbs into the base of her skull. It hurt. But gradually it eased the tension and the pain lessened.

She stepped out of the bathroom to be met by the aroma of freshly brewed coffee coming from the kitchen and the sound of Elgar coming from the living room. Of course it would have to be the *Enigma Variations*. Thornton's sense of humour? Or was he just feeling particularly the Edwardian gentleman this morning? A brand new sparkling white towelling robe was now substituting for the old schlep around the house one which had been left half in, half out of the bidet to soak and she realised that, despite Thornton's outlandish ideas as to what constitutes a good breakfast, she was ravenous. Not that she would tell him that, he'd probably go out and shoot a horse, if he could find one. The kitchen, she noticed in passing, was in exactly the same state as it was before she had gone to the bathroom and Thornton, relaxed in an easy chair in the living room, was reading a newspaper. He looked up at her and smiled.

'Well there you are then. All squeaky-clean. Feeling better?'

Sometimes Thornton reminded Holly of the kind of dog that, if you go down the road for a pint of milk, greets you on your return as though you had been on an expedition to the North Pole, but she agreed she felt better. 'It's amazing what a shower can do for a body,' she said, glancing around the room. 'I take it you tidied up in here.' Thornton nodded. 'And in the bedroom?' He nodded again. 'And I won't be able to find a thing until I do it all again.'

'I just put everything away in what seemed a logical place.'

'That explains it. Then how about applying some logic to the kitchen.'

Thornton sighed and dropped the paper. 'A woman's work is never done,' he groaned as he heaved himself out of the chair and headed for the kitchen.

'Forget it, Thornton,' Holly said, 'I can do it later. In fact I'd rather do it myself.' He turned back with obvious relief. Creating a mess is one thing, cleaning it up another. 'There is something you can do for me though.'

'Name it, old girl. Just name it.'

'Throw away the kidneys and kedgeree...'

'Can't. Polished off the lot I'm afraid.' He looked slightly sheepish. 'While you were in the bathroom. Was feeling rather peckish. After all it was a hard night. In more ways than one. Your couch is not exactly the most comfortable, not for stretching out on anyway. Think I maybe trapped a nerve somewhere between the third and fourth rib.' He winced slightly for emphasis.

'There's no need to apologise. I don't begrudge you a single mouthful of either kidney or kedgeree. But, while I'm getting dressed, please make me lashings of toast and make sure the coffee's piping hot. I can't bear lukewarm drinks, ice cold or boiling hot, nothing in between. Think you can manage it without Mount Etna erupting in there again?'

'No sooner said than done, my dear.' He resumed his interrupted trip to the kitchen. Holly smiled as he passed her.

'And, Thornton,' she said quietly, 'thank you.'

He stopped again; turned, and looked at her, 'What for?' he asked as though he didn't know what she was on about.

'Saving my life. You obviously did save my life didn't you?'

He seemed to be thinking for a moment and then he said, 'Yes, we have to talk about that. But, as for thanking me...' He shrugged. 'I happened to have been on hand, that's all.'

'My hero!' Holly gushed, pressing her hands together and fluttering her eyelids a la Betty Boop. Then she pointed towards the kitchen. 'Now really prove your worth, Mr King, and kindly do not burn the toast this time.'

'Gordon Bennett!' He threw back at her as he went, 'you're a worse actor than Cord Wainer.'

'Not possible. He's dead.'

'Precisely.'

****

Holly was reading aloud from the newspaper, It wasn't for Thornton's benefit as he had already scanned most of the morning press anyway, but she still harboured a feeling of disbelief and reading aloud somehow made the news of Cord Wainer's death more tangible. 'The well-known film star was found by a member of his staff. Details of his death have not been released as the police are pursuing their enquiries. A spokesman for the studios told me that they were almost at the end of shooting his latest picture, *To Dice With Death.*'

'And he lost.' Thornton sipped his coffee. 'Well that's given some executive a jumbo-sized headache.'

Holly shook her head, folded the paper, and dropped it on the table. 'They'll be insured,' she said, lifting a piece of toast from the rack and digging her knife deep into the butter.

'Insurance executives don't have headaches? No, maybe not. They just up the premiums.'

'You can say that again,' she replied with some vehemence. 'Do you know what my car cost me before I gave it up? Was forced to give it up?' She slapped the butter across her toast as if she were attacking it.

'That's your fault for (a) living in London, (b) driving a high-powered sports car and (c) sharing the road with every other driver, ninety percent of whom are either maniacs or total idiots. You're better off without it. Now can we forget Cord Wainer for a minute and talk about last night?'

But Holly couldn't forget Cord Wainer that easily.

'But what will they do about the picture?' She asked as though Thornton was the be all and end all of cinematic knowledge.

'Oh, they'll finish it one way or another I suppose. Long shots with a look-alike, over the shoulder shots, that sort of thing. It's been done before. Unless, of course, it's a real turkey, in which case maybe they'll be glad not to finish it. I only hope the poor names at Lloyds, who've already lost their all over the world's recent disasters, aren't expected to stump up for it. Hey!' He snapped his fingers. 'Maybe it is a turkey Maybe they didn't want it finished. Do you think that could be the reason he was bumped off?'

'Don't be ridiculous.' Holly jabbed her knife into the marmalade.

'Why not? People do all sorts of things to claim on the insurance if they're in a tight financial spot. Or even if they're not come to that. You know. Set fire to buildings, sink boats, murder supposed love ones. There was that case in West Africa where a plane went missing with a cargo of diamonds.'

Holly said nothing. She had a mouthful of toast and marmalade, but she looked interested, or so Thornton thought, so he went on.

'Evidently the president of the country the diamonds were going from, and the president of the neighbouring country the diamonds were flying over en route for Europe, got together and with the connivance, and pay-off of course, of the plane's crew, conveniently lost both aircraft and cargo over the bush. They claimed on the insurance and, having been paid out in full, sold the plane to a third African country, put the diamonds on another flight and made a killing. Quit a few killings in fact as the pay-off for a number of witnesses was to be permanently silenced. That's the way I heard it.'

Holly snorted and stared at him sceptically. 'You don't just lose an aeroplane,' she said, 'the insurance companies would want evidence.'

'Oh, they got it,' he replied. 'There are plenty of old junky planes lying around in Africa fit only for scrap. I remember when I had to fly to the Cote D'Ivoire one time, we put down in Guinea and, as we were coming in to land, our pilot informed us that, except for passengers disembarking, no one should attempt to leave the plane, and under no circumstances should anyone try and take photographs. All cameras were to be kept strictly out of sight. So we hit the runway, the entire length of which on either side was littered with junked aircraft. It was like a graveyard for planes. Then, as we taxied up to the buildings, I saw the reason for the warnings. You've never seen so many combat clad trigger happy thugs in your life and we had to sweat it out in that damned plane for a couple of hours before we were ready for take-off again. This was when socialism in Africa was still an excuse for dictatorship and all arguments were settled with a bullet. It still is in some places unfortunately.'

Holly grunted, whether in disbelief or because he had convinced her he wasn't sure, but she picked up the paper and looked at it again.

'Cord Wainer, who would have thought it? Such a lovely man too.'

'As you and a hundred million other females all over the globe thought alike that's what made him a star, that and his boundless conceit. Come on, Holly, admit it, he was the world's worst actor. In heaven he won't even rate a bit part, not even a walk-on. That's if he gets there in the first place.'

'Do I sense a hint of jealousy in those remarks?'

Thornton took the paper from her, opened it and disappeared behind it.

'Isn't this cosy? We could be an old married couple.' She took another nibble of her toast and addressed the paper. 'I've been trying to piece everything together, Thornton, and I come up with a complete blank. Do you really think he was number six?'

Thornton turned over a page but didn't look at her as he replied. Obviously the jealousy jibe had stung. 'Maybe. I could think of any number of people who might have liked to have done it. Ex-wives? Ex-mistresses? Maybe he had Mafia connections. He wouldn't be the first Hollywood actor to have dubious friends. Who knows?' He turned another page. For a while Holly munched on her toast and stared at the newspaper without really focusing on it. Then she focused and reached for the coffee pot. 'More coffee?' There was no answer. 'Thornton! More coffee?'

A hand appeared from behind the paper, the fingers groped around the table, found the edge of the saucer, lifted up cup and saucer and held them out. Holly was sorely tempted to pour coffee in the wrong place, a lap for instance, but she resisted the temptation.

'Like I said, we could have been married for years,' she repeated, pouring the coffee and remembering her parents in the garden breakfast room of her Purley childhood.

The paper was lowered. 'That's the second time in two days marriage has been mentioned. There isn't a conspiracy afoot by any chance?'

'Who else mentioned it?'

'The princess. What made you say that anyway?'

'Memories. Are we going to talk? Or are you just going to sit there reading the paper until it's time to go to the office?' She sounded exactly like her mother.

'It was time to go to the office hours ago.' He looked into his refilled coffee cup. 'Thank you.' Lifted it and took a sip. 'And it's time you hightailed it to the hospital for that check-up.'

'I feel fine!' Holly snapped. 'Now, come on, Thornton, let's talk about last night.'

'Oh, you're finally ready, are you? I was only waiting for you to do it in your own good time.' He put down the cup. 'But why don't we do it in the cab?'

'Cab? What cab?'

'The one that'll be taking you to Bart's.'

'I'm not going.'

'Coward. All right, suit yourself. But Adrian's going to be awfully mad at you.'

'Too bad.'

'What if there are complications? What if you were to have a relapse or something? I'm not going to feel very happy either if something happens.'

'Oh, something is going to happen all right. You don't presume for one moment that the status quo is going to stay status do you? Or quo for that matter. An attempt has been made on my life and I want to know why. Not only why but by whom?'

'You don't know who?'

'Oh, it was Ninette, if that is her name, who tried it on, but who was behind it? Will there be another attempt? And, if so, when? And how? But, above all, Thornton King, why?'

'It would seem we've asked these questions before,' he said, blandly. 'So tell me about last night.'

Chapter Six

Thornton opened his mailbox, took out a fistful of envelopes of various sizes, slammed the box shut and started up the well worn wooden stairs, sifting through the mail as he went. Just as he expected, the post consisted entirely of ad mail and bills, including the dreaded ones in red. He could have wished *The Kismet Tandoori* wasn't situated in the adjacent building. The smell of curry seeped through the cracks in the wall, permeating the stairwell. Fortunately, he noticed as he let himself in, it didn't penetrate as far as his office. Either that or it was overwhelmed by the smell of damp.

The landlords really ought to get that gutter fixed. The fungus was beginning to look like something out of a horror movie. Then, on the other hand, why should they? The fabric of the building meant nothing to them. Make as much money as possible while it stood then let it fall down and sell off for redevelopment. He threw the mail on the desk, took off and hung up his coat and scarf, and switched on the kettle. Then, while he waited for it to boil–it would take a long time considering the amount of fur that had to be heated up first–he called his answering service; no messages, and started on his mail, slitting open the envelopes with his wooden West African paper knife. Pity the fireplace had been boarded up. The amount of junk mail he trashed would create a fair amount of heat even if it did add to the greenhouse effect.

He had yet another chance to win, £5000. A very friendly letter from the competitions organiser to a most valued customer informed him how favoured he was. He had already come through the first two stages of the draw and, in a separate folder, he would find his six lucky numbers which he should return for the third and final stage, preferably in the YES envelope (no stamp required) ordering the current offer, *Favourite Hits of The Forties* on long play or cassette. And, if he replied within seven days, there was the chance of a bonus and a mystery gift. He found a smaller envelope and discovered he could win a Peugeot, a Volvo, or a BMW (so much for the British car industry) if the toy number plate included in the package matched that of one of the cars. Naturally he hit the jackpot with the most expensive, the BMW.

The question then arose, remembering Holly's complaint, could he afford to insure it? Could he afford to run it? Well, he could always take the cash in lieu of. Let's face it; there weren't too many people around who could afford to sniff at the chance of a four figure windfall though he could do without the favourite hits of the forties. He looked to see what the alternative was. *Best Loved Classics*. He could do without those as well. It would be the usual pot pourri of *Eine Kleine Nachtmusik, The Four Seasons, Elvira Madigan Theme*, as it had come to be known. Mozart would turn in his grave. *Overture to William Tell* of course, a couple of pieces by Strauss - Johann, not Richard – the Pachelbel *Canon* and naturally *The 1812*, complete with cannon effects. He threw it all in the wastepaper basket, all except his six potentially winning numbers which he put in the NO envelope (stamp required and no mystery gift). £5000 was £5000 and, although it never happened to him or anyone he knew, it was like the pools or Premium Bonds, someone had to win, though usually the wrong person in his opinion. At least that was the way he looked at it and, in his financial state, what was a measly stamp anyway?

The kettle boiled. He got up, made his coffee, and returned to the desk to see what else was there, apart from the bills that, in a

Micawberish gesture, he set to one side. He wondered if his bank manager might be in a good mood and would consider raising his limit. Maybe not. With all the mega-bankruptcies and bad debt around this was no time to be asking favours. Leave it till next week. Who knows what may turn up? Maybe by the time the bailiffs came hammering on his door he'd be dead anyway. Thornton dreaded any contact with his bank manager in the same way Holly dreaded the thought of anyone messing around with her eyes. He lifted the phone and dialled her number. Slitting open another envelope while he waited for her to answer, he extracted the contents, a consumer guide. The ringing stopped.

'Yes?' It sounded like a yap. Holly was always curt on the telephone. She hated them. Couldn't understand why people would want to talk for hours on end.

'This is your friendly security service,' Thornton greeted her, 'Just checking.'

'I'm fine thank you, Thornton, and no I have not been to the hospital, Thornton, and no I am not going to the hospital, Thornton, and I am in the middle of cleaning up after the tornado that struck my kitchen a few hours back, Thornton, so thank you for your solicitous enquiry and, if you haven't got any answers yet, good-bye.' She put down the phone. He did likewise and turned to his new consumer's guide. He hadn't quite reached the limit on his credit card and, despite recession and heavy interest charges, he'd long since given up any serious attempt to pay off the outstanding balance. He flicked open the guide. Ah, this looked promising, a multi-lingual talking translator, five languages at his fingertips. He wondered if it would be tax deductible. He might need it for all those jobs he was destined to do in the countries of the Common Market: France, Spain, Italy, Germany. But then, knowing his luck, the first language required of him would be Turkish and Turkish was not included. He passed over the pages of collections on cassette at knock-down prices for the reason already stated, decided he had no need for an electronic dictionary, hair remover, manicure set, or a skin toning system at a mere £125 including creams, but a horoscope computer might prove useful. Perhaps he could compute the birth dates of the dead six, Holly, and himself, and come up with a few answers from the stars. The consumer guide followed the YES envelope into the wastepaper basket. He took up his copy of *Yellow Pages*. Cosmetics... Fenella... Fenella... Fenella... No such company naturally, not in *Yellow Pages*, not in the telephone directory, not in the companies register.

Maybe the princess would know something. He rummaged through a drawer in his desk and came out with a three year old personal telephone book, looked her up and dialled, sipping his coffee while he waited. The phone was answered.

'Chinique,' a sultry voice whispered in Thornton's ear. Thornton brightened perceptibly at the dulcet tones, redolent with sexual overtones. For some reason he had a vision of a saronged beauty lying on golden sands beneath whispering palms. It was a ridiculous image brought about by a Hollywood vision of the South Seas.

'Good-morning,' he chirruped, 'May I talk to the princess please?'

'Of course you may, sir. Might I enquire who is calling?'

The saronged beauty, golden sands, palms and all disappeared. This just had to be a pert little blonde with legs stopped only by the buffers of her butt, and the rosiest of rosebud mouths. Thornton sucked in his breath at the thought. It was just as well he wasn't on vision phone; she might not have lived up to his fantasy.

'Of course you might,' he crooned right back, 'Thornton King.'

'If you'll just hold the line one moment, Mr King, I'll see if she's available.'

Thornton took another sip of coffee before the princess came on the line.

'Thornton, dear boy!' She gushed in her unmistakable accent, 'How nice to hear from you. What a pleasant surprise. Have you news?'

'News?' He frowned. 'News of what?'

'That dreadful business at François.'

'Oh, that! No, no news.'

'Then to what do I owe the pleasure of this call, dear boy? Oh, of course! You received my invitation. Now don't tell me you are being naughty and saying you cannot come.'

'Invitation? What invitation?' He started a quick search through the rest of the mail.

'To my show of course. Oh, don't say it has not arrived. It was mailed express, Thornton.'

'That means it takes twice as long. Ah, what's this?' He had found a plain envelope nestling among the bills and turned it over in his hand. 'Yes, I think I have it.' The envelope was quite large and stiff. 'It's not a bomb, is it?'

'Bomb? Why on earth should it be a bomb? What makes you say a thing like that?' She sounded quite put out.

'It was a joke, Princess, a joke. I just thought you might not have got out of your old Bolshevik habits.'

'Thornton, you know very well I was never a Bolshevik and I am not in the habit of sending bombs to my favourite people, of whom you are one. You could go to gaol for making jokes like that. Now be a good boy and don't disappoint me. You come to my show and enjoy it. Goodbye, Thornton.'

'Hold on hold on!' Thornton almost shouted into the mouth-piece. 'I haven't talked to you yet.'

'There was something else? Be brief, Thornton. I am particularly busy at the moment.'

'I'll be brief. Do you know, or have you heard, of a cosmetics company by the name of Fenella?'

There was a rippling laugh at the other end of the phone. Thornton thought it sounded more like Titania in the woods than Tatiana in her office.

'Called what?' The laughter continued.

'Fenella. Fenella.'

'Thornton, this must surely be another joke. No reputable company producing fine cosmetics would have such a name. I mean, how does it sound next to Channel, Fabergé, Givenchy, Dior, Chinique? Are you sure you're not thinking of lingerie? It sounds more like lingerie.'

'So you've never heard of them.' He doodled on his novelty memo pad that showed the drawing of a couple copulating and carried the message, "Important Things To Do Today." The rippling laugh echoed over the phone. 'I take it that means negative.'

'Why do you want to know, Thornton?'

'It's not important.'

'Aha! Don't tell me it is not important. You wouldn't be asking me this question if it were not important.'

'It really isn't important, Princess. I had a girl in here today applying for a secretarial job, that's all, who said she had worked for them. But, as I don't intend to employ her anyway, it really doesn't matter.'

'Then why ask?' She was like a terrier with a bone. For some reason Thornton was doodling a skull and crossbones on his pad.

'Curiosity. And please, no remarks about cats.'

'Thornton, Fenella is probably a transvestite who sells cheap scent off a barrow in Whitechapel Market.' And, with a really ripping laugh that forced Thornton to hastily distance the receiver from his ear, she hung up.

As he dropped the phone he found himself grinning over

the mental picture of Fenella the fella behind her barrow in the Whitechapel Market. Why was it always tall bony guys with big hands, feet, and prominent chins of blue who went in for cross-dressing and looked like so many caricatures? Come to think of it, it might not be such a bad idea. Maybe that's what he really ought to be doing. Not the cross-dressing bit but the selling. He could flog off a few cases of Chinique that just happened to fall off the back of a lorry and make some real dosh. It would be a damn sight better than sitting in this dreary hole, submerged in debt and trying to gain the interest of an unmindful and uncaring world. How come some people seemed to have all the luck? One of the singular drawbacks of having been part of a secretive organisation, living a portion of your life in the shadows, quasi-incognito as it were, when you came out into the light or, as in Thornton's case, were pushed out with what amounted to a copper handshake and a "Well, good luck, old chap," hardly anyone except a few who were a part of your shadowy world had any way of assessing your value. Maybe he should have taken a crash course in marketing techniques before trying to set up in business and not simply relied on the network that, in his case, seemed to have totally broken down.

He pushed himself out of his old swivel chair and strolled over to the window to look down into the narrow street. In his small forecourt across the way, Harold Norris was lovingly, gently, stroking the bonnet of one of his cars, a Ford station wagon with panels painted to resemble wood, as he talked to a prospective buyer. Thornton could imagine the patter. Lovely little runner, Harold would be saying in that gravelly voice of his, full road licence, immaculate condition, low mileage, one lady owner, only used it for shopping and taking the kids to school. Low cost finance could be arranged, easy monthly payments. And, yes, he would take part exchange, depending on the car of course.

Certain models no call for, only good for spares.

Harold Norris looked for all the world as if he were auditioning for a bit part as a World War II spiv in an ancient Ealing comedy. Maybe he'd got stuck in a time warp. Perhaps it was the black market that got Harold started and nostalgia for the good old days kept him sartorially fixed in the forties. It wasn't so much the suit. Although a little heavy on the stripes and lapels it was beautifully cut and tailored. Not Saville Row. Probably one of Harry's East End pals or, maybe, Shepherds Bush. Of course it could have been that he'd had the suit since World War II. Harry was as skinny as a beanpole, always had been, always would be and, with advancing years, really had no need for new clothes to accommodate an advancing girth. No, it was the ridiculous pencil-line moustache and the slicked down hair that really did it. Thornton wouldn't be surprised if Harry still had a goodly supply of wartime Brylcream stashed away somewhere. He just knew he could never bring himself to buy a second hand car from Harold Norris despite the good deal constantly on offer. He watched as salesman and customer headed for the office obviously to complete the paperwork, Harry striding out confidently in his suede shoes, the customer diffident, glancing back a couple of times at his intended purchase, maybe with a feeling of pride over his acquisition, maybe a slight angst at the thought that he might not be doing the right thing and should he get the AA to check it out first?

Was this all life amounted to? Was this the one and only great purpose, what it was ultimately all about? Buying and selling, wheeling and dealing, the world nothing more than one great marketplace and survival in the market place the sole object of existence? Some revelation! It all started in infancy of course, the exchange of nice poo-poos and a spot of peace and quiet for a little love and the nipple, and it carried right on from there. You bartered with your strengths and your weaknesses. You played on the strengths and weaknesses of others. You got the best price you could for your muscle and expertise, your talent, imagination, knowledge, ability, sex. It wasn't for nothing that some nations describe ejaculation not as cumming but as spending. You traded on ambition, hope, cupidity, you battened on people's needs, real or imaginary; their pain, their fears, real or imaginary. If you had nothing concrete to sell you sold ideas. You traded in myth and magic all nicely packaged and bound up in dogma, ritual, mystery and despite some pretty bizarre and painful catches along the way like ritual mutilation, sepuku, martyrdom, people bought it. The only cheap plentiful commodity in never ending abundance in this vast marketplace was life itself. Whoever came up with the absurd notion that life is precious needed his head examined. Other commodities might sometimes be in short supply or simply nonexistent but human beings were fruitful and multiplied at an alarming rate. The feral inherit the earth until the fecund destroy it and when it finally goes out it won't be with a bang but whimpering and choking under an avalanche of shit. And if there is anything metaphysical to existence in all probability it still boils down to a matter of buying and selling like Faust striking his bargain with the devil.

Thornton turned away from the window and went back to his chair. It complained bitterly as it took his weight. It wasn't only the chair complaining. The night on Holly's couch had left him with a crick in the neck and what felt like a trapped nerve, not between his third and fourth rib but beneath his left shoulder blade. He rolled his shoulders to try and release it but all the manoeuvre succeeded in producing was a spasm of pain and another wince. He tried a long hard stretch but that didn't help either. It looked like a visit to the osteopath was going to be the order of the day. The relief of pain, that was the business to be in.

That's what the market boiled down to. Think of the profits of the drug companies, the manufacturers of homeopathic remedies, the distillers, the drug dealers, the inventors of contraptions like motorised massagers, inhalers, support pillows, sound wave gadgets, a thousand nostrums, elixirs, balms, palliatives, treatments to ease the thousand natural shocks that flesh is heir to. The Victorians had climbed on that bandwagon in a big way with their universal panaceas. There was that nurse from New England, Mrs. Winslow, with her soothing syrup. Now, if he could invent something like that, wouldn't he be sitting pretty? "Mrs. Winslow, an experienced nurse and female physician, presents to the attention of mothers her soothing syrup for children teething. Greatly facilitates softening the gums, will allay all pain and spasmodic action, and is sure to regulate the bowels. Never has it failed in a single instant to affect a cure when timely used. All are delighted and speak in terms of highest commendation of its magical effect and medical virtues. It not only relieves the child from pain but invigorates the stomach and bowels, corrects acidity, and gives tone and energy to the entire system. It will almost certainly relieve griping and wind colic and overcome convulsions which, if not speedily remedied, end in death."

Feeling a bit like death himself at that moment, Thornton decided he could do with a dose of Mrs Winslow's syrup despite the fact that, according to The Family Doctor of the time, it consisted of nothing more than cane sugar, oil of aniseed, water, and absolute alcohol. He wondered how many Victorian alcoholics had acquired a taste for the hard stuff through being weaned on Mrs Winslow's soothing syrup. It was his father who had told him all about this famous physic, and it was his grandfather who, having taken the stuff, told his father. A devotee of the Music Hall and a great admirer of the Lion Comique, George Leybourne, he would sing the chorus of one of Champagne Charlie's songs which Thornton's father sang to him in turn and which even now he still remembered.

'When baby's had his little bath, and mammy's wiped him dry, And powdered him with what I've seen my wife use on the sly, She gives him just a little dose, which sends him off to sleep, And thanks to Mrs Winslow's art, all night he'll quiet keep.'

Thornton smiled at this memory of his childhood but was brought out of his reverie by seeing the skull and crossbones on his pad. He leaned forward in his chair. It creaked alarmingly. So did his neck. At least his osteopath was male. Remembering Ninette he didn't feel he could trust his body to a female right at this moment, she might be inclined to snap his neck like a rabbit's. That particular procedure, neck cracking, always made him apprehensive anyway. Beneath the skull and crossbones he had now doodled the figure 8, the ballpoint going over and over the pattern. Could he be number eight? And if so, why?

He was really too nice a guy for anyone to want to make a serious attempt on his life. Wasn't he? The cold war was over, ancient history, the files were closed. A whole lot of people were still at each other's throats through ancient ethnic hatreds but democracy rules, ok! So all right, if nice wasn't exactly the word to describe him, how about average? The average man in the street didn't get himself killed unless by accident, a brutal mugging, or a double decker bus, something like that. Now he had scribbled the word Fenella with a great deal of embellishment around the F. So who was it who was buying Ninette's expertise? Or that of the girl in the restaurant? Presuming she was the agent who brought about Shoggi's sudden demise. And why this seemingly absurd mix of killings which, on the face of it, seemed to have no connection? Except that all the victims were male... wrong again, one intended victim was female, and all the assassins female. All? Surely that was jumping to a too hasty conclusion. How many constituted all? Two? Three? Six? The female theory was only surmise. Certainly it must be said that none of the dead could be described as average, or particularly nice. Thornton had to admit that he wasn't deeply grieved at the loss of any of them. Probably not many other people were either despite their fame, wealth, or eminence. A scientist who conducted experiments on animals could have been the target of animal rights campaigners. That was a distinct possibility. Beagles are much more appealing than crusty old scientists. A fat cat diplomat from a country ruled by a ruthless corrupt gang of thugs with Swiss bank accounts swollen by the guilt-ridden handouts of the ex-colonialists might have been the victim of equally ruthless lean cats eager for their share of the booty. Though they might have missed the boat as, hopefully, the ex-colonialists seemed to be wising up at last. The admiral, the ultra-jingoist, no candidate for sainthood there with his membership of the hang 'em, flog 'em, castrate 'em brigade. Gay Rights? They weren't known for resorting to that sort of violence no matter how hardly done by. The IRA? The admiral had never been in any way connected with Ireland or the six counties. Not that that necessarily made a difference. It wouldn't be the first or the last time the IRA had blundered, or quite deliberately and coldly disposed of someone on the basis of some cruel flawed logic terrorists make all their own. On the other hand maybe the lady wife had finally cottoned on to the admiral's peccadilloes and decided to do him in herself.

Cord Wainer, an egotistical pain in the arse with the personality of a retarded randy adolescent, who would want to risk a life sentence for him? With the passing years he would have naturally faded away with his fading looks. His lack of talent didn't give him the sustaining power of a long distance runner, though it was always possible he could, for nostalgia's sake, have been cast in something as dreadful as one of those hospital soaps. Or was it a crime passionel? Maybe some crazy, starstruck, love-hungry fan finally going over the top.

Shoggi, dealer in death, happy so long as people were killing each other and anyone who happened to get in the way and who were paying him handsomely for the means with which to do it, someone who definitely didn't believe in the life is precious theory and, there you are, maybe in the end paid for it with his own.

And last, but not least, the supposed dealer in diamonds but, in fact, another agent of death, a modern shaman peddling dreams that turned into nightmares, for whom the accumulation of vast wealth, no matter how obscene the means, was his sole never to be satisfied obsession. How many Rolex watches does one person need? But, as to his killer, as with all the recently deceased, the identity was anybody's guess, as were the motives.

Thornton took a deep breath and blew out with such force it set his lips vibrating like a shying horse so that they tickled and he had to scratch them with his teeth, first the bottom, then the top. He picked up his paper knife in one hand, the plain white envelope in the other, and was on the point of inserting the knife beneath the flap when he suddenly froze.

'Oh, my God!' He whispered. Strange how in moments of crisis, or assumed crisis, or impending crisis, one automatically invokes a deity one doesn't believe in. It had only been a joke but many a true word as the old saying has it. His heart was thumping against his ribs. Every hair on his body seemed on end making his skin feel like it wanted to crawl across the floor. The envelope felt much thicker than it did when he first picked it up so casually. It felt like padding. He put down the knife, put down the envelope, very slowly, and stared at it lying on his desk just beneath the skull and crossbones and the figure 8. He realised he was breathing hard through the mouth and forced himself to relax. Suspicion was one thing, fact another. Surely he was just imagining things. Should he dial 999? A right idiot he would look. What did she say it was? An invitation to some kind of show. Gently he picked up the envelope again, trying desperately to control his trembling fingers. He held it up to the light but nothing could be seen. Slowly he got to his feet. His legs were as wobbly as those of a newborn foal.

It wasn't as though he hadn't been in dicey situations before. As Mr Miller might have said, they came with the territory, and the first territory in which he had experienced just such a situation was Zimbabwe, or Southern Rhodesia as it was then. He was driving out to dine at a friend's tobacco plantation close to the Mozambique border when one of 'our boys in the bush' sent a sniper's bullet whistling passed his windscreen. Thornton was only a kid at the time but, in the face of extreme danger, he behaved impeccably in the truest John Wayne tradition. The track was steep and pitted with deep ruts and in the dark he had been going very slowly which was fortunate because he nearly ran off the road and into a tree. He felt perfectly calm and, thinking that to move on would invite another shot, he took up the pistol that lay on the seat beside him and waited to see what would happen next. Nothing happened. He must have sat there for fifteen, twenty minutes perhaps. The lone gunman obviously thought that either he had put paid to his quarry or, if he hadn't, he wasn't going to get any closer to find out and, in fact, must have slipped away into the bush. Thornton decided it was time to move on.

It wasn't until two hours later, sitting down to dinner, that the shock hit him. He had taken a leisurely bath, dressed, joined the party in the drawing room for a very dry sherry and chat, mostly about the situation, the old country, how civilisation was crumbling and the world generally going to the dogs, and was everyone aware the Thompson's had had another little girl? They called her Hope. The drawing room, with the curtains drawn so that one did not see the floodlights and the barbed wire, might have been somewhere in the home counties and the underlying tension could have been domestic rather than that of living in a siege situation. A boy in white uniform and sporting a scarlet sash informed the assembly that dinner was ready and everyone put down their glasses and trooped into the dining room, all warm wood, fine china, and glittering crystal. The heavy shutters kept out the menace of the night. Thornton took his seat and lowered his head to hear grace, studying his fellow guests all the while, cool as a cucumber. "For what we are about to receive," having been said, he spread his starched napkin across his lap and lifted his spoon to take his first sip of consommé, wondering if he could avoid the half-submerged lightly poached egg without giving offence and, if he couldn't, whether he would be sick. As it was the question never arose because it was at that moment that he lost it. The spoon fell from his nerveless fingers to hit the bowl with a splash, spattering the damask tablecloth and his immediate neighbours with soup and yolk of egg, and he sat there, a trembling, teeth chattering wreck. The local police captain who, with his hen like wife, all brown in antique lace and amber beads, happened to be among the guests, looked up from his own suspended spoon and calmly remarked, 'You've been shot at.' Thornton was in too much shock to answer.

And here he was again, now a seasoned pro, almost in the same condition, and all because of his vivid imagination. He put up a hand to rub his head and almost yelled out loud as his fingers hit his stitches and his neck went into spasm. He walked slowly over to the filing cabinet and switched on the kettle again, not for coffee this time, but to carefully steam open the envelope. It seemed it would take some time to come unstuck until Thornton cottoned on to the bright idea of keeping his thumb on the kettle's automatic cut-off.

Gradually the flap curled back until it was free but not before he had added a scalded thumb to his list of injuries. He blew on it, which only seemed to make matters worse but, as he didn't fancy walking all the way down to the toilet to run cold water on it, he went back to his desk and with the envelope face down he inserted the tip of his paperknife and carefully investigated the contents. Deciding there was nothing suspicious, he eventually eased out the princess's invitation. It was no wonder the envelope felt padded. The invitation to *A Presentation of Fashion at The Princess Spitskaya School of Modelling* was in the form of a full-scale poster in swirling psychedelic colours the production of which must have cost a small fortune. The princess was obviously not short of a bob or two, something Thornton had long been aware of without really giving it much thought. So now the old girl had opened a school of modelling. Were funds beginning to run a bit low? Had the recession affected her business? Or was it merely a way of keeping herself occupied in those tedious moments between toy boys, now that her double-dealing, double-crossing days had been brought to an end? Maybe the toy boys were the reasons for funds running low. Toy boys, like their opposite numbers, could come expensive.

A smallish, elegant, gilt-edged invitation card was lightly gummed to the poster. Having kowtowed to the trendy, this was more in Tatty's style, being embossed with what Thornton presumed to be the Spitskaya coat of arms and the double headed imperial eagle. She could never forget her Russian origins and never wanted the world to forget either, especially her family's links with the Romanov dynasty no matter how tenuous these had been and Thornton guessed they were pretty tenuous.

With the defeat of the Whites the family had managed to flee what was once Holy Mother Russia and join their fellow émigrés in Paris though, thanks to a couple of Fabergé pieces they managed to smuggle out with their precious lives, they never had to resort to driving taxis or acting as doormen at restaurants. In fact they carried on much as before except in a different locale and the young Olga Tatiana Katarina, an avowed beauty from whose slipper any man would want to drink champagne, grew up wild and wilful in a Europe about to be plunged into turmoil where she could flirt not only with royalty in exile, preferably with coffers not too badly dented, international financiers, wealthy manufacturers and members of governments. Blessed with a shrewd intelligence, a streak of ruthlessness and a remarkably retentive memory, she collected, along with a constant supply of handsome presents, a constant stream of information, which was to prove extremely valuable both to her and those to whom it was for sale. Maybe she wasn't included in the list of grand horizontals but Olga was an expensive lady to know, perhaps not quite as expensive as those particular ladies of La Belle Époque but twice as dangerous. Not counting the casualties of war, both hot and cold, whose fate she sealed, at least two husbands had been thrown to the wolves and one princeling who, having bankrupted himself on her behalf only to find her in the arms of another, tried, like Brahms throwing himself into the Rhine, to emulate the great composer by throwing himself into the nearest river which happened to be the Seine. Like Brahms he was fished out but unlike Brahms who was committed to an asylum, he suffered little more than a chill from which he quickly recovered. It was a silly thing to do. Had he really wanted to kill himself he should have jumped off the Eiffel Tower. No one catches you half way down.

However, he got his wish a few months later when, fleeing to Monte Carlo where he hoped to recoup his losses and mend his broken heart, he ended up blowing his brains out with a borrowed revolver. Well borrowed isn't exactly the right word. You can't return something once you're dead and the unfortunate owner of the weapon, unaware of its disappearance, was arrested and indicted for murder. He turned out to be none other than the princeling's erstwhile rival. Such was the fate of those whose paths crossed that of the princess. Thornton wondered whether she would think of taking a sentimental journey to the imperial city of St. Petersburg. Somehow he didn't think so. Conditions in the changing Russia were likely to be rough for some time and living rough was not the princess's style.

Deciding the poster would brighten up his dull surroundings, he found a pack of blue tack in a drawer and positioned it over the fireplace, nodded his approval and went back to his desk where he could admire it from a distance. It was hardly a Chagall but it was bright and decorative. He lifted the telephone and dialled Holly's number. He was on the point of giving up when the receiver was lifted at the other end.

'Yes?' She snapped.

'How would you like to go to a fashion show?' He asked.

'I haven't a thing to wear,' she said.

Chapter Seven

For a girl who hadn't a thing to wear she looked ravishing in a wide-lapelled, waist-hugging woollen suit of honey-gold with velour fedora to match, a silk scarf in russet and the band of the fedora in the same colour. A cashmere poncho kept the autumn chill at bay. Thornton gave the outfit an appreciative once-over and Holly knew exactly what he was thinking.

'It was a birthday present,' she said, not meaning to sound defensive, 'from daddy. At least the cheque was from daddy. The choice was mine.'

'Nice daddy,' Thornton said, 'nice choice.'

He hailed a passing cab that drew up at the kerb, opened the door for Holly and, having informed the driver of their destination, climbed in after her, as requested sitting well back in his seat for comfort and safety.

'Where exactly are we going?' Holly asked.

Thornton reached inside his breast pocket, withdrew the invitation card, and handed it to her. Holly read it out loud.

'"Mr. Thornton King... The Princess Spitskaya requests the pleasure of your company at a presentation of fashion."' She gave him a sideways look as she returned the card. 'Very nice, Mr. Thornton King, but it makes no mention of me.'

'Of course it does,' he corrected her, 'you're my guest. One never visits the zoo on one's own. Not half the fun.'

'Isn't it a bit strange,' Holly ventured, 'getting two invitations from the princess so close together?'

'Coincidence.' Thornton shrugged. 'I don't think she was instrumental in getting me invited to the *Grise*. She just made that up on the spur of the moment, but seeing me there put her in mind to invite me to this, that's all.' He glanced again at the card. 'With a polite request not to be late which, judging by the traffic, is exactly what we're going to be. And I tell you this, Miss Day, if any of those models are half as beautiful as you I will buy you the entire collection from *The House of Schnoof*.'

'Schnoof?'

Thornton took another look at the card. 'Schnief.'

'Well thank you for the compliment, Mr King, but I won't hold you to it.' Holly laughed.

'And why not?'

'Because it's the Judgment of Paris again, my dear. You have to proclaim me belle of the ball or earn my undying enmity. And, should you crown me queen of the bimbos, you couldn't afford to buy me a single accessory from *The House of Schnief*, let alone a whole Spring collection. You, after all, do not have a rich daddy who occasionally beefs up your exchequer; unless you've been leading a secret life we know not of.'

'No ready repartee about to spring to my lips all I can do is deny that insinuation most emphatically. Pink was never my colour, politically or sexually.' Thornton gave her a supercilious look as though she could even think such a thing.

'There are ladies who pay for favours, or didn't you know that? It is the age of equality after all.'

'Oh, come off it, Holly, look at me! Would anyone pay me for services rendered?'

'It takes all kinds,' Holly said, 'and some people have very peculiar tastes.'

'Thank you. I don't think I'm all that unattractive.'

'Getting a bit long in the tooth maybe, a beamish boy no

longer, but some girls do go for the older man...'

'Only if they're father-fixated and then usually if the daddy they're fixated on is rich, preferably mega-rich but don't imagine I can't still pull the birds if I want to.'

'You're tying yourself in knots, Thornton.' She took his hand and twined her fingers in his. 'And I'm only teasing. You are actually a very attractive man.'

'Is that so? Just think how well I would have done in Corsica then.'

'Corsica?' Holly opened her eyes very wide. 'You see yourself as a latter-day Napoleon do you?'

'Don't be silly. He left Corsica. Ah, the Mediterranean. I'm such a romantic at heart.'

'You and Barbara Cartland both. You think the Mediterranean is one big erogenous zone do you? Romance and sex aren't necessarily the same thing you know.'

'Maybe not, but think what the former has done for Barbara Cartland and what the latter has done for the handsome young lads of Corsica.'

'What? Not that I can't guess but, as it looks as though we're going to be stuck in traffic for a thousand and one nights, be my Sheherazade and entertain me.'

'Well, it was like this...'

'Is this a "once upon a time" story?'

'Well I don't know if it still goes on, do I? May I continue?'

Holly squeezed his fingers and nodded.

'News got around amongst the blue-rinse widows of Miami that there were some pretty hot young studs in Corsica who were game for anything, and news got around the Corsicans that there were some pretty rich pickings to be made from the blue-rinse ladies of Miami. We're back in the old market-place again aren't we?'

'What market-place?'

'Skip it. Anyway, as usual in such a situation, an entrepreneur was bound to appear, right? In this case a wily old jeweller who persuaded the lads to take presents in lieu of cash in exchange for their favours. So the blue-rinse ladies were wheeled along to the jeweller's shop, a very expensive one needless to say, where the lads received handsome presents which they promised to wear or keep for ever but, before the ladies' planes had even taxied to the runway, they'd hotfoot it back to the jeweller's and sell him back their presents, minus discount of course. Then they set out to repeat the process. So there you are, a good time was had by all. The old girls went home happy. The boys were happy. The jeweller was happy. One lad was given the same gold bracelet so many times he saved up enough to buy himself a farm and then, when he got married to a local girl, the jeweller gave him the bracelet as a wedding gift. It was like winning a trophy so many times you eventually get to keep it. A neat little racket, huh?'

'Pretty good,' Holly agreed. 'But I don't believe that last bit, about the wedding present.'

'All right, I admit I made that up. But, like I said, I'm a romantic at heart and there's nothing I enjoy more than a happy ending.'

'You and Barbara Cartland both. But you can give up your story telling now, Thornton, it looks like we're on the move again.' And, indeed, the cab was nosing its way along Newgate Street towards Holborn Viaduct.

'That was the shortest one thousand and one nights in the annals of fiction,' Thornton huffed.

'And this is going to be the longest ride in the annals of London transport. This city is choking itself to death. And, speaking of death...'

'Who was?'

'...have you unravelled the mystery yet?'

'No. Have you?'

'No. Any leads?'

'No.' There was a long silence. 'And you?'

Holly stared out of the window.

'We make a great team,' Thornton said.

Half an hour later the cab pulled up outside the cream coloured portico of a large Regency house. Thornton was feeling decidedly irritable. Naturally they were late and Holly, on getting out of the cab, had stepped on a dog turd. A brass plaque on one of the columns at the head of a flight of steps assured them they were at the *Spitskaya School of Modelling* and the steady thump thump thump of ear-bending, mind-numbing rock pulsating from the interior reaffirmed their tardiness and that the show was already in progress.

Thornton paused on a step to study the plaque while Holly, leaning against the pillar with one hand, lifted her foot and tried to clean her patent leather shoe by means of a diminutive tissue.

'What I don't understand...' Thornton started to say before Holly interrupted.

'What I don't understand is why you're not offering to help a lady in distress. And, God, I hate the English and their bloody dogs!'

'What I don't understand,' Thornton repeated, his eyes still on the plaque and still ignoring Holly's predicament but then interrupting himself with, 'Why don't you take your shoe off, Holly? It would be much simpler.' He returned to his train of thought. 'What I don't understand is, why should Tatty start a crummy school of modelling ...?'

'Crummy? What kind of ancient public school expression is that?' Holly tossed the soiled tissue into the area and produced a second from her pocket. 'The butler can pick it up,' she defended herself, referring to the first as it fluttered downwards.

'Never went to a public school,' he protested. 'Nor Oxbridge for that matter. Manchester Grammar and Redbrick I'm afraid; degree in Political History. And what makes you think all models are bimbos? Some of them could be girls of the highest intelligence.'

A laughing couple, arms around each other's waists, waltzed past them and up the steps, stopping to stare at Holly bending over her crooked leg. She glowered back at them. 'Dogshit!' She barked. The couple moved on, the girl turning to look over her shoulder before they disappeared, giggling, inside.

'As I was saying, when she must be making a small fortune with Chinique anyway,' Thornton finally finished.

'What? What are you on about, Thornton?' Holly was in a very bad mood as she tried to get the tissue into the crease between the upper and the sole where the mess was firmly imbedded. 'You can say what you like about New York,' she growled, 'but at least they don't let their dogs foul the bloody pavement. They might mug and murder, plaster the place with graffiti and commit general mayhem but the sidewalks are clear of dogshit and that is something to be extremely proud of. Anyway, who says she's making a fortune?' She discarded the second tissue.

'She heads an established and flourishing company doesn't she?'

'Really? You've been privy to the company's books recently have you? We're in a recession, Thornton. How do you know they haven't got cash-flow problems? How do you know they aren't mortgaged up to the hilt? How do you know they aren't about to go bust? You attended the last board meeting did you? How do you know the head isn't about to roll?'

'All right all right all right, you've made your point.'

But Holly was on a roll of her own and not about to stop. 'How do you know there hasn't been, or there is about to be, a palace revolution? You don't know what the situation is within the company so don't talk through the top of your hat.'

'I'm not wearing a hat. I'm wearing five stitches.'

Thornton didn't enjoy being put down and this was meant to remind her she was talking to the man who, albeit inadvertently, had saved her life. For the nonce she was singularly unimpressed.

'It's an expression, Thornton. Now, are we going in? Or are we going to stand here chatting all afternoon?'

'You could be right,' Thornton sighed. 'Knowing Tatty, her fees per term for this circus would probably keep a first-born at Eton for the length of his school career.'

The place was packed and they had to content themselves with standing in the hall and trying to get a look-in through the double doors that opened into what was once a spacious drawing room where the action was taking place. Flashes were popping, fashion journalists were trying to scribble their notes, the jostling crowd who didn't have seats were pressed together shoulder to shoulder, lights pulsated to the music. A catwalk had been erected down the centre of the room with the girls making their entrances and exits from a ramp built at right angles and extending through another set of double doors leading to the back room. The chandeliers quivered and, as the girls strutted their stuff, hips swaying, pelvis thrust forward, knees knocking, faces blank, the catwalk parade reminded Thornton of a nature programme on stick insects in *National Geographic*. Whatever happened to the anti-diet movement?

'Why, Thornton, old boy! How are you?'

Thornton felt a clap on the sore shoulder hard enough to make him wince. He turned around to see, standing behind him, an employee of the department who hadn't been made redundant and who was no doubt feeling very smug about it. He could have wished for the sight of someone he considered more congenial so instead of returning the hail fellow well met greeting he merely said, 'Why are all those girls wearing suits made out of municipal plastic bin bags?'

'Search me, old boy,' his one time colleague shrugged, pulling his mouth down at the sides and cocking his head, a piece of body language that made him look like a rather perplexed poodle. 'Guess some people are just into bin liners; it takes all kinds.' And he smirked in the way Thornton remembered and had always hated.

'What have we missed?' He asked, and then, remembering his manners, 'Oh, you know Holly, don't you? Holly? Do you know Mike Aliff?'

'No,' Mike drooled before Holly could open her mouth, 'I haven't had the pleasure.' He extended a podgy hand that Holly reluctantly took. For her it was dislike at first sight. She just knew this was the kind of guy who carried pornography and condoms in his wallet and joked about willy warmers (giant ones) in his Christmas stocking. 'How do you do?' He gave her hand a little squeeze and the intonation in his voice, to say nothing of the leer that now made him look like a decidedly randy perplexed poodle, confirmed all her suspicions. She attempted to return the smile but it didn't work. All she did was give the impression that she had bitten into a rotten tomato and was about to throw up quite violently. Thornton, meanwhile, was surveying the comings and goings in, out, and around the hall and up and down the splendid staircase, as he wondered why Mike Aliff had never been considered a security risk. But then the department's record on security risks, going way back, hardly bore scrutiny anyway.

'Shouldn't we be watching the show?' Holly yelled in an effort to be heard above the music, which after a relatively quiet spell was belting forth mega decibels again. 'There might be questions afterwards.' She slipped out from between the two men and moved around to Thornton's other side to get away from the pushy presence of Mike Aliff. Pelvis pressure, as many a girl (or boy) in the underground in the rush hour could vouch for, could lead to attempted groin gropes and one couldn't be too careful in a crush except that, out here in the hall away from the main action, there wasn't exactly a crush and therefore no excuse for intimacy except innate horniness. Holly shuddered and pretended to be thoroughly absorbed in the cavorting on the catwalk.

'Who is this man, Schnief, anyway?' Thornton asked.

'What?' Holly shouted.

'What?' Shouted Mike in unison.

Thornton looked from one to the other and jerked his head to indicate they should move further away so that they could talk without the danger of a strangulated larynx or developing nodules on their vocal cords but Mike seemed reluctant to move. He was dribbling visibly over a girl wearing a harness that covered nipples and pudenda and little else.

'My God!' Thornton exclaimed to himself as no one else could hear him. 'Where is she supposed to wear THAT in the spring?' Then, taking in the thigh boots, 'Sherwood Forest maybe?' He grabbed Mike by the arm and pulled him away before the man could make an exhibition of himself. He was breathing much too hard and had that look on his face that only a sexual partner or a mirror should see. Quivering like a gun dog or a stallion that smells the mare, he was either about to hyperventilate or suffer premature ejaculation and his cigarette, when he lit it, trembled between his goldfish lips, the lighter shaking in his hand. Thornton looked at Holly. Holly looked at Thornton. Each raised an eyebrow. Mike took a long drag at his Benson and, as the nicotine buzz hit him, seemed to relax a little. 'Did you see that?' He squealed. It was a rhetorical question but he repeated it simply because he did not know what else to say. 'Did you SEE that?'

'It was about the only thing I didn't see.' Thornton said. 'Who is this Schnief anyway?'

'Oh, everybody's talking about him, old boy,' Mike said, taking another drag at his cigarette and rearranging his crotch.

'I'm not surprised,' Holly said.

'Definitely one of the up and coming...' Mike looked straight at Holly to make sure she got the double entendre, as though she could miss it... 'generation of budding designers.'

'Of budding perverts,' said Holly.

'The princess has taken a tremendous interest in him. That's why they arranged this show. Good publicity for both of them.'

'So...' Holly glowered at Mike... 'Does he design clothes for women? Or to indulge the sexual fantasies of sexual prigs like you?' She had meant to say 'pricks' decided to change it to 'pigs' and it came out as 'prigs', one of which Mike certainly wasn't.

'Now steady on, old girl...' Mike started but was cut short by a snarl.

'I am not an old girl!' Holly growled, looking and sounding exceedingly dangerous.

'... there's no need to come the old feminist claptrap with me.' Mike had gone a sort of purply colour. Thornton decided it was time to step in before blood was split.

'So you're a friend of this Schnief are you?' He said, laying a gentle but restraining hand on Holly's arm.

'Good grief, no!' Mike looked positively shocked. 'Not in a million years, old chap. Wouldn't be seen dead with him. The fellow's a raving woofter!'

Holly found herself immediately warming to Mr Schnief. He was probably very sweet despite his bizarre designs no normal person would consent to wear even in private. But then, in her opinion, most practitioners of modern so-called art, in all its disciplines, were a bunch of no-talent charlatans anyway, conning the gullible pseuds and getting away with it to the tune of an obscene amount of money.

'So you're pally with the princess then?' Thornton went on with his questioning.

'No, not really,' was the reply. 'Know her casually but wouldn't actually call myself a friend.'

'You do have friends I suppose.' The contempt in Holly's voice couldn't be disguised.

'So why are you here?' Thornton asked hurriedly. 'Just along for the ride?'

'No, actually I came to see Ninette.' He was looking around for somewhere to stub out his cigarette so didn't notice the startled reaction.

'Ninette!' The exclamation came from both of them.

'Tall, green eyes, red hair?' Holly asked.

'Tall, blue eyes, and a fantastically beautiful brunette,' Mike replied. 'Excuse me.' There being no ashtray in sight he headed for the front door to flick his stub out and onto the pavement.

'Could have been a wig,' Thornton ventured.

'Could have been tinted lenses,' was Holly's added guess.

'Maybe we ought to get back in there and watch the rest of the show.'

But, before they could move, Mike was back.

'So where is she then?' Thornton asked. 'This fantastically beautiful brunette.'

'That's what I don't understand,' Mike replied. 'I thought she was supposed to be modelling today and...'

'She told me she wanted to be a model,' Holly hissed.

'... there's been no sign of her. Still, no shortage of scenery to admire, old chap, hey? So shall we mosey back in and enjoy, hmn?' He rubbed his hands together and once again there was that suggestive smirk.

They moved back to the door just as there were hoots, yells, whistles, cheers, stamping of feet and a great deal of applause from an obviously excited audience. The show was over. With fixed smiles on their faces the girls stood on the catwalk. With them was the slenderest of porcelain young men in the soberest of pinstripe suits and collarless shirt buttoned up to the neck. Unsmiling, he stood there, the pale slim fingers of one hand enfolded in the larger, bonier, bejewelled ones of the Princess Olga who, gazing at him adoringly, raised her free hand in an imperious gesture and the applause died away. She turned from her protégé to survey the assembly.

'Ladies and gentlemen,' she beamed, 'thank you so much for being here at this parade of fashion from the *House of Schnief*. May I say how proud and honoured we are that Monsieur Schnief so graciously granted us the privilege of giving you this preview of his spring and summer collection. I am sure you were both amazed and delighted by his original and imaginative creations: so artistic, so unique.'

The applause broke out again and Monsieur Schnief took a diffident bow. He was wishing the princess wouldn't squeeze his fingers quite so hard.

'For those of you who can stay a while longer,' she continued, 'refreshments will now be served in the room directly above.'

There was a concerted rush for the door and, not quick enough to avoid the human tide, Holly, Thornton, and Mike were swept up the stairs.

The waiters, in red boots, baggy trousers, and peasant blouses looked as though they had been recruited from a visiting dance ensemble.

'I hope they're not going to burst into song,' Thornton remarked as he accepted two glasses of Leningrad champagne and handed one to Holly. 'Don't see any balalaikas.' He surveyed the room. 'Funny looking lot,' he said.

'The guests or the waiters?' Holly asked.

'Both.'

'Good afternoon, Thornton.'

He turned to see Princess Olga standing behind him. There was no sign of Schnief. He was probably in the bathroom soaking his bruised fingers.

'And Miss Day,' she trilled. 'How good of you to accept my invitation. Did you enjoy the show?'

'Amazing! Absolutely fabulous!' Thornton lied.

'Very nice,' was Holly's less enthusiastic but more honest comment. The princess eyed her coldly for a moment and then turned back to Thornton.

'What on earth have you done to your head, dear boy?' She stretched out a hand as though about to touch it but stopped before actually doing so.

'I didn't do anything to my head,' Thornton informed her. 'Someone did it for me.'

'Oh! Really?' A note almost of teasing crept into her voice. 'This wouldn't have anything to do with that mythical cosmetics company you were enquiring about, would it? What was its name?'

'On the ball as always, aren't you, Princess?' He raised his glass.

'Not always, Thornton,' she smiled sweetly, 'not always. I am certainly not on the ball right at this moment because I should be circulating. There are some extremely influential and interesting people here I should be... what's the expression?'

'Buttering up?'

'If you say so. But don't leave, dear boy. I am sure there are some influential and interesting people here for you to meet as well. Circulate, Thornton, circulate. Who knows? You might make some important contacts for business. Word has it you're not doing too well at the moment.' And, with that, she swept into the crowd that respectfully parted for her like the Red Sea for Moses.

'She's a bitch,' Holly said.

'I don't know why we use that expression.' Thornton intercepted a passing waiter holding a tray of savouries, made his selection and with his teeth eased a cocktail sausage from its stick. 'It's an insult to bitches. I know some very nice bitches, much nicer than humans.' He stretched out a hand and placed it on another passing waiter's arm. The theatrical character paused and Thornton took caviar and cracker in exchange for his cocktail stick which he left on the silver salver. The waiter raised a disapproving eyebrow and, with a slightly curled lip of disdain, moved on.

'Now that...' Thornton said, 'is what you could call a bitch.'

But Holly didn't hear, she was staring over his shoulder. 'Thornton, don't look now but she's here.'

'Ninette?' he said with a mouth full of cracker and caviar.

'No, the other one, the one from the restaurant.'

Thornton swallowed. 'Are you sure?'

'I didn't follow her half way across London and not get a good look at her.'

'Who's she with?'

'Some of the other girls. They've just come in in a bunch. She must have been on the catwalk and we didn't see her.'

'Unless she was kept off the catwalk for obvious reasons. But then why reveal her now? Or maybe she's staff. Or maybe she's a guest, or a friend of one of the girls. Whatever, there's only one way to find out who she is and that's to ask so why don't we, in the words of the unmentionable, "mosey over there" and engage in conversation?' But, before they could move any further than the trestle table makeshift bar, a hand gripped his arm.

'Ah, there you are, old lad. Been looking for you.' Mike held his glass out to one of the barmen. 'Fill it up will you? White.'

'Speak of the devil,' Thornton said, 'and just why were you looking for us when we were about to go looking for you?' He reached out to a passing tray and eased another sausage from its stick. He was quite partial to baby wieners. There wasn't any caviar in sight and he didn't fancy bacon, cheese, and pineapple chunks.

'Well, to speak the truth, old son, don't you find all these trendies just a little bit boring? They don't find each other boring of course because they're all puffed up with their own damned conceit.' He received his refilled glass from the barman without giving the man so much as a glance.

'Maybe you're a little out of your depth,' Holly suggested as she and the barman exchanged sympathetic looks. Thornton cleared his throat. Holly turned from the barman to look at him.

'Bit went down the wrong way,' Thornton said.

But the ruse didn't work. Mike was not to be sidetracked. He turned to Holly. 'Darling, paddling in shallows is hardly out of anyone's depth. I've been to more get-togethers than you've had hot dinners, too much cheap sherry, too much cheap talk.' He took a hearty swig of his wine and looked disapprovingly at the glass. 'And I would have thought the princess would have come up with a better plonk than this. What is it? Chateau Loo?'

Thornton stepped in hastily before Holly could open her mouth. 'You're not in a very good mood, Mike, are you?' He observed. 'I thought you enjoyed the show. You certainly gave that impression.'

'Yes... well...' He drained his Chateau Loo and scowled. 'Fact is, old boy, I'm a bit put out I suppose, Ninette not being here. And none of the other girls seem to be in the mood to be chatted up.'

Holly choked on her drink.

'Careful,' Thornton chided gently, then turned back to Mike. 'As a matter of fact, old boy, talking about chatting up, I was just about to do that. There's a girl I'm rather interested in.'

'Really?' Mike seemed to suddenly come to life again, vicarious pleasure being better than no pleasure at all. 'But I thought...' He glanced at Holly.

'Oh, don't mind me,' she said, 'as the saying goes, we're just good friends.'

'Really?' He became even more interested and, after a quick leer at Holly, looked around the room. 'So which one is it?'

Thornton too surveyed the room and, spotting the girl, pointed her out. 'That one.' He said.

Mike craned his neck and finally found the group indicated but couldn't make out exactly where Thornton was pointing. 'What? The oriental one?'

'No, the one standing to her left.'

'Oh, yes. That's Anya. Nice girl. A little on the shy side but very nice.' His tone indicated that he had made a pass or two at Anya and got nowhere. Perhaps a tinge of jealousy crept in at this point with the thought that Thornton might succeed where he had failed and he quickly went on. 'Ah, but here is someone you really must meet, Thornton, old boy.' He extended his arm and waggled his fingers towards a girl standing close by talking to an elderly gentleman in a Harris tweed suit. At least that's what Thornton thought until the gentleman turned around to reveal himself to be a full breasted lady in a Harris tweed suit, obviously one with a penchant for young girls. She curled a sour lip and tossed her head as her young companion left her and smilingly approached the trio.

'Thornton, this is N'tombi.' Mike put his arm around the girl's slender waist and gently pushed her towards Thornton. 'N'tombi, I'd like you to meet Thornton King.'

'How do you do, Mr King?' She extended her hand.

'Oh, no!' Mike enthused, 'not Mr King. Call him Thornton.'

'Yes, please do,' Thornton agreed as he took the proffered hand. 'And this is my friend, Holly.'

N'tombi turned her smile on Holly. 'Did you enjoy the show?'

She asked.

'Well, to be quite honest...' Holly started.

'I'm afraid we didn't really get to see much of it,' Thornton hurriedly finished. 'There was rather a crush and we were sort of stuck outside. Being late. London traffic. Couldn't do a damned thing about it. Pity.'

'Oh, that's too bad. I'm sure you would have enjoyed it.'

'Oh, we did enjoy the little we managed to see,' Thornton assured her. 'At least Mike here certainly did. Didn't you, Mike?'

But Mike wasn't rising to the bait. Hoping he had diverted the interest of his rival stag he pursued his own with Holly. Mike was not one to be that easily discouraged. 'I tell you what, Holly,' why don't you and I socialise a bit?' He suggested, 'and leave these two to chat, what? They're going to get along like a house on fire, I can tell.'

'I've got a much better idea,' Holly countered. 'Why don't you and I go and look for Ninette?'

'Ninette?' N'tombi sounded surprised. 'I'm afraid Ninette isn't here.'

'What do you mean, not here?' Mike looked even more surprised.

'Well, I don't know whether I should really tell you this but she's been sent home.' She looked at each of them in turn. 'You see, she wasn't up to it. Couldn't make the grade.'

'You mean she's been expelled?' Mike sounded highly indignant.

'Not expelled exactly.' N'tombi was looking decidedly uncomfortable. 'She just... well... sort of... flunked.'

'Flunked what exactly?' Holly persisted.

But N'tombi, glancing beyond the group, hastily but politely excused herself and moved away. Without excusing himself, Mike followed her, obviously to pursue the matter further, and the two of them stood in earnest conversation a short distance away.

'Pity I never learned to lip read,' Thornton said. 'I suggest we go and talk to Anya.' But, before they could move, the reason for N'tombi's sudden discomfiture was upon them.

'Well, Thornton,' the princess crooned, 'still not circulating? Must the mountain come to Mohammed? Is that man a friend of yours?' She was staring at Mike.

'No friend of mine,' Thornton answered quite truthfully. 'I thought he was a friend of yours.'

'Did you?' There was a hint of acid in her voice. 'Well, all my girls are quite capable of taking care of themselves and I don't suppose I can really be held responsible for their moral welfare. It would be an insult to chaperone them anyway, they're not children.' She stopped staring at the couple and turned to Holly. 'Miss Day I have to tell you, I am most gratified. Judging from the generous comments I have heard, and the shower of compliments paid to me personally, the show was a great success and my girls passed with flying colours. Is that the correct expression, Thornton? Now I have done all I can for them, their future is out of my hands.'

'How about taking on Holly as a student?' Thornton suggested half jokingly.

'Oh, I think not, Thornton.' Then, seeing Holly's reaction, 'for two very good reasons. Firstly, unless Miss Day's papa is in the multi-millionaire class or she herself earns a great deal of money, I doubt she could afford my fees.'

'No problem,' Holly said airily, surveying the room in the manner of one who could purchase the entire establishment and still be left with change.

'Oh!' For a moment the princess looked somewhat nonplussed but quickly pulled herself together. 'Secondly,' she said, 'we are at the end of term and, as for next term, I am fully booked. My girls, you may have noticed, are all from abroad. The school, I am happy to say, is internationally famous and it is not at all difficult to keep it absolutely exclusive.' The last word was positively exploded in Holly's direction. 'Once the girls have finished the course they return to their own countries ready to take up their new careers.'

'As models?'

'What else, Thornton? What else?' Princess Olga smiled benignly and then turned her smile on a gentleman bearing down on them. 'Ah... Colonel...' She indicated Thornton. 'You know each other I believe?'

'Indeed we do!' Thornton grinned and shook the other's hand vigorously. 'Ever since the colonel was a subaltern in my father's regiment. How very good to see you again, sir.' There was no doubting the genuine warmth of Thornton's greeting.

'Long time no see, Thornton, my boy,' the colonel huffed, obviously equally as pleased at the meeting. 'What've you been up to, hey? Hear you've been in the hush-hush department, is that right?'

'That's right. Past tense I'm afraid. With the warming of the globe's atmosphere I have been made redundant. So I've launched out on my own.'

'Stout fella, that's the spirit.' He placed an avuncular hand on Thornton's good shoulder and turned, beaming, to Princess Olga. 'Remember this lad as a wee kiddie, Olga. Stout little fella even then, regular tyke. His family were very good to me, treated me like one of their own. Remember those garden parties, Thornton? Remember the time...' But Thornton interrupted his reminiscence. 'Colonel, please allow me, this is Miss Holly Day. Holly? As you can gather, an old friend, Colonel Montcliff.'

'Delighted, my dear. Delighted.'

'Thank you, Colonel,' Holly returned the smile and retrieved her hand.

'As I was saying,' the colonel continued, 'we were all out on the lawn this one time, refreshments on the tables, quite a large party it was as I remember. And suddenly people started to laugh. Quietly at first you know, but then more joined in. Thornton's dad couldn't work out for the life of him what the joke was until he looked around the corner of a table and there was Thornton drinking from a bottle of pop, leaning nonchalantly against the table as he was drinking and letting it out at the same time. Standing there holding his little wee-wee and making room for more pop.' And the colonel burst into a peal of laughter that killed conversation in the room stone dead as every head turned in their direction.

'Yes, well...' Thornton murmured, flushing slightly and waiting for the room to return to normal, which it did almost immediately. 'And how is your charming wife, Colonel?' He asked.

'Dottier than ever I'm afraid.' Colonel Montcliff shrugged and smiled with obvious affection at the thought of his Margery. Then the smile faded. 'Poorly too, more's the pity. But why complain? Doesn't do any good and age advances on us all. That's the only enemy these days, Thornton.'

'You do have plenty of time for your golf though, Alex,' Tatty chipped in.

The smile returned. 'Indeed I do.'

'You should take Thornton on,' she suggested.

'Yes. What a splendid idea. Forgot you were a golfer, Thornton. What's your handicap now? Tell you what, how about tomorrow? Hey? The opposition's let me down and I'd resigned myself to spending the afternoon in the morning room with *The Times* crossword. That really makes me feel like a senior citizen.'

'I'm sure Thornton would be delighted,' Tatty gurgled. Thornton thought she sounded like his mother when, as a small boy, she tried to urge him to entertain guests while he silently wished he were anywhere but where he was. Maybe it was the colonel's story that had brought it to mind.

'Well...' he frowned, 'honestly, Colonel, I haven't played in such a long time my game must be as rusty as my clubs. I'll be a pushover. No fun for you at all.'

'Nonsense, dear boy, you'll soon get back into the swing of it.' The colonel chuckled. 'No pun intended, hey? What?'

Holly closed her eyes for one brief moment, getting the wrong idea. Were all men the same?

'Oh, come now, Thornton,' the princess urged, 'don't tell us you're that busy, and you were never one to back down from a challenge.'

'Is that what it is?' Said Thornton softly. 'Tomorrow then.'

'Wonderful! Wonderful!' The colonel took Thornton's hand again and shook it vigorously. 'Tee off after lunch. Meet you at the club, my boy, two-thirty suit you? Fine.' Then it was Holly's turn. He took her hand. 'Delighted to have met you, young lady,' and finally the princess. 'Thank you, Olga. A friend in need, what? Jolly good show you put up today. Yes, indeed. Must tell Madge all about it. Two thirty, Thornton, and what on earth have you done to your head? But, before Thornton could answer, the colonel was gone, followed by the princess.

Thornton turned to look at Holly. 'Care to caddy?' he asked.

Chapter Eight

'To quote the old cliché, Thornton, a penny for them. I'm tired of sitting here looking at trendy young things enjoying their cocktails while you sit there and brood. You haven't touched your drink and it was a very expensive drink. The colourful umbrella triples the price.'

'Yes,' he growled, not looking up from his glass, 'I hate rip-offs. What price the cherry do you think?'

Holly looked around the bar, its decor already faded and dated, only its prices keeping up with the times.

'I'm sorry.' He looked up and smiled. 'It's just that I'm trying to add up and nothing makes sense.'

'Neither does it make for very good company.'

Thornton lifted the little paper umbrella from his glass, twirled it between his fingers, stopped and pointed. 'See that? At the end of each of those spokes is a death. And all the spokes, as spokes do, go to the centre.' He touched each tip in turn. 'Scientist, admiral, diplomat, film star... you might just as well say tinker, tailor, soldier, sailor... Holly... Thornton.'

'Oh, come off it!' She scoffed. 'I don't see where you come into this. No one's tried to bump you off, except by accident, because you happened to get in the way.'

'Holly, do me a favour, will you?' He dropped the umbrella and picked up his glass. 'Call in sick tomorrow and come out to the golf course with me. I'll prove I'm right.'

'I hate golf! It's a ridiculous game.'

'Don't let any golfer hear you say that. That's sacrilege. Anyway, make the sacrifice.'

'What sacrifice? If what you say is true I'm liable to make the ultimate sacrifice.'

'No,' he chuckled, 'I don't think so. I just have this gut feeling that it's me who is being set up here. I want someone to watch my back. You can stay in the clubhouse and just keep your eyes open.'

'A fat lot of good that will be. You're on the eighteenth hole and I'm in the clubhouse?'

'It won't go as far as that.'

'What makes you believe all this anyway?'

'Too many coincidences that aren't coincidences.'

'Like what? Come on, Thornton, spell it out for me.'

'Like being in at the death at *L'Éminence Grise* and Tatty just happening to be there as well. Like an attack on you, with obvious intentions to kill, by a perfect stranger named Ninette. Like one of Tatty's girls having the same name, Ninette, but this Ninette for some reason or other no longer being around. Like being invited to Mr. Schnief's fancy dress parade and finding Mike Aliff there who I wouldn't trust further than I could rocket to the moon on a wet fart, who just happens to be looking for the aforementioned Ninette, and who prevents us from talking to Anya who happened to be the girl dining with the victim in the restaurant, but who makes a big thing of my being introduced to a girl named N'tombi.'

'Oh, come on, Thornton. She just happened,' she laid particular emphasis on the word, mimicking him, 'to be standing near us in the crush. It could have been any one of them. It could even have been Anya for that matter and that man, being the raving sex-maniac he is, thinks every other man is like himself and he was doing you a favour.'

'He was making sure she got a bloody good look at me, that

135

is what he was doing. Of that I'm absolutely sure.'

'But why? Aren't we being just a little bit melodramatic? Paranoid even? These things might all arouse slight suspicions, but hardly deep ones.'

'Maybe. But I have this feeling in my water, as my sainted grandmother used to say, that tomorrow on the golf course Nemesis awaits me.'

Holly burst into a peal of laughter that had the occupants at the nearby tables turning around and wondering if they could share the joke. 'A pretty mundane place for Nemesis to wait,' she quipped.

'No more so than any other place she waits, and I'll have you know that the fairway is a sacred stairway to paradise and some people, a great many in fact, find golf very exciting.'

'I'm sure some people get a kick out of shove ha'penny. Do people play shove ha'penny anymore? Some people get their kicks out of watching animals being torn apart or a couple of brainless birds pecking and spurring each other into a bloody mess or two men trying to knock each other's brains out.'

'Ah, yes, but there's a great deal of money involved there.'

'There's a great deal of money involved in everything. I'm led to believe that golf is a pretty expensive pastime. Do you want to take a bet on tomorrow?' She regarded him quizzically.

'A bet on what? The match?'

'Don't be silly. It's an absolute cert you'll lose that.'

'Thank you very much. It's a great confidence booster when your friends are so supportive. How do you know I'm not a brilliant player?'

'You're out of practice, Thornton, you said so yourself.' She took a sip of her cocktail. 'And in more ways than one. Anyway, if you were such a brilliant player you'd be in it for the money as well as the excitement.' She giggled. Obviously the mysterious excitement of golf would remain forever a mystery as far as Holly was concerned. 'No,' she put down her glass and leaned across the table, chin resting on top of her interlaced fingers, 'I'll bet you that nothing untoward will happen. Unless the game is rained off, or you cheat, or slip a disc, all will proceed as peacefully as a church fete.'

'Do you know what goes on at a church fete? Blood can be...'

'Thornton!' She stopped him before he could take flight. 'Nothing will happen. And I will have sat there the whole afternoon, bored out of my tiny mind for no reason but to lay your fanciful imagination to rest. So make it worth my while. Bet!'

'You're on.' They clinked glasses and each took a sip, Thornton forgetting to push his umbrella aside and nearly gouging out an eye.

'Have you been to the hospital yet?' He asked, putting down his glass.

'Don't change the subject.'

'All right, how do you collect your winnings if I'm proved right?'

'You could always put it in a kitty.'

'You're a mercenary bitch! These could be my funeral expenses I'm hazarding here.'

'You should worry.'

'I've a better idea. I'm going to take precautions anyway, however sceptical you are, and they're going to cost me. So, if I win the bet, you pay my expenses, if I lose I pay them.' He frowned at that prospect. 'Somehow,' he added gloomily and didn't want to think about it anymore.

'Done.'

'Daddy send you another cheque?'

'As a matter of fact, yes. There aren't that many shopping days to Christmas.'

****

Thornton stood in Harold Norris' forecourt and surveyed the half dozen or so cars that comprised Harold's current stock in trade. Their paintwork gleamed and the polished chrome glistened in the rays of a bright morning sun. There was a definite nip in the air though and Thornton turned up the collar of his Burberry and dug his hands deep in what was left of its pockets. Not having a wife or mother prone to getting rid of favourite clothes before they had outlived their usefulness it was a garment he had worn for more years than he could remember. It was an old old friend, shabby but comfortable as old friends sometimes are. He had half a mind to be buried in it. But, if she really were going to be waiting for him at the golf course that afternoon, there wasn't time to add the codicil to his will.

Harold, in silk scarf and vicuna overcoat, complete with pockets, materialised beside him. If there was no money in used cars there was certainly money in something. Thornton found himself wondering why the Harolds of this world always wore silver ties. He could understand it for a Bar Mitzvah or a wedding, but for work?

'Thornton,' Harold croaked, 'to what do I owe this pleasure? Going to buy a car at last? I can make you a good deal, the very best.'

'No way, Harold, sorry. Tell me, just what is the point of owning a car in London?'

'The point, Thornton, my boy, is to get you from point A to point B and maybe back again, that is the point.'

'We have a not too highly inefficient, uncomfortable, and expensive municipal transport system to do that but alternatively cars get nicked, cars are vandalised, cars get stuck in tailbacks, cars in town guzzle gas, cars have to be insured, cars minding their own business suddenly sport expensive tickets on their windscreens or end up in the police pound. Cars, not to put too fine a point on it, are very heavy on the bank balance.'

'If you don't want to get a ticket you could always hire yourself a chauffeur.'

'Chauffeurs make it even heavier on the bank balance.'

'Or get a Rottweiler.'

'Rottweiler's drive cars?'

'To bite the shit out of the vandals, what else?'

'And probably bite the shit out of me as well.' Thornton shook his head, 'Or rip up the seats or eat me out of house and home.'

'So go on already, tell me more, I'm all ears. Cars pollute the atmosphere. Cars kill people. Repairs cost an arm and a leg. I'm glad you're not my PR man, Thornton. I'd be out of business. So what is your business? Or is this a social call? Or have you come to tell me I'm anti-social because I'm in the used car business?'

'I need a favour, Harold.'

'Oh, yes,' was Harold's noncommittal reply, not even inflecting it as a question and, producing a yellow duster like a magician out of thin air, he started to gently polish the already gleaming portion of bonnet closest to hand.

'I need a couple of minders for the afternoon.'

'Oh, yes? Been a naughty boy then, have you? Got up some-body's nose then?'

'Oh, shit, Harold! It's too long and involved a story and I don't understand the half of it myself but I need a couple of guys to watch my back.'

Harold sucked his teeth and gazed at Thornton for a long time with rheumy eyes. Then he lifted his right hand and pointed his forefinger at Thornton's temple, thumb sticking up and three fingers curled into his palm.

'Yes?' He said.

'Maybe,' Thornton nodded.

'Hmn...' Harold frowned and for a few moments watched the comings and goings in the street. 'You should get yourself a shooter, Thornton. A man in your trade needs a shooter.' He went back to polishing the bonnet. 'I can get you one cheap.'

'I don't want a shooter, Harold. Shooters are dangerous.'

'Of course. That's why men in your trade have them.'

'People who have them tend to want to use them.'

Harold seemed lost in thought then, 'Exactly. That's what I mean.' He frowned again. Was that what he meant? The conversation was getting a little confused.

'The minders, Harold?'

He turned from the bonnet back to Thornton. 'It'll cost you,' he said.

'It's covered,' Thornton answered.

There was another silence while Harold went back to surveying the street then, deciding that Thornton was a man of his word, he nodded slowly. 'I'll make some calls,' he said.

'One other thing...'

Harold turned back, chin lowered, eyeing Thornton suspiciously.

'... Could you lend me a motor for the afternoon?'

'Lend?' Harold made a noise that was as close as he would get to a laugh. It sounded rather like water gurgling down a drain. 'You have got to be joking.'

'All right, hire then.'

'That's covered too?'

Thornton nodded.

'For business or pleasure?'

'It's to carry my golf clubs.'

'Golf clubs. But, Thornton, tell me, is it in danger of being vandalised?'

'On a golf course? Never!'

'So which one do you want?'

'I rather fancied the Lagonda.'

'Now I know you're joking.'

****

Thornton looked around the small almost bare room; a table on which stood a tape recorder and a couple of files, three chairs and a bench on which sat a young constable of androgynous appearance. Judging by the childbearing width of his hips he'd sat there far too long, or maybe it was just the cut of the uniform that gave that impression.

Detective-sergeant Venables glared at Thornton from across the table. He reeked of Vicks. 'All right, Mr King,' he wheezed, 'let's have it again. And let's try add make it a bit bore believable this tibe shall we?' He leaned back in his chair, stretching out his legs beneath the table, rummaged inside a trouser pocket and withdrew a wrinkled and grubby handkerchief on which he blew his nose and then sniffed loudly. For a moment he sat and contemplated the results like a high priest of Wotan studying the runes then folded the handkerchief carefully and put it back in his pocket. He now produced an inhaler, took two long snorts, one in each nostril and this, having relieved his discomfort somewhat, a packet of cigarettes and a zippo appeared from another baggy pocket. He lifted a cigarette from the pack and then, as an afterthought, extended the packet across the table. Thornton shook his head.

'No thank you, I don't. And you shouldn't either. It's a filthy, unhealthy, disgusting habit, even more so at the moment with that cold.'

'Look, you self-righteous little hypocrite...'

Thornton, at six foot one, wondered how he could be described as little, and just how he was being hypocritical when all he had done was state an honest opinion.

'... I dote deed lectures on my health from you. If I want to smoke myself to death I'll do so without eddy dagging from every Tob, Dick, and Harry. I get enough of that frob the wife.' He took a drag and exhaled in Thornton's direction. Thornton suffered in silence, stoically resisting the urge to wave the smoke away from his face and giving Venables the satisfaction of seeing his discomfort. Venables meanwhile fell into a coughing fit that would have finished off a lesser man. Had he been anyone else he would also have fallen into a fit of cursing but being an upright Baptist and a staunch pillar of the church, swearing was a sinful luxury he did not allow himself. Sergeant Venables' greatest hero was the Chief Constable of Greater Manchester and his one regret in life was never to have had the honour of serving in that division under that great full-bearded giant of a man. Still, he was proud to boast that in his own patch it was a well known fact that perverts had a pretty grim time of it the second they stepped outside the law by as much as a little toe and, as his manor was in the great metropolis, perverts came two a penny. Venables thanked his God morning, noon, and night that he had never had inclinations or leanings of any sort. There was nothing bent about his sex-life; it was entirely normal; wham, bam, and thank you, ma'am, and if God had seen fit to burden him with an unresponsive wife, God knew what He was doing. Rita hadn't been totally frigid as the existence of two children he detested testified, but she had a catalogue of excuses as long as The Encyclopaedia Britannica for putting off the distasteful and messy act. Not that she would describe it to her spouse as such but that was the way she felt. Despite her reluctance to behave as a dutiful wife he'd been faithful, had never once messed around, and he'd spent many an anguished hour wrestling with the temptation to indulge in self-abuse. He'd resisted it as a spotty teenager, having read *A Boy At Fifteen* and taken to heart the book's dire warnings, and he would be damned if he was going to give in to the urges as an adult. He used the word damned in its literal sense.

He was somewhat guilt-ridden by his active dislike for the fruits of his own loins and sincerely wished he could, if not actually love them, then at least like his very own teenage brats but, in his eyes, they were not only revolting to look at, they were revolting in their behaviour and he just knew in his bones they would turn out to be no good possibly even, perish the thought, perverted. But, right now, though thoughts of perversion were never very far away, it was murder he had on his mind.

'Right,' he said, 'shall we start at the beginning then?' The inhaler had done its work.

'What for?' Thornton objected. 'You must be bored with this story by now. I've told you everything as I saw it and I don't want to have to go on and on repeating myself.'

'Oh, believe me, lad, I never get bored with a good story.' He turned to look at the constable. 'You never get tired of a good story either, do you, Roper?'

'No, sergeant.' The constable grinned sheepishly.

Venables had wondered about those hips himself, and the complexion. He had harboured doubts about young Roper ever since the day he had come out of court and found the youngster, hands in pockets, deep in conversation with a solicitor's clerk of dubious sexual orientation. In his opinion the pair had been standing much too close to each other, and now here he was, surveying Thornton with what seemed more than usual interest, though maybe it was because, in his short career, he'd never actually come face to face before with a suspected murderer.

Venables settled for that and turned back to Thornton.

'Well?' He barked, and sniffed again, screwing his mouth to the right. Obviously the left nostril was still giving some trouble.

'Could I have a cup of tea?' Thornton requested politely.

'Tea's off.'

'Where is my car?' Was the next question.

'Your what?' Venables almost yelled. He was wondering how Thornton had got from tea to car. Was he trying to throw him? Fat chance.

'I'm a little bit worried about you, sergeant,' Thornton said, sounding solicitous. 'That cold could be making you a bit mutt and jeff.'

The nostrils immediately closed up again. 'Dote try to be clever with me, lad. There's dothing wrong with my hearing. The reason I sou'ded surprised was because I didn't think eddyone would want to admit to owding a junk heap like that. Got its licence has it? Idsured is it? It'd better be. How log have you had it?'

'Why?'

'Because,' Venables took another couple of snorts and his smile broadened, 'according to our records the last person registered as the owner of that particular vehicle was a Mr Doddy Bates...' Damn it! He snorted the Vicks again. Could one become addicted to this stuff?

'Doddy?'

'That's what I said.'

'Noddy,' Roper volunteered helpfully. Venables glared at him. Roper blushed and lowered his head.

'Doddy Bates, a gentleman who, with any luck, will shortly be going dowd for a dice log stretch id de Scrubs. Bought it off him did you?'

'No.'

'So where did you get it thed?'

'I hired... borrowed it, as a matter of fact.'

'Bake up your mind, lad, hired or borrowed?'

'Borrowed.'

'Ad from whom did you borrow this magnificent vehicle?'

'Harry Norris.'

'Oh?' Venables' forehead crinkled as he raised both eyebrows. 'Oh, dear, oh dear, oh dear me, fide company you keep, Mr King. I thought you said you borrowed it.'

'That's right, I did,' Thornton insisted. He was pretty sure Harold wasn't in the car hire business, only buying and selling, and didn't want to be the cause of getting him into any trouble with the law on that account.

'He lent it to you as a favour did he? Out of the goodness of his heart?'

'That's right.'

'Ad just what were you going to give Mr Dorris in return for this little favour? Harold Dorris doesn't do eddything out of the goodness of his heart.'

'Oh, yes he does. For friends.'

'Oh! So you're a friend of Harold Dorris's are you?'

'Well, no, not exactly.'

'Ad what is that supposed to mean? "Dot exactly." First of all you tell be you hired a car. Thed you tell be you borrowed a car. Thed you tell be you're a friend of Harold Dorris. Thed you tell be 'dot exactly'. In other words you're lying through your teeth add you're trying to cover up. What are you trying to cover up? Is it possible those aren't the only little porkies you've beed telling?' His nose started to run. It tickled and his eyes started to water. He hastily fished out his hankie and blew into it long and loud. It was sodden. He returned it to his pocket with a sense of deep disgust but there was nowhere else to put it, and at least the nose was sort of clear again, though not quite. Venables was beginning to wonder if his cold might not be psychosomatic. Maybe he was allergic to Thornton. He wouldn't be in the least surprised. Thornton on the other hand was beginning to wish he hadn't tried to keep Harold out of trouble.

'You're getting in deeper and deeper by the minute, lad. Well, for your information ad just to set your mide at rest, as you're so worried about the motor you borrowed from your fred, it's id the yard, ad it's going to stay with us till foredsics get through with it, all right? I'b sure if they dote fide traces of eddy explosive substads, or eddy other idcribinating evidence, they'll come up with quite a few mechadical faults, so the least we'll be able to do is book you for driving ad udsound vehicle.'

'Am I under arrest?'

'What? Good lord, no! No, dot at all, perish the thought. Whatever put that idea id your head? You're dot udder arrest. You are assisting the police with their edquiries, that's all. If you were in a position to turd on the TV todight that's what you would hear, "A mad is assisting the police with their enquiries." You must have heard that phrase before.' He screwed up his face, leaned back in his chair again and rummaged for his hankie but, before he could get to it, hastily turned away his head and sneezed violently.

'Bless you,' Thornton said. 'You really ought to be in bed with that cold you know.'

Venables finally extracted his handkerchief and wiped his hand and then his nose. 'That.' He said, glaring at Thornton venomously, 'is where I'd like to be.' He put away the hankie, took a final drag of his cigarette and stubbed it out in an ancient, upturned coffee bottle lid from the time when they were still made of tin and which by the look of it had obviously been used for the purpose many times before. 'Have you ever been in the cells below a courtroom, lad?' He asked. The sneeze seemed to have finally cleared his nostrils.

Thornton wished the sergeant would stop referring to him as a lad. He supposed it was just the man's way but his answer to the question was to sigh deeply.

'They have a very peculiar smell all of their own,' Venables went on. 'It isn't just sweat, or toe-jam, or urine, escaping gas and worse, though it includes all those. No, it's something else as well. Do you know what it is?'

Thornton regarded Venables stonily. The man was a semi-educated pompous ass and this was getting extremely boring.

'I'll tell you what it is,' Venables sniffed. 'It's fear, the smell of fear. Have you ever smelled fear, Mr King?'

'This may come as a surprise to you, sergeant, but the answer is yes, I have. I've been in some pretty dicey situations in my time but this isn't one of them. So can we please just get on with it and let me get the hell out of here?'

'But that's what I've been wanting you to do, get on with it.' Venables spread his arms wide, a figure of infinite patience.

'All right, for the last time, this is how it was. The reason why I don't like going over it is because the colonel was an old friend of the family and I was very fond of him, and his wife, Marge,' he quickly added seeing the look on Venables; face. "Marge!" Thornton suddenly looked very concerned. 'Has she been told?'

'She's been informed and she's being looked after so don't worry on that score.' He tapped the inhaler a few times on the desk then unscrewed it, applied a thumb to one nostril and took a good long sniff just for the hell of it.

'Poor old Marge.' Thornton shook his head. 'I've been so busy thinking of... I hadn't... What's she going to do without her Teddy?' For a while he sat in silence, staring at the table, not seeing it, seeing only a red brick weathered house with diamond pane windows and mock Tudor chimneys: seeing only an old fashioned

English garden and a little old lady almost all skin and bone, trug in hand, secateurs at the ready, pottering among her delphiniums, her dahlias, and her especial favourites, old-fashioned bearded yellow irises.

Venables waited. Finally Thornton looked up. 'If you suspect me of murdering the colonel, give me a reason. Why would I want to do such a thing? I want to see his killer brought to justice even more than you do. No, that's a terrible phrase. I'd like to see his killer punished.'

'Most commendable, but you're not getting on with it.'

Thornton breathed deeply, blew out hard, and began. What he wanted to do was explode, vent his rage in some useless violent action but, instead, his voice was low, so low that Venables had to lean forward across the table in order to listen, his gaze never leaving Thornton's face and Thornton meeting his gaze almost without blinking. 'Yesterday I went to this fashion show at Princess Spitskaya's School of Modelling...'

'The same princess who was with you at the restaurant?'

'She wasn't with me. I just happened to pass her table and join her for a while, but, yes, the same princess and, at the reception afterwards, I met the colonel who, in fact, I hadn't seen for quite some time.'

'How long a time?'

'I really can't remember but quite a few Christmas cards ago. Anyway, I was really delighted to see him again.'

'What would a man like that be doing at a fashion show? He had an interest in fashion? Doesn't seem the type to me. Military man.' Was perversion raising its ugly head again?

'I don't have any particular interest in fashion but I was there.'

'Yes.' Venables inserted a little finger into a nostril to relieve another tickle and then tugged at an earlobe. 'Exactly why were you there?'

'Because I was invited, why else?'

'No other reason?'

'Free food and the chance of a booze-up.'

'You're being smart again.'

'All right, curiosity, sergeant, curiosity.'

'About what?'

'The latest trends of course.'

'But you just said you weren't interested in fashion. You see, lad, you're hiding something from me and I want to know what it is.' He regarded Thornton for a while. 'What do you do for a living?' He suddenly asked.

'That's my business,' Thornton snapped.

'I know it's your business, but I'd like to know what business your business is.'

'I work for the government. That is, until a short while ago I worked for the government. I was made redundant. Satisfied?'

'Not really.'

'Well that's all you're getting.'

'Fine. It won't be difficult to find out, so...'

Thornton squirmed. His bum was getting quite sore on the hard seat, another reason for getting this over with. 'So we arranged to play a round of golf this afternoon. We met at the course. The colonel teed up at the first and was just addressing the ball when Holly... Miss Day... came out of the clubhouse and shouted that I was wanted on the phone. She said it was urgent so I excused myself and started for the clubhouse. The colonel must have decided to go ahead and take a swing at the ball. There was this explosion and that was it. Someone called emergency and we waited for you and the ambulance to arrive. That is all I know and that is all I can tell you.' Thornton folded his arms on the table.

'And I don't believe a word of it,' Venables said.

'Why not?'

'Because you've left too much out that's why not. Look, King, we've had more killings these last couple of weeks than I normally see in six months or more and something has to be done about it and fast. We're getting a reputation for murder second only to Washington DC and we can do without it.'

'Yes,' Thornton nodded. 'At least in Washington they know what the murders are all about. These seem to be for no reason, have no explanation, but there has to be a connection.'

'Serial killer?'

'No.'

'Really.' Venables lit another cigarette. 'You seem to have given it a great deal of thought.'

'I read the newspapers don't I?'

'Now come on lad, you don't believe everything you read in the papers do you?' He blew out a cloud of smoke, this time carefully avoiding Thornton's direction. 'Well we won't find the answers while witnesses, for reasons unknown, hold out on us. In case you didn't know it, though I'm sure you do, that is a criminal offence, obstructing a police officer in the course...'

'I'm being as helpful as I can be.'

'What was Miss Day doing there?'

'She wanted to come along.'

'Just for the ride? Curiosity I suppose. Why did she stay in the clubhouse?'

'She wasn't feeling too well. As a matter of fact she called her work that morning to tell them she wouldn't be in because she was sick. You can check if you like. Then, in the afternoon, she felt better and thought the outing might do her good. But she decided to stay in the clubhouse.'

'I've got to hand it to you, lad,' Venables toyed with the end of his cigarette on the edge of the tin lid and eyed the result, 'you're quick on your feet, but I'm getting just a little bit impatient with all this shadow boxing. She was in the clubhouse because that's where you wanted her to be. Because, from there, she could conveniently call you to answer a nonexistent phone call which would get you a safe distance from the explosion. Excluding Miss Day there were four in your party. Who were the other two?'

'Caddies of course.'

'Did you know them?'

'Never saw them in my life before. The colonel arranged the whole shooting match. Shit!' It wasn't exactly the most tactful way of putting it.

'And, of course, he can't corroborate that. Why did they disappear so fast?'

'I have no idea.' Thornton shrugged.

'Give me a description.'

'I've already done that!' Thornton sounded really exasperated.

'Give it me again.'

He remembered every feature of the two minders Harold had provided for him but he wasn't too sure he could remember the false descriptions he had given Venables earlier and a mistake now could really compromise him. 'I've given you a description. If you want to refresh your memory look up your notes,' he said with a tone of finality.

'You gave me a description of two of Snow White's dwarfs.'

'Aren't most caddies on the shortish side? That's the impression I've always had.'

'You've got an answer for everything haven't you?' Venables sneered. 'That, my friend, is one of the reasons I don't trust you and why I don't Adam and Eve a word you say. The last time we met, also at the scene of a suspicious death as you will recall, you told me you were a doctor.'

'Oh, no! No, no, no, I did not. Someone else told you that.'

'Because that's what you told theb.' The unblocked nose was

blocking up again. "To prevent panic" I think was the reason you gabe at the tibe. I believe I am correct in that assertion. Or do you wad me to look up my notes?'

Thornton shrugged.

'So dow shall I tell you what I really believe? I believe you told them you were a doctor so that you could, without arousing suspicion, leave your table add exambid the gentleman at close quarters to bake sure he was a goner.' Venables' head never stopped nodding throughout this exposition as though what he believed would brook no argument, but Thornton, if this was to go on much longer, decided that argumentative he might as well be.

'If that were the case why did I try resuscitation?' He countered.

'I don't know that you did that, lad.' Venables sniffed long and loud and swallowed. Thornton saw his Adam's apple rise and fall and winced, not just at the sniff and the thought of what was going down the man's throat but because he had reverted to addressing him as lad instead of my friend.

'That could have been all an act. You could have been squeez-ing the last bit of life out of him for all I know. Ad, as I remember, Miss Day was with you on that occasion as well ad Miss Day did a neat disappearing act just like your two caddies.'

'I don't believe this,' Thornton said with real feeling. 'She came forward later to make a statement didn't she? You know why she disappeared. She went after that girl. The one who was sitting with Shoggi when he collapsed, the one who really did do a neat disappearing trick.'

'That's right. We haven't traced her yet. But we will, we will. The big mystery is, why should Miss Day take it upon herself to go chasing after the girl in the first place?'

'I didn't say she chased her. I said she went after her.'

'Yes, but why?'

'Didn't she give a reason when she made her statement?'

It was Venables turn to stare at Thornton, the stare meaning that Thornton knew exactly why Holly had gone after the girl and he had better come up with the answer. But Thornton pretended he didn't understand and kept his mouth shut. Venables finally broke the silence. 'Ad I suppose your two caddies will turd up out of the blue ready to bake statements. Let's see, what were their dames?' He opened one of the files lying on the desk and took out a sheet of paper. 'Dave and John. Short for David and Jonathan do doubt. Accents?'

'What?'

'Did they speak with an accent?'

'Oh. Dave had a Scottish accent, Glaswegian I think. Not that I'm an expert on Scottish accents. Don't recall the other one saying very much. You know what?'

'Surprise me,' Venables said without enthusiasm.

'I think they could have been off-duty squaddies earning a bit on the side. Maybe they were from the colonel's old regiment, doing him a favour. It isn't that long since he retired so he wouldn't have lost contact. Why don't you try his ex-batman or something like that? Could be your man, one of your men.' Thornton smiled encouragingly.

'You would recognise them again then?' Venables ventured.

'Of course.' Thornton sounded quite bright. He had a feeling this ordeal was about to end.

'Thed what would you say if I brought out a dozen books of mug shots and had you go through them?'

The smile was wiped from Thornton's face. 'I'd say I'd be here till breakfast,' he said with doleful resignation.

Venables sneezed violently. It seemed to momentarily clear all his symptoms because, instead of the blocked nostrils and the gruff wheeze Thornton had got used to, the clear girlish voice he remembered came back.

'We serve a very good breakfast,' it squeaked.

****

Holly looked around the small almost bare room: a table on which stood a tape recorder and a couple of files, some chairs, a bench against a wall on which a young woman police constable sat, trim in her blue uniform. She was very pretty and Holly had come, of late, to distrust pretty girls, even in police uniform.

Venables' sidekick from the restaurant, Ron Pocock by name, smiled at Holly across the table. 'Run it by me one more time,' he said using trans-Atlantic jargon, a legacy of watching too many American series on television. Perry Mason was his particular favourite. He never missed an episode. It was really neat. He watched cop series as well. Francisco, New York, Chicago, Miami, Hawaii, or Boston, wherever they were set, not because they all followed the same format and used the same old clichés but because, for excitement, they simply had the edge on their English equivalents and he rather resented that. In the final analysis it was the guns that did it. Even when an English cop was armed it wasn't the same. How could a guy who had to go and sign for his weapon over a counter be as romantic and heroic a figure as one who carried a cannon under his armpit twenty-four hours a day and blew people away with careless abandon? Ron was very much a boy of the concrete jungle at heart with a yearning for violence and sentimentality. He had come up with a few good ideas himself for television series and sent them off to the various companies but they always came back with thanks and regrets, sometimes without the thanks.

'What do you want me to run by you?' Holly asked.

'Everything.'

'Why?'

'Oh, there might just have been something you left out, forgot, you know. If you go over it again it might bring it back to mind; some little detail, could be something vital, no matter how small or trivial it might seem to you.' Ron had his patter off pat.

'I've got a better idea,' Holly countered, 'why don't you run it by me one more time? And, if I remember anything else, I'll stop you.'

'Okay.' Ron leaned forward, opened a file and studied the statement he pulled out and laid on the table in front of him. After a moment he glanced up. 'I'll skip the preliminaries and go straight into it, okay?'

Holly shrugged and nodded. The policewoman attempted a smile in her direction. Holly ignored it. Ron fiddled with his pencil for a while, tapped it a few times on the table and started to read.

'Mr. King and I arrived at the golf course at approximately two-fifteen...'

'It was two-thirteen according to my watch,' Holly interrupted, 'but Thornton looked at his watch and said, 'Dead on time'. That's why I've said approximately you see. Our watches didn't synchronise.' The policeman stared at her in some amazement. 'I just thought I'd make that point absolutely clear,' Holly said, smiling sweetly, 'in case there are any question about it later or it causes confusion.'

'Thank you.' Ron looked down at his paper again. '... and met up with Colonel Montcliff in the clubhouse where he was waiting for us.'

'I should have said we parked the car first, shouldn't I?' Ron sat in silence for a moment, his eyes glued to the statement, before he looked up again. 'That is,' Holly continued, 'Mr. King parked the car.' She gazed at him solemnly. 'In the car park.'

Ron was getting a little confused. He wasn't quite sure what was happening here. His frowning silence gave her the opportunity to continue so she took it.

'As usual we had a hell of a time finding a space I can tell you. Isn't it always the way? No matter how large the parking lot you're always the one going around in circles trying to find a place, and when someone pulls out someone else seems to appear out of nowhere and gets in before you.'

'Yes,' Ron agreed, 'but I don't think...'

'We had a lucky break though,' she went blithely on, 'because we were sitting there wondering what to do when a man did pull out and made room for us. I don't mean he pulled out to make room for us. I mean he was leaving, having obviously finished his game and, at the time, there was no one else looking for a space.'

'Okay, okay!' Ron hurriedly interrupted, 'so you parked the car.' He sounded quite snappy.

'Well you said if I'd left anything out and I had hadn't I?'

For a moment they gazed at each other across the table almost like a pair of lovers, which, as Holly was being foxy and Ron was beginning to lose his cool, was totally misleading. The WPC was biting a cheek and studying her fingernails. Ron looked down again, found his place, and went on, going back a little for the sake of continuity.

'...Where he was waiting for us. He and Mr. King then left the clubhouse ...'

'We had a quick drink first,' Holly said. 'Well not that quick. I mean we didn't gulp it down. I mean, I still had mine when the men went out to play.'

There was a strange strangulated sort of sound from the bench. Ron kept his eyes on the statement. When he eventually looked up they still appeared a little glazed. He finally pulled himself together and cleared his throat. 'You know something?' He said, and he didn't dare stay looking up, 'I'm not sure this was such a brilliant idea. Why don't you keep your interruptions till the end?'

'I'm not so sure that's such a brilliant idea either,' Holly objected. 'I mean, I read this article called "How Reliable A Witness Are you?" and, of course, most witnesses are notoriously unreliable, aren't they? I mean no two people see the same thing do they? If you go to a movie, or the theatre, it's the same isn't it? You can sit side by side with someone but both of you will get different impressions. No two people ever see the same thing do they? Or they forget things. Or they put the wrong interpretation on them. Or put them in a different sequence to what actually happened. Or they exaggerate.'

"What gives with this woman?" Ron thought, "rabbiting on like a bloody maniac."

'And,' Holly continued with emphasis, 'I might remember something but, if I have to wait till you've finished, I might also forget it again.'

'Are you finished?' Ron barked.

'I was only making a point.' Holly looked and sounded truly hurt by his abruptness. 'There's no need to get angry. It's a perfectly valid point and, if you miss out something because I've forgotten it, don't blame me.'

'All right, I won't blame you. Happy now?' Ron wasn't too sure of the logic behind her statement but all he wanted to do was get this over and done with. 'Now can we get on?' he pleaded.

'Could I make a phone call first please? I am, I believe, entitled to make a phone call and I haven't done it yet.'

'I'm sorry, no phone calls.' He looked a bit embarrassed and glanced at the WPC who was studying her hands again, clicking her fingernails with her thumb.

'What?' Holly was suddenly hostile. Gone was the little girl lost act.

'I said, no phone call.' He hastily raised a hand, palm towards her as he saw her mouth open about to object, an objection he surmised that would take at least five minutes. 'There is really no need for you to call anybody,' he said and was about to go on by way of explanation when she interrupted him again.

'How do you know that? I could have an important appointment. I could have a date. Somebody might be waiting for me and getting extremely worried wondering where I am, what is happening to me.'

"Gordon Bennett!" He thought. "Does she have to spell out everything?" Aloud he said, 'No, what I mean is, you have not been arrested. You have not been formally charged with anything. The Duty Officer hasn't read you your rights. Has he read her her rights?' He turned to the WPC who looked up from her hand and shook her head. She appeared to be smiling but she couldn't say anything because she had both cheeks firmly clamped between her teeth. 'And, anyway, although I am fully aware that you are legally entitled to make one phone call, there are exceptions to the rule.'

'There always are,' Holly said. 'What's this one?

'Well, in cases involving terrorism...'

'Terrorism!'

Holly's sudden shriek caused Ron to visibly wince. The WPC lost both her smile and her fascination with her hand as she suddenly sat bolt upright. In the corridor outside a colleague passing the door at that moment nearly dropped a tray of teacups. As it was most of the tea was slopped onto the tray and, in other offices, heads were lifted and conversations stopped dead. It took quite a few seconds for the station to return to normal. Ron's heart was thumping. He hoped nobody thought there was a case of GBH in the interview room, especially against a woman. He breathed deeply and went on almost in a whisper, 'In cases involving terrorism a phone call can be denied for reasons of security. Orders from the Super you understand.'

'No, I don't understand.' Holly glared at him.

'Well, let's put it this way, you are a member of a terrorist organisation ...' That was obviously not the way to put it because Holly shrieked again.

'I'm what?'

'I'll rephrase that,' Ron said hurriedly. 'You are suspected...' Seeing her mouth open again he winced in anticipation but managed to stop her this time by raising both hands placatingly. 'All right, all right! I'm making it a hypothetical case. You are suspected of being a terrorist, okay? I'm not saying you are one but it's possible you might be. We let you make a phone call; it's to your lawyer you tell us. During the call you give a coded signal to whoever you're talking to to tell them you've been nicked. They quickly pass the word on and, before we can make a move, the rest of the cell have scarpered, gone to ground. Got it? We can't afford to take that chance so, no phone call.'

'And you suspect me of being a terrorist. But just a minute ago you said I was no more than a witness,'

'Yes... well...' He was losing patience again, 'what I am saying now is, if you let me finish reading this statement back to you, and if you then sign it, we can wrap this up and you can go home can't you? It shouldn't take that long so there is no need to delay proceedings by making a phone call. Now, may I please be allowed to get on with it without interruption?' He sighed, picked up the statement, and continued to read from where he had left off. The WPC went back to clicking her nails. Holly, after a glance at the wall clock, switched off. Ron's voice became a distant murmur. In fact she didn't even see him anymore as she mentally went over the afternoon's events.

****

Having stepped out of the car, Holly waited as Thornton collected his gear from the boot. She stood shivering, hands deep in pockets, surveying the landscape until he joined her and, clubs slung over his shoulder, sports bag in hand, he put an arm through hers and they headed for the clubhouse. She snuggled into him. Mad dogs and Englishmen might go out in the midday sun. Mad dogs and total maniacs went out in weather like this to chase a little white ball all over the place and drop it in a succession of holes. She gave him a sideways glance and a wet smile, wondering what got into otherwise seemingly normal people that they wanted to go through the torture of these weird outdoor rituals when it was cold enough to freeze the fur pants off an Eskimo and the best place to be was in front of a roaring log fire, a gas fire, an electric fire or, failing any of those, at least cocooned in the comfort of central heating or snuggled under a duvet. She hunched into her upturned collar and was about to put this point to Thornton when, ahead of them, two men stepped out from behind a car and stood between them and the way to the clubhouse. "Oh, my God!" Holly thought as she clutched Thornton's arm, "it's High Noon!" Neither man looked particularly prepossessing, not quite B horror movie material, they were nevertheless the kind of characters you might, if you were of a nervous disposition, cross the road to avoid, especially on a dark night. Only here there was no crossing of roads. Thornton, though, didn't seem too perturbed, quite the opposite in fact.

'Stay here a minute,' he said and, as Holly, needing no second bidding, stopped where she was, he advanced to meet the pair. They talked quietly for a few moments and then Thornton looked back and waved Holly on. The men regarded her in passing, unsmiling, but with looks she knew would follow her all the way to the clubhouse as they strolled behind, veering off at the last minute to head for the first tee via the terrace. Out of earshot she turned to Thornton. 'Who are they?' She whispered.

'Call them the back-up team,' Thornton said.

'Where did you find them?'

'A fairy godmother waved her magic chequebook.'

'Oh! I see. Well not yet she hasn't. And by the looks of it she isn't going to. Have you ever witnessed a more peaceful scene?'

'Somebody said those exact words in a garage in Chicago once... on Saint Valentine's Day.'

They found Colonel Montcliff at the nineteenth hole that, as usual, he'd hit before the first and he slid off his stool to greet them affably. 'Thornton, my boy!' They shook hands. The colonel was a great one for shaking hands. Having finished with Thornton, he extended his horny paw towards Holly. 'And Miss Day! What a pleasant surprise. So glad you decided to join us. Come along to watch me thrash your man have you?'

'I'd hardly call him "my man," colonel. But I'm sure he'll not prove much opposition He's dreadfully out of training. Look at that.' And she gave Thornton a playful karate chop in the midriff, which as a matter of fact was as flat as an ironing board and as hard. But he reacted as he was meant to and having dutifully clowned being in agony and winded he smiled indulgently.

'Is he, by Jove? That's too bad. Won't do. Won't do at all. So what's your poison, Miss Day?' He was already signalling to the barman.

'Oh, Colonel, please! Do call me Holly.' She reinforced the invitation with a beguiling smile and a flutter of the eyelids. Coming into the warmth of the clubhouse Holly was feeling quite light-hearted as well as light-headed. She was convinced the afternoon would pass without incident and, if she stayed in the clubhouse on the colonel's tab, the brandy and ginger ale she was about to ask for would lead to a second, maybe even a third, by which time she would be suffused with a warm glow that would last all the way home where she could spend a nice relaxed evening in front of the telly, if there was anything worth watching. 'And, if I may, I'll have a brandy and ginger ale,' and she gave a little shudder to show how the winter cold had set in, 'to chase the chill from between my shoulder blades.'

'Of course you may, my dear,' the colonel nodded affirmation to the barman who was standing by and who immediately set about getting it. 'Waste of good brandy though. Ginger ale? Tch tch! Thornton, old fellow m' lad, what's yours?'

Ron Pocock's voice brought her out of her reverie. 'The men went off to change and Colonel Montcliff also said he had to visit the pro-shop because he needed new balls.' He looked up as Holly started to giggle. 'Something is funny?' He asked.

'Just the thought of the colonel needing new balls,' she said and giggled again, this time even exchanging a glance with the WPC who had stopped biting her cheeks, which by now were pretty raw, and was currently gnawing at her lower lip. Ron looked sternly from one to the other.

'May I remind you, Miss, this is hardly a laughing matter. We are conducting a murder enquiry here. A man has been killed.'

'I know I know! I'm sorry!' She was desperately trying to suppress the laughter. 'It's just that, well, it could have been put differently. Perhaps you ought to insert the word golf just to make it absolutely clear what balls we're talking about.'

'I don't think that will be necessary,' he snapped. From the look on his face and the tone of his voice his reply was obviously meant as a severe put-down. He seemed genuinely upset, or disgusted, maybe both, or he was faking it beautifully. Holly, deciding he was genuine and really rather nice because of it, conceded to herself he had every right to be both upset and disgusted. The colonel's death was no laughing matter. It had been horrible. And the laughter she was now desperately trying to control was no more than the old banana skin reaction, a safety valve. What she really needed right at this moment was that second brandy. She remembered how she had carried her drink over to the window to look out across the terrace and watch as the men made their way to the first tee where the minders stood waiting. There was a long conversation, Thornton no doubt explaining the presence of the two men to Colonel Montcliff. The old man finally shrugged, turned away, bent down, and teed up. Then he waved the rest of the party away and addressed the ball.

'It was then,' Holly heard Ron reading, 'that I heard Mr. King being paged to take a telephone call. I thought at first of taking the call myself, on his behalf, but then said I would fetch him. I went out onto the terrace and shouted to him that he was wanted on the phone. He said something to the colonel, excusing himself I suppose, and started towards the clubhouse. The colonel stood watching him for a moment and then must have decided to take a few practice swings while he waited. He hit the ball. There was a flash and a bang and he was thrown backwards. Mr. King ran back to him and I started to go towards them but Mr. King waved for me to stop. Then he came back and told me the colonel was dead. He took my arm and we returned to the clubhouse. People had come to the windows and out on to the terrace to see what had happened. I don't know who called the emergency services. We went back inside and waited.' Ron looked up from the statement. 'Is there anything you want to add?' He asked. His tone was still acid. Obviously she had not been forgiven for the levity. She gazed at him solemnly.

'No,' she said, 'there's nothing to add.'

She wondered how Thornton was doing. Would he have told Venables about the minders? Should she have mentioned them? But to have done so would have opened a whole new can of worms. She just hoped their statements tallied more or less, enough not to raise too much suspicion, but her fingers trembled as she signed it.

Ron, who was hoping Holly really was an innocent, thought that if he cracked a funny she might lighten up a little after her ordeal.

'Mind you,' he said, 'at his age I'm not surprised he needed new balls.'

WPC Bryson let out a whoop and stomped her feet. She was later brought up on a serious disciplinary charge.

Chapter Nine

London's teeming millions, both visiting and native, were well into the morning's business when Holly and Thornton, looking and feeling like death, emerged from the station. Thornton, still dressed for the game of golf he was never destined to play, cursed and shivered violently as the icy wind, felt even more keenly due to lack of sleep on a concrete bunk, refused to be cheated by his light windcheater and cut right through it. Why hadn't he had the foresight to change? Or at least collect his overcoat before they marched him out to the police car? He hadn't had the foresight because he had been too shaken up to think of anything that practical, too much the object of curiosity coupled with sympathetic gestures, solicitous enquiries and suspicious glances and, when he and Holly had managed to get in a huddle, too busy trying to sort out this latest development and, as usual, coming up with a big fat blank. They had sat in the clubhouse as far away from the windows as possible. He had no wish to be in a position where, even from a distance, he could see the colonel's mutilated corpse sprawled on the grass. The memory of it was firmly fixed in his mind as it was.

'So you were right,' Holly had whispered after a lengthy silence.

'Half right,' he replied. 'Though why, in God's name, it had to be the colonel I really don't know.'

'Are you sure it was? It could have been intended for you.'

'No.' He shook his head. 'It was definitely poor old Teddy. But who in the world would want to kill him, and for what reason, is totally beyond me. They say if there's a bullet with your name on it, that's your lot, but to have your name on a golf ball! How infra dig.'

'Did he ever have anything to do with security?'

'If by security you mean our lot then the answer is no; just a regular soldier, but I should think the last place he saw active service or at least was in a hot spot, would have been Aden, Cypress, maybe Kenya, somewhere like that, and that is going way back.' They sat for a while, each engrossed in their own thoughts, and then, 'How much do I owe you?' Holly asked.

'What?' Thornton looked up from scowling at a tabletop.

'I lost the bet,' she said with a little shrug.

'Shit, Holly! This is no time to be flippant.'

'I'm not being flippant,' she defended herself. 'You've got some pretty hefty expenses coming up from this afternoon's little exercise.'

'Well I don't want to talk about it now.'

'I'm sorry.'

'And I'll sort it out myself. You don't owe me anything.'

'We'll see.' Holly said, and once more they lapsed into silence until she picked up the conversation again with, 'They disappeared pretty fast, didn't they? Your back-up team.'

'Well what would you expect? The cops are on their way and those boys, I shouldn't wonder, both have records as long as your arms, their last known address being Wandsworth or the Scrubs. There's no way they were going to hang around. It was stupid of me to even get them out here in the first place.'

'Yes.'

He wasn't sure if that meant he was stupid or that the boys were wise to scarper. She looked at him for a moment before she went on. 'There's something else puzzling me though.

'What's that?'

'Why you stopped.'

Thornton frowned, obviously puzzled in turn by her remark.

'When I called you, you started towards the clubhouse but then you stopped, just a second or two before it happened. I thought you were going to turn back even before the explosion.'

'It suddenly struck me as peculiar, if peculiar is the right word, that I should be getting a phone call here. Who would be calling me? The phone in my office has been as dead as a doornail for days, weeks even, and who knew I was playing, supposed to be playing, golf this afternoon? And where. Only you, and Tatty, and the colonel. Madge too of course.'

'And anyone who happened to be within earshot at the reception. Mike Aliff for example?'

'Was it a man calling?'

'I didn't take the call, Thornton. But it wasn't a man.'

'How do you know?' Thornton raised an enquiring eyebrow.

'Because, while I was waiting for you, while you were looking at the colonel, I happened to notice a car pulled up on the main road overlooking the course, so I took a closer look ... with these ...' She produced a pair of field glasses from beneath her coat. 'There was a girl in the car and I could see her full-face, looking in our direction, but too far away to recognise the features again. In fact, at first, I thought it was a young man because, whoever it was, was wearing a cap and it wasn't until she took it off and the hair came tumbling down that I realised it was a woman. Then she drove off.'

'Car phone?'

Holly nodded. 'That's my guess. And, if she were disguised as a man, it would have been for one purpose only I imagine, so that she could get into your changing rooms, or wherever, without arousing undue suspicion. You didn't notice a young man hanging around by any chance?'

Thornton shook his head. He looked around the clubhouse bar. It was almost like a re-run of the scene in *L'Éminence Grise* on the day Shoggi snuffed it. Sometimes the human face scared the shit out of him. He turned back to look at Holly.

'It's time we turned up the wick,' he said.

****

'Are we going to stand here all day, or what?' Holly's voice and a particularly nasty gust of wind brought him back to the present. He tapped his breast pocket to reassure himself that his wallet was still there. He might have just enough credit left on his card for a modest purchase and, he thought, he owed himself an early Christmas present. 'I'm going to crash out,' he said, 'but first I'm going to buy an overcoat. Want to come with and help me choose?'

'No thank you, Thornton.' She turned up her coat collar, blew on her hands, and rubbed them vigorously. 'I feel thoroughly dirty, disgusting, and degraded. I am going to do an energetic workout followed by a sauna as hot and as long as I can stand it. And do you know what I am going to do then? I am going to get my hair done and it's going to cost a small fortune, every penny of which will be a penny well spent.' With which she hailed a passing cab. 'I'll call you later,' she shouted above the noise of traffic, slammed the door, and the cab pulled away. He saw her lean forward to give the cabbie directions.

'She could have offered me a lift,' Thornton said to no one in particular and sounding mightily aggrieved. Then he turned and walked away. He had decided to head for the men's shops in Regent Street but when he reached the top of the Burlington Arcade, changed his mind and turned into it, making for Piccadilly instead. The change of direction was an automatic reaction, like finishing a bar of chocolate just because it's there and you haven't the will power to leave a piece for later. The arcade had always been one of his favourite places for window-shopping, mainly because most of the pricey merchandise on display, although way beyond his means, were right up his street taste wise. Occasionally a tie or scarf and once, in a moment of rashness, an extremely expensive cravat pin were about all he could even contemplate. Anyway, he reasoned, Regent Street would be crammed with Christmas shoppers fighting for their share of the pavement and the arcade would at least lend him some protection from the wind. He found it also crowded and the peripatetic owners of Hermès and Gucci accessories weren't there just to window shop.

There was obviously plenty of money about in some quarters, Thornton thought, why did none of it ever head in his direction? He paused to look at a collection of meerschaum pipes with their intricately carved heads, then at some netsuke, some Georgian silver, a collection of chess sets, some barley-twist stem glasses and, thus, zigzagging his way from side to side, from one enticing window to another, he slowly made his way to the Piccadilly end intending to visit Simpsons to see what they might have on offer in the way of greatcoats. It was probably too much to hope for but there might just be a few sale items. Retail sales were well down after all and shopkeepers couldn't wait for the January bargain jamboree. To his surprise the Piccadilly pavements were as crowded as he knew the Regent and Oxford Street ones must be and so was the actual street. Why in God's name did there have to be a demonstration just when he needed to insulate himself against the British weather? He squeezed, nudged, elbowed, and shouldered his way to the kerb and, for a few moments, watched the banner bearing marchers, keeping a hand on the pocket in which his credit card nestled. The dips must be having a field day.

The doom and gloom brigade were hotfooting it along loudly

proclaiming ecological disaster. There were Green slogans, Save The Whale slogans, anti-nuclear slogans, save the forests, save the world: and while they marched on the loggers were still logging, manufacturers were still manufacturing, consumers still consuming, the money makers still making money, the breeders still breeding. Was this rag tag and bobtail army of idealists fighting a rearguard action doomed to failure on an already doomed planet or was there some hope yet for life on earth? How does one bring to an end man's rapacity? His seemingly unbounded ability to destroy? Hold an Earth Summit and talk talk talk and sign meaningless treaties while mealy-mouthed, self-seeking politicians carry on politicising? Thornton didn't want to think about it as he grew steadily more chilled with each passing banner.

The obvious answer to his immediate problem was to walk to the Circus, cross the road via the subway, and walk back to Simpsons along the opposite pavement, but Thornton was in no mood for the obvious. He decided to cut a swathe through the marchers and, having so determined, stepped off the kerb. He managed to make a couple of yards into the massed ranks before being gradually shunted sideways until he was turned to the left and swept along with the tide. At least he was heading in the right direction and maybe he could make the other side by the time they reached Simpsons. But an arm on either side, suggestive of solidarity if nothing else, linked with his and held him fast. Glancing to his left he was slightly disconcerted to find himself in the grip of an ageing pretty obvious, that is obvious but not pretty, homosexual: skinny, sporting a droopy moustache and clad in leather and chains from boots to peaked cap. A pair of watery eyes met Thornton's look and the ancient licked his mousy nicotine-stained moustache with the tip of his tongue. He was obviously clinging to a long past raunchy youth spent in gropey cinemas, cottages and bars, with side trips to Amsterdam and

New York for visits to the baths, back rooms and piers. He was definitely a forerunner of what was to become the clone and he was beginning to bear a distinct resemblance to Peat Bog Man. Thornton turned his head to see who had a hold of his right arm and was greeted with a ravishing smile from a diminutive pixy in a chunky purple polo neck, red and white striped ski cap, a very expensive looking sheepskin-lined suede coat, and whose face Thornton seemed to know.

'You must be absolutely freezing to death,' the insulated midget said, blowing out a cloud of steam with every word, 'and I'm not surprised, dressed in a skimpy little thing like that. I mean!' He lowered his gaze, leaning forward and then arching back before looking up again. 'It's all very well wanting to advertise and show off the goodies, and they look as though they're worth showing off, but not, my dear, if you're going to catch pneumonia doing it. There will be other days, other ways.' And he gave Thornton's biceps a little squeeze before releasing the arm in order to remove his sheepskin coat. 'Here,' he said.

'No!' Thornton heard himself shouting in sudden panic, and then, not wishing to seem rude and ungrateful, 'It's hardly my size.'

'Just drape it over your shoulders,' the pygmy ordered. 'I know they're broad but they're not that broad,' and he threw the coat over Thornton who clutched at the lapels and only then noticed the large badge which, even when read upside down, blazoned forth its message in stark black and white - GLAD TO BE GAY!

Thornton looked around the massed ranks behind him and up at the banners. He gulped visibly. Apart from those that proclaimed gladness and pride quite a few read GAYS AGAINST POLICE HARASSMENT. This was a new phenomenon. Since when was the gay community so bold? Since Wolfenden? "Oh, my God!" Thornton thought, invoking the nonexistent deity again in a moment of crisis, "What if Venables should see me now?"

Thornton was not homophobic. As far as he was concerned it was each man to his own, if that was the right expression to use, but there were times and situations when he could have wished nature weren't so wilful and this was obviously one of them.

They marched by an unprepossessing group of lager louts to be greeted by tribal yells, jeers, and a hail of derogatory comment to which Thornton's stouthearted little companion, surrounded by friends and protectors, gave twos-up in return. Thornton had the feeling that, even if not surrounded by friends and protectors, he would probably have reacted in the same way and more than likely have been viciously mauled by the pack for his effrontery. Woofter he might be, wimp he certainly wasn't. But then woollywoofterism and cowardice did not necessarily go hand in hand as many a giant name in history has testified. It always struck Thornton as faintly amusing that one of them, until fairly recent times every English schoolboy's hero though, with the state of modern education, the current generation had probably never even heard of him, sat astride his horse in Westminster and went by the name of Lionheart. What would poor old Venables have to say if he realised that Richard's lover was a French prince and that he was abjured by the church to give up sodomy and evil practices lest he bring down the wrath of the Almighty on the kingdom? Forgetting his anxieties for the moment regarding that plainclothes gentleman wrestling with his conscience and an almighty conundrum back at the station, and easing the pressing fingers from his left arm, Thornton smiled down at the pixy. 'It seems to me I know your face,' he said, 'what's your name?'

'Adrian. Adrian Spangle. What's yours?'

Thornton thought quickly. 'Charlie Thorpe,' he said.

'You don't look like a Charlie,' Adrian giggled.

'I certainly feel like one,' Thornton muttered to himself. And then, out loud, 'Adrian Spangle... the photographer?'

'Huh-huh.' Adrian nodded.

The verbal abuse from the louts was now followed up by the lobbing of a couple of lager cans which, as they were empty, didn't cause any particular damage although they did add to London's litter problem, which they would have done anyway. A couple of bobbies stood smilingly by obviously regretting the cans were aluminium. A few good old-fashioned beer bottles might have drawn blood or, at least, raised a few pigeon's eggs on a few heads. They also regretted the old-fashioned time when a few of these nancy boys could have been snatched and whisked off to the station for a not so peaceful lesson in how not to disturb the peace. Being a policeman did have its fun moments. Now, unless things got really out of hand, all they could do was stand by and watch or some goody-goody would be down on them like a ton of bricks and, if the gay they happened to snatch also happened to be black, they were really up shit-creek without a paddle.

'The trouble with that lot,' Adrian said, nodding towards the louts who, Thornton noticed with a distinct feeling of unease, were keeping pace with them, 'is that no one, but NO one on this earth, fancies them: not man, woman, nor dog, not even their mothers, and naturally they feel very bad about it, poor things.'

Thornton couldn't help smiling although he anticipated an incipient riot and the glimpse of a strategically parked police bus with reinforcements only added to his insecurity. He was so concerned that he hadn't noticed they were well passed Simpsons and almost at Piccadilly Circus. It was his turn to take Adrian by the arm. 'Let's get out of here,' he said urgently, and Adrian, mistaking his motives, was only too happy to oblige. They managed to work their way to the edge of the parade on the south side and Thornton almost flew down the subway steps. Half way down he stopped to slip off the coat and hold it out to Adrian. 'Here,' he said, 'thanks for the loan but I won't need it down here.'

But Adrian pushed away his hand and the coat with it. 'No, no, keep it,' he ordered, brooking no objection, 'until you're really warmed up.'

'In that case,' Thornton said, starting to unpin the badge, 'do you mind? Ouch!' He yelled as, in his haste, he stabbed his finger with the pin, drawing blood.

'You're not still in the closet are you, Charlie?' Adrian's enquiry carried a hint of disapproval.

'In the darkest corner,' Thornton replied, sucking his wounded finger, 'with both doors firmly closed.'

'Then how come you were on the march?'

'That would take a lot of explaining.'

'Humph!' Adrian was torn between disgust at his new friend's pusillanimity and the desire to play Florence Nightingale. Miss Nightingale won. 'Here,' he said, proffering a snowy white handkerchief, 'bind it up with that.' Thornton did so. Better his blood on a handkerchief than on an expensive suede coat. He slipped the badge into a pocket and they continued in silence down to the concourse. At the ticket automat Adrian turned to him. 'Your place or mine?'

'What? Oh! Oh, yours,' Thornton replied, 'definitely yours.'

They arrived on the westbound platform just in time to see the tail lights of a departing train as it sped into the tunnel. Thornton was a little disconcerted realising that, until the arrival of the next train, he would have to make some attempt at conversation and not too sure how he should go about it in the circumstances. He had never picked up a man before. It was a unique experience. The platform emptied of the passengers who had alighted only to make room for new arrivals from the outside. Thornton studied them closely and, although no one looked overtly suspicious, he had a nasty feeling in the pit of his stomach. Maybe it was the company he was keeping that made him uneasy. 'Let's move further up,' he said, and started to walk. Adrian dutifully followed.

'So where do you live, Charlie?' He asked as he padded along.

'East London,' Thornton said, 'in the socialist republic, nuclear -free zone of Hackney.'

'Oh,' was Adrian's response, meaning Thornton could have said he lived in Timbuktu or on Mars for that matter for all Adrian knew of the East End, though he had been told of one or two interesting pubs, especially if you were into rough trade; which he was. They stopped and Thornton turned to survey the platform. It looked peaceful enough but then, with another influx of humanity from the outside world, his heart missed a beat and then seemed to double its pumping speed. He realised Adrian was speaking to him. 'I'm sorry. What was that?'

'I said, don't they keep up with the times?'

'Who?'

'The people you're talking about.'

'What people?'

'Where you live!' Adrian was exasperated.

'Bigotry and hate, and ignorance, are difficult to eradicate, Adrian,' Thornton replied, 'especially when they are so deeply entrenched and even more so when they are donned as armour against a guilty conscience.'

'What on earth are you talking about?' Adrian looked truly perplexed. 'You've lost me completely.'

'And I wish this little lot had got lost. I have a feeling they're either from the same place or, worse, East Ham! They must have followed us.'

Adrian turned to look and they stood rooted to the spot as a half dozen members of the lager lout brigade approached them in decidedly bellicose fashion, chanting their homophobic slogans interspersed with scatological remarks which in their tiny befuddled minds passed for wit.

'I would have put them down at birth,' Adrian said, 'it would have been a kindness, and to think this lot are going to father the new generation.'

With the instinct of the pack, there having been no obvious signal given, the louts stopped their advance a few feet away and stood silently regarding their quarry. A few curious bystanders cast glances in their direction and then, suddenly losing their curiosity, moved discreetly away, switching their interest to the advertising or burying themselves in their newspapers.

'Fucking poofter!' One of the louts said, finally breaking the silence.

'Bloody queers!' Said another.

'Yeh,' said the third.

'Fancy me then do you, darlin'?' said the fourth with a leer.

'Like I would a dose of clap,' Adrian responded mildly. He looked very boyish in his chunky sweater and red and white striped ski bonnet with its pom-pom and Thornton couldn't believe what he was saying.

"Oh, my God!" He thought, placing a restraining hand on his companion's arm, a gesture immediately misinterpreted by the bovver boys who hooted in unison and for a few moments camped themselves silly in what they fondly imagined was an imitation of fag behaviour. "Please don't provoke the buggers," immediately went through Thornton's mind. He felt a bit like Chamberlain waving a piece of paper after Munich, which is why he didn't actually voice his thought. He also feared that saying it out loud would have exactly the effect of provoking the buggers. The camping stopped and the fifth youth's face, already a deep shade of acne spotted red, grew even more mottled as the leer was replaced by a menacing scowl. He moved forward, fists clenched, Doc Martins gleaming below his rolled up jeans. Thornton raised his other hand, intending to point a finger of warning, forgetting the finger's recent contact with a sharp point. It had bled profusely for so small a wound and, at sight of the red stained handkerchief, the lout stopped dead. Nobody would ever know what sparks suddenly flickered in its brain. Perhaps it was the sight of drawn blood that he had not had the satisfaction of personally drawing which surprised him but it was in that moment of indecision that she struck. Thornton had no idea where she had come from but suddenly she was between them and, with a high kick that would have done credit to a can-can dancer, the hard point of a dainty shoe connected with the underside of the youth's jaw closing his gawping mouth with the snap of a sprung trap and sending his bottom teeth grinding into the upper with such force the roots practically invaded his nasal cavities. He didn't actually stagger back. In some miraculous kind of way his feet left the ground and he seemed almost to fly as he sent two of his compatriots sprawling and the others leaping for safety. Then she turned to Thornton and smiled sweetly.

'Mr King,' she said as he gazed at her blankly, 'how nice to see you again. You remember me? N'tombi. We were introduced...'

'What? Oh. Oh yes. Yes, of course.' His stare strayed from her to the prostrate youth surrounded by his anxious companions and then back to her again. 'How are you?' Was all he could think to say, and then, to his great relief, a train came thundering out of the tunnel. 'Are you catching this one?' He shouted. N'tombi shook her head.

'As a matter of fact I'm going the other way,' she said and with a cheery wave she tripped away. Thornton and Adrian leapt for an open door and stood there prepared to repel boarders. One of the youths looked up.

'He needs an ambulance,' he cried.

'Then call one,' Adrian shouted back. The doors started to

close. 'And I hope it's a boy!' He added.

For a while they travelled in silence. Thornton was reliving what could have been an extremely nasty chapter in his life. Adrian was sulking. Thornton didn't know this until, passed Green Park, he turned to Adrian and asked where they were going? Receiving no answer, he repeated the question. 'Adrian, I said, where are we going?'

'Knightsbridge!' Adrian snapped. 'Sloane Square is closer but, as we're not on the right line, Knightsbridge will do.'

'Is something wrong?' Thornton asked.

Adrian gave him a sideways glance and then studied an ad for Odour-Eaters.

'What is it?' Thornton persisted. 'You thinking about what happened?' That was exactly what Adrian was thinking about but not in the way Thornton envisaged.

'Who was that woman? She a friend of yours?' From his strap hanging position Adrian scowled down at a youth desperately searching for his girl friend's tonsils with his tongue while she dug her nails into his blue-jeaned thigh. "Gross indecency," Adrian thought it, revolting, the kind of thing you would expect to see going on in a rip-off sex establishment on the Reeperbahn maybe, or in some dingy backroom club to where the *News of the World* was always sending its reporters to make their excuses and leave at the critical moment. It was not the sort of carry-on expected in the London Underground in full view of women, children, and respectable homosexuals.

'Just someone I met at a party the other day,' Thornton replied.

'She called you Mr. King.'

'Well of course she did,' Thornton agreed affably, 'that's my name.'

'Oh, no, it's not!' Adrian hissed, 'its Thorpe, Charlie Thorpe; at least that's what you told me. Or do you have a different name for everyone you meet? Is this all part of being in the closet?' Adrian's voice had got louder and Thornton looked around anxiously to see if anyone was listening but no one was. Adrian meanwhile hadn't taken his eyes off the couple below him who were oblivious to everything except their own intimacy. To make matters worse, at least as far as Adrian was concerned; the young man in question was to his way of thinking decidedly dishy, eminently havable, and a burgeoning beneath the blue jeans was beginning to make itself only too evident. This in turn brought about a stirring in Adrian's own loins until finally he could stand it no longer and turned to face Thornton. 'Well?' He snapped.

'It's a long story,' Thornton said.

'I bet.' Adrian glanced back at the jeans and dragged his eyes away again. Surely she wasn't going to stroke it, in full view of everybody?

'But I'll tell it anyway even if you don't believe me. I go by both names you see.'

'Really? Why?' He sounded genuinely interested.

Thornton launched into a long story about the divorce of his parents while he was still at a tender age, how his mother's maiden name was Thorpe and as he was close to his mother: his sweet, adorable mother, and hated his father; his cold, tyrannical father, a point Adrian could sympathise with as it was much the same in his own case, he preferred to use his mother's name rather than his legal one. However, if he were introduced as King then people used that name and there was really very little he could do about it was there? He silently hoped his parents, especially his sweet, adorable father, would forgive him and that Adrian had swallowed the lie: which he had; hook, line, and sinker, mainly because of the sweet adorable mother bit just like his own. Fortunately there were aspects of his own mother's life of which he was blissfully unaware but he felt emotionally much closer to Thornton as they left the train at Knightsbridge although he couldn't resist a last glance back before the doors closed.

'Did you SEE the SIZE of THAT?' He said with awe.

'The size of what?' Said Thornton in all innocence.

'And definitely TBH,' Adrian added.

Thornton noticed there were bars on all the windows of the little mews house as Adrian slipped his key into the double mortise, flung open the door, and with a theatrical flourish, ushered him in. 'Well here we are,' he chirruped, 'home sweet home.'

Thornton stepped straight into the front room. In fact, apart from a narrow galley-like kitchen at the back, the only room on the ground floor, and Adrian closed the door behind them. 'Welcome to "Bijou Cottage,"' he said as he took his coat from Thornton's shoulders and threw it over the back of a chair. Then he made as though to put his arms around Thornton's waist. Taken by surprise, Thornton jumped back.

'Hey, hey!' he said, holding Adrian at bay. 'What's the rush?'

'The rush, my dear,' Adrian said huskily, 'is time's winged chariot.'

'It's still standing in the stables,' Thornton replied.

'Oh. I see.' Adrian grew coquettish which made Thornton even more uneasy. 'You like to take things slowly do you?'

'The slower the better.'

'Fine by me, I've got nothing else in my diary. I left the day free for the march and whatever came out of it, and I like what came out of it.' His voice had grown husky again as he advanced on Thornton who slipped around a couch. Adrian stopped his advance. 'Perhaps you would like a drink,' he suggested, 'help to, you know, relax you a bit.'

'To tell you the truth, Adrian, there's nothing I would like better right at this moment.'

'Yes, you really are very tense, aren't you?' Was it the run-in with those hooligans?' Then, before Thornton had time to answer, 'What's it to be then?'

'What have you got?'

'Aha!' He wagged a finger. 'You'll have to wait and see what I've got. But, in the meantime, what would you like to drink? Name it.'

'Scotch, please. Straight.'

'One Scotch coming up.' Adrian shimmied over to a large gilt-framed mirror and gazed at his reflection for a moment. 'Mirror, mirror, on the wall, who's the fairest of them all?' And then, adopting a deep base answered, 'Not you, you silly bitch.' He broke into a peal of laughter, which ended in a mock sigh as he reached out for one side of the mirror. 'Ah, well, looks aren't everything as the actress said to the bishop. One has to be philosophical about these things.' He slipped his fingers behind the frame and pulled. The mirror swung out and concealed lighting automatically switched on to reveal a well-stocked and equipped drinks cabinet, the glass shelves backed by yet another mirror. Adrian deftly upturned a tumbler and reached out for a Waterford decanter to pour his guest a generous drink, chattering on gaily as he did so. 'My dear,' he said, 'if burglars ever did get into Bijou Cottage and I am told nothing, but nothing in the world will deter the determined burglar, not even the alarm and my barred windows, at least they won't find my Aladdin's cave. I can come home to find I've lost my all; my little nest has been soiled, despoiled. I can be totally distrought but at least I will be able to drown my despair in consoling alcohol while I wait for Lily Law to come and tell me that, not only is there precious little chance of catching the thief, or thieves, but even less chance of recovering my possessions and, as you can see, I do have a few bona things.' He handed Thornton his drink.

'Thank you,' Thornton said, wondering if Adrian ever stopped to draw breath. He raised his glass. 'Cheers!'

'Bottoms up!' Was the response. Thornton's hand paused half way to his mouth then continued its journey and he took a hefty swig at his scotch.

'The only consolation would be...' Adrian slipped off his shoes and padded across the deep-pile white carpet to a music centre where he ran his fingers along the spines of a row of LP's, selected one, and took it out, '... firstly, if I were in bed when the burglar called and he just happened to be very very dishy in a butch kind of way or, secondly, when Lil turned up she turned out to be even prettier even though totally clueless in the detection department.' He put on the record and performed a few languid dance movements to the music. 'Sarah Vaughan, a megastar if ever there was one, a diva, a prima donna, my dear. Don't you just love her voice? Most poofs go for fag-hags like Judy and Bette and Barbara, all wonderful lustrous creatures I admit, but I've got more class, dear. All my favourite singers are women, and all BLACK! All except Barbara Cook that is. I just adore Ella, and Sarah, Jessye and Lena! Now THERE'S a WOMAN for you! Have you ever in your life seen such a beautiful animal? As for the so-called pop stars of today...' The word pop popped out of his mouth like a mini-explosion, '... bumped up with all their technical shit. Take away the amplification, the echo chambers, the backing, the hype, and all the rest of it and where would they be? Give them a real song to sing and they'd fall flat on their tiny faces so hard their fannies would stick to the floor. You're not drinking.'

Thornton looked down at his glass. True. After the first panicky swig he had been so absorbed in the flow of chatter he had totally forgotten the glass in his hand. He looked up again as Adrian waltzed back across the carpet. 'It's too good to rush,' he said, wondering just how many delaying tactics he could think up and how long he could spin them out before Adrian decided it was time to get down to the nitty-gritty. There were many things he had done in the line of duty but biting the pillow and thinking of England wasn't one of them... look what it had done to Lawrence! Anyway, England had unceremoniously given him the boot. This was personal, he felt he owed it to the colonel, but even for the sake of auld lang syne bedding down with Adrian was really taking things too far. Not even for an old family friend would such a sacrifice be in order.

'I bet you say that about everything,' Adrian simpered.

'What?' Thornton had forgotten what he had said.

'Too good to rush,' Adrian reminded him.

'Oh. Yes, I suppose so.' He took a more genteel sip of his whisky. 'And I was admiring your pretty things.' He added, looking around the room.

'Well don't take too long about it. There are other pretty things to admire you know. Oh, my goodness! YOU'RE not a burglar are you?'

Thornton burst out laughing. It was a great relief to laugh. It seemed he hadn't laughed in a long while. He shook his head and watched as Adrian tripped back to the drinks cabinet to mix himself a snowball. If Adrian's orientation wasn't always obvious to the world outside it was certainly abundantly clear inside his own house. No one could be so naive as to mistake it for anything other than a tiny temple of phallus worship in the heart of Belgravia. The walls were hung with a number of theatre costume designs, all of young men in a state more of semi-nudity than costume. Bronze copies of Greek statuary were dotted about together with a number of modern pieces that were nothing if not homoerotic. Still, as Adrian was always delighted to point out, what the French call 'The English Vice' is not only universal but also as old as mankind itself so what was all the fuss about? Thornton wondered if Adrian's mother ever visited.

'I suppose as you're such a slow starter,' Adrian was saying as he sliced into a lime, 'I might as well join you in the drinkies stakes. I don't usually indulge before early evening but I guess there is always the exception to the rule and today is it.'

'Isn't it dangerous? Thornton asked, 'picking up strange men and bringing them home?'

Adrian turned wide eyes on his guest. 'What a weird question!' He said. 'Where have you been all your life? Oh, yes, of course, I forgot, in that dark dark closet. Haven't you heard, my dear? Life IS dangerous. Have you forgotten already that not more'n an hour ago we nearly, as our American cousins would say, had the shit beaten out of us? If it hadn't been for your little lady friend we could both now be prostrate in hospital beds or on slabs. So, if you're trying to frighten me, forget it. I can take care of myself.'

'I'm sure you can,' Thornton said.

Adrian went back to his mixing. Then another thought struck him and he turned back to look at Thornton. 'My God!' he shrieked. 'You're not a virgin are you? Not at YOUR AGE!'

Thornton laughed again. He was beginning to like Adrian. 'No, my dear,' he said, 'I am not a virgin. And I am certainly not trying to frighten you. Nor am I a burglar so you don't have to be anxious on that score. Relax.'

'Who said I wasn't relaxed? I'm so loose all I want to do is flop out somewhere on the horizontal.' Having mixed his snowball and dabbed with a glass cloth at the mess he had made by his over-enthusiastic use of the Soda siphon, he threw himself on the couch and patted the seat beside him. 'Do come and sit down, Charlie,' he said invitingly, curling his legs up beneath him.

Thornton put down his glass on the marble topped coffee table, carefully avoiding the glossy magazines that artistically adorned it. 'I need to use the loo,' he said.

Adrian took a sip of his snowball and pointed upwards. 'Up the stairs, first on the right. Go straight on by the first door you come to or you'll be right back in the closet. Oh, I forgot. You haven't come out of it have you?'

Thornton wondered if he detected a hint of acerbity in Adrian's voice. 'I won't be long,' he said.

'Promises, promises. Take your time, honey. But remember; shake it more than three times and you're playing with it.' Adrian sniffed loudly and took another sip of his drink. 'I'll just sit here, look beautiful, and listen to the divine Sarah until your return when you will play on me like a twelve string guitar.'

Feeling there was no answer to this, Thornton mounted the flight of open treads and found himself on a small L-shaped landing. The first door, so he had been informed, was to a closet. Ignoring the second and third, he stepped quickly to the end of the landing and carefully opened the fourth door to peep into what was obviously the spare bedroom. It was very small with hardly enough room for a single bed, American Colonial, and a mahogany chest of drawers on which stood a Victorian ewer and basin and soap dish decorated with tiny pink roses. The chamber pot belonging to the set stood on the windowsill and held a pale yellow chrysanthemum, an appropriate colour Thornton thought.

The pictures were discreet, a Hockney print and a couple of stark black and white photographs of New York, and not a priapic object in sight. He closed the door as gently as he had opened it and retraced his steps to investigate behind the third door, which had to be the main bedroom. This was a total contrast to the first room, which by Adrian's standards, was almost a monk's cell in its simplicity. Here there was only one picture, a photographic reproduction of Lord Leighton's *The Hit,* but there were mirrors everywhere. One wall was lined with fitted closets completely faced with them. The bed was enormous and littered with dolls, teddy bears, and cuddly toys of every size and description and all reflected in an enormous Baroque mirror angled slightly downwards at the head of the bed. The purple carpet was, if anything, of a deeper pile than the one below and the drapes, even on this dull day, were a shimmering white. In one corner a spiral staircase led to a room above. A studio? A darkroom?

Something, anyway, not normal in a mews house and it was up there Thornton surmised that he would find whatever it was that had led him here. The question was how to go about snooping around without Adrian's knowledge. He took a last look around the room. Apart from a couple of small Gallé lamps, one either side of the bed, the only source of illumination appeared to be a chandelier hanging from its rose in the centre of the ceiling. Naturally, Thornton noticed as he closed the door, it was on a dimmer. He moved to the second door, took a deep breath, and braced himself to face the bathroom.

He opened the door and stood stock-still. The colour scheme was chocolate, white, and gold. The bathroom suite and tiles were reproduction Edwardian with the fittings in gold. The pictures were alarming. There were a couple of Beardsley's more anatomically bizarre creations in Hogarth frames, a series of pornographic cartoons by Rowlandson complete with accompanying ditties, and a series of sepia blow-ups, photographs of naked boys every one of whom was hung like a horse. Thornton stepped back and closed the door, stepped forward and opened it again, crossed over to the toilet and flushed it. Then he left and, closing the door once more, descended the stairs to find Adrian exactly where he had left him although the glass in his hand was now empty. Adrian looked up and smiled.

'Find it all right?'

'Yes thank you.'

'Feel better?'

'Yes thank you. That's er... some bathroom you've got there. Did you take the...' Thornton paused... 'er the pictures of the boys?'

'My, my! You really are an innocent abroad aren't you? Goodness gracious! Have you never seen those photographs before?'

Thornton shook his head.

'They're famous, my dear! Fabularoso and famous. I copied them and printed the blow-ups of course but the originals are like a hundred years old or more. Not sure exactly. Couldn't you see they're period pieces? A Hun, a certain Baron von Gloeden, took them. He fled Prussia or wherever when his proclivities were discovered, though they're all in the same boat there so I am told but, like you, it's kept hush-hush, and he went to Sicily where he could photograph, and no doubt do delicious things, with boys to his heart's content, or something else's content anyway and, without doubt, she was a size-queen to end them all, dear, but don't they absolutely make the bathroom?'

Thornton nodded, took a deep breath, and reached for his drink. Adrian regarded him for a moment.

'So tell me, Charlie, if you're not a burglar, what do you do?'

'Oh, I work for a company in the West End.'

'Doing what exactly?'

'Buying and selling.'

'Buying and selling what?'

'Are you grilling me, Adrian?'

'I'm interested, darling.'

'Information.'

'How intriguing! What kind of information? Tell.'

'Oh, mostly industrial stuff, not nearly as intriguing as you think, quite boring really.'

'Right. Twenty questions over.' Adrian suddenly leapt to his feet. 'Time for beddies.' He crossed over to the drinks cabinet and put down his glass and already had a foot on a stair when Thornton stopped him.

'Adrian.'

Adrian turned.

'Aren't you forgetting something?'

'Am I?'

'Well, if it's all right with you, would you mind if I took a shower before... before...' He couldn't actually bring himself to say bed, 'and, if you don't mind my saying so, I would prefer it if you took one as well.'

'Watersports! I love it!' Adrian shrieked.

'No! No, I'm sorry, it's just that I happen to be very particular about cleanliness. Hygiene.'

'Oh.' Adrian couldn't conceal his disappointment. 'Fine. I'll wear surgical gloves and a mask, and we'll use tweezers.'

'I've offended you.' Thornton tried to look contrite.

'Not at all,' Adrian assured him, 'come along, let's shower. You can scrub my back and I'll do yours.' He resumed his ascent of the stairs.

'Er... no.'

Adrian stopped and turned to look down. He was frowning.

'Solo showers if you don't mind. Would you like me to go first?' And then, before Adrian could answer, 'No, I tell you what, I'll bring my drink upstairs...' He stepped up to Adrian's level, '... and finish it while you're showering.' He took the other's hand. 'Then I'll take mine.' He gave Adrian a peck on the cheek to allay suspicion and hand in hand they mounted the stairs, Adrian leading all the way to the bedroom door, which he pushed open and, with a flourish, ushered Thornton in, closing the door behind them.

'Wait in the boudoir,' he breathed, 'I'll be a little while making myself hygienic.' There was a suggestive pause before he emphasised the final word. 'I have to milk the ass first.' It would have been his turn to deliver a peck but somehow a glass of whisky just happened to get in the way so, with a last lingering look, he took the communicating door to the bathroom.

'Phew!' Thornton blew out hard, finished his drink, and put the glass down on the bedside cabinet. He heard the water running as the shower was turned on and quickly crossed the room to shut the bathroom door. Then he moved back and looked around. He smiled as his glance took in the bed with its accumulation of toys and, reaching out, he picked up a King Charles spaniel by its ear. Tiddly, a dog prone to no movement that didn't result in ingestion let out a staccato succession of soprano barks interrupted only for a second as he sunk his sharp little teeth into Thornton's finger. Thornton's instant reaction, as he leapt in a number of directions at once, was to drop dead of a heart attack. His second reaction was to dive for the floor where he managed to catch a Gallé lamp one inch above the carpet. Clutching the precious object in both hands, he lay there for a while eyeing the bathroom door, fully expecting it to fly open and a naked, possibly dripping Adrian to come bursting through. But nothing happened. The yapping had ceased and he could still hear the sound of the shower, which must have drowned out the noise in the bedroom. Valuable moments were slipping away. He got to his feet and, resisting the temptation to smash the objet d'art over the animal's head, he gingerly replaced the lamp on the cabinet. He was only too aware that, on its own, it was well worth any burglar's attempt to gain entry. As one of a pair he dreaded to think of its value. He retrieved the whisky glass which had also been knocked off and replaced that, then he stood and glowered at Tiddly who, seemingly satisfied that he had seen off his assailant and no counter-attack would be forthcoming, flopped down among the toys, gave his balls a quick lick, curled up, and promptly fell asleep again. Thornton inspected his finger to see that it was bleeding quite badly from a nasty rip brought about by a too hasty withdrawal from those snapping jaws. Thank God it hadn't happened above the white carpet!

He reached into his pocket for Adrian's already bloodstained handkerchief and, binding it around the fresh wound, made for the spiral staircase.

Reaching the top he found himself in a small studio. A quick glance around and he headed for a light box on which lay a number of transparencies. He switched on the light. The pictures were obviously from a modelling session and, as far as Thornton was concerned, he'd hit the jackpot. The location was the forecourt of the Midas Building. He switched off the light and, slipping a selection of slides beneath his jacket, headed for the stairs, managed to descend swiftly and without mishap, crossed the bedroom, moved quickly along the landing, pausing for an instant to listen to Adrian's warbling in the shower, before flying down the stairs and out of the house. He closed the front door gently behind him.

In the steam filled bathroom, the Baron's Sicilian boys' dead eyes and their more obvious attractions hidden in the mist and condensation, an expectant Adrian, looking forward to a happy hour or two of lubricity in every sense of the word, soaped his pits and, in true Garland style, gave a not too excruciating rendition of *The Man Who Got Away*.

Chapter Ten

Apart from a detour to see the other Adrian who was luckily on call at the hospital and obliged him with a quick anti-tetanus jab and three more stitches, Thornton allowed himself the luxury of a cab to take him straight home. The way he felt and after all he had been through he was not going to risk public transport. The cabby eyed him suspiciously.

'Been in the wars have you, mate?'

'You might say,' Thornton replied wearily, 'I have been defending my honour.'

'I hope you won,' the cabby said as they pulled out into the traffic.

Once inside his flat, Thornton made straight for the phone and called Holly. There was no answer. He assumed she was still luxuriating at the hairdressers. Ripping off his clothes and taking the phone with him he padded along to the bathroom where he ran a bath as hot as he felt he could bear. Easing himself into it with Oooh's and Aaah's, a couple of gasps and a wince or two, he almost immediately got used to the temperature and ran some more hot water. Then, with his newly bandaged hand hanging over the edge, he sunk to his chin beneath the surface and, like Tiddly, but without the preamble which, for him, would have been a physical impossibility anyway, promptly fell asleep to be awakened a chilling fifteen minutes later by the sound of the telephone ringing. It was the police to tell him he could collect the car. There being no point in even trying to warm up the now tepid water, he gripped the chain between his toes and yanked out the plug. Then he hauled himself up and reached for a towel.

Comfortable in slippers and his old towelling robe, Thornton rummaged through the fridge for something to fill the gap. He found some pâté, which had a decidedly suspicious green tinge to it, and a piece of old cheddar. Tossing the meat in the pedal bin, he settled for the cheese and some equally old water biscuits. He spread the transparencies on a table and, lifting them one by one to the light, examined them as he munched on hard cheese and soft biscuit. There was a girl in the pictures, a dog and, in one of them, a man standing in the background looking towards the girl, but they really needed blowing up to be examined properly and he did not have the means. Holly had a projector. Damn it! Why didn't she call? He glanced at his watch and decided to make a call of his own.

****

Thornton pressed the doorbell with a wool-covered finger. Woolly gloves were hardly the correct thing with a three-piece pinstripe suit but as leather could not be persuaded to stretch over wounded fingers, wool it had to be. He looked around as he waited. There was plenty of movement in the street and on the pavement but nothing seemed to be stirring inside the house. He rang again and, shielding his eyes with his gloved hand, he peered through the etched glass and the ornate iron grille behind it. A figure was approaching across the hall. Thornton stepped back. The door opened to reveal a hirsute colossus in a Petroushka costume. He looked down at Thornton, his face expressionless. Thornton smiled.

'The Princess Spitskaya please,' he said.

The giant shook his massive head slowly from side to side.

Thornton felt the hair should have moved about a bit as well. It didn't. Maybe the man had a permanent set but what was the gel? Glue? He decided he was not going to be put off by a mere six foot five twenty odd stone.

'The princess is not in?'

The man shook his head again and started to close the door. Thornton placed the end of his umbrella between the door and the jamb which was a mistake. He lost the end of his umbrella as the door slammed shut. He examined it ruefully. It was his best umbrella, a true Englishman's umbrella, long and shiny black and beautifully wrapped around the shaft. He aimed the broken tip at the bell, jabbed, and kept it there. It took a while but the door was finally flung open and the giant reappeared, stepped out and lifted Thornton a foot off the ground in what could only be described as a Russian bear hug. Then he carried him down the steps and deposited him, still standing, on the pavement, folded his arms and stood staring at Thornton, defying him to make another attempt.

'The trouble is, chummy,' Thornton said, still smiling affably, 'I think you'll find that I can run faster than you.' He suddenly crooked the handle of the umbrella behind the giant's leg and, with a simultaneous push and pull, upended him. Then he raced up the stairs, leaving his umbrella between the man's legs, and slammed the door behind him just as the giant made it and hammered on the woodwork. Thornton made sure the door was locked and sturdy enough to withstand the assault before he gave a little wave through the grille and moved away across the hall, heading for the room in which the fashion show had been held and from which came the sounds of some sort of activity. He opened the door and looked around. The activity immediately ceased as every head in the room turned towards the door.

'Good afternoon, ladies,' Thornton said, raising his hat. 'Please don't stop on my account.' Smiling, he surveyed the bevy of cat suited and leotarded beauties of various sizes, shapes, colour, contours, and features who gazed back at him, unsmiling. What does one call a group of fashion models? A mob of models? Singularly inappropriate. A modality of models, a molarity of models, in this particular instance perhaps a Moira of models was most apt. Or should it be Moirai? What he was really looking for as he scanned their faces was one who could pass easily for a boy. His gaze lighted on a bob-cut blonde, suitably gamine, but then he remembered Holly had said something about hair tumbling down and he moved on with a nod of recognition to N'tombi in passing, to a girl; tall, slender, with an abundance of raven hair tied up in a red bandana. It seemed she did not like his looking at her as she turned her head away to gaze at nothing in particular.

'Thornton, dear boy! What a pleasant surprise. Did Ivan let you in?' Tatty had left her seat against a wall and, stick in hand, was advancing on him. Although she appeared to be smiling, there was something chilly in her greeting.

'He did his best not to,' Thornton said, keeping his eye on the girl in the red bandana who had now turned her head to look at nothing in particular in the opposite direction.

'You must forgive him, Thornton. He guards my girls jealously and sometimes he can be a little too zealous. The hungriest wolves are not necessarily Siberian you know. To what do we owe the pleasure of your visit, dear boy? Have you come to see Mira?'

'Mira?' He turned to look at Tatty who was now standing very close and breathing garlic all over him. He wondered if she had been lunching at *L'Éminence Grise* again.

'That's Mira, is it?' He looked at the girl again but she still avoided his gaze.

'I only ask because you seem to be taking such an interest in her. Are you interested in her? Or have you come for some other reason?'

Thornton thought quickly. There really was no reason for him to be there and to say he was looking for a girl who could pass for a boy would sound ridiculous and distinctly suspect. If he couldn't come up with something legitimate it was quite likely that Ivan the Terrible would be let loose and, if allowed free rein, wouldn't be quite so gentle with him next time around. 'Actually, Princess, I've come to see N'tombi.'

'All right, girls,' the princess thumped the floor with her stick, 'carry on.' She took her unexpected guest by the arm and led him towards her chair. 'I might tell you, Thornton, I don't appreciate classes being interrupted, for whatever reason. You are a naughty boy.' She patted his hand, a gesture that, for some reason, made his flesh crawl. He looked back at the girls, none now quite as beautiful as a few moments before.

'Weight lifting, Princess?' He raised an eyebrow. 'For models?'

'But of course. There is nothing like it, Thornton, for the development of strength, suppleness, and agility. Provided of course it is done in moderation and does not build unsightly muscle I strongly recommend it.'

'What about golf? Do you recommend that?' He wondered if it was his imagination or did her fingers tighten momentarily on his arm before she let it go?

'Ah, yes... golf...' She thumped the floor suddenly with her stick as she was distracted by the activity. 'Keep that bar straight, Zena!' Then, obviously satisfied her instructions were being obeyed, turned back to Thornton. 'I trust you had an enjoyable game with the colonel... Mira! Swing from the hips, girl, from the hips... She pronounced it "zee eeps..." 'Who won?'

'Nobody won. We didn't even get started.'

'He didn't call it off!'

'Somebody else did.' Thornton was looking around the room again. He caught Mira's eye but it was only an instant before she looked away again.

'Oh, that's too bad.' She sounded genuinely disappointed for him.

'I take it you know nothing about the accident?'

'Accident? What accident?'

'The colonel is dead, Princess.'

'Oh!' With a little cry and her hand on her heart, the princess sank onto her chair and stared at Thornton with wide eyes. The woman was either a consummate actress or she genuinely did not know anything about it and Thornton couldn't tell which was the truth. She was breathing hard. He could see the rise and fall of her chest, which was somewhat disconcerting. 'Oh, no!' She looked beyond him as though conjuring up her last memories of the colonel. 'How? Why?'

'Why? That's a strange question.' Thornton turned again to look at Mira. 'Because somebody wanted it that way. Tell me,' he turned back to the princess, 'has one of your girls been keeping company with the colonel recently?'

'No, of course not. I mean, not that I know of. No, I hardly think so.'

Thornton decided it was time to stop pussyfooting around, this was getting him nowhere. 'Tell me, princess,' he said, 'in strict confidence of course, between old friends,' he leaned forward so that his face was level with hers. He was aware that every pair of eyes in the room were focused and every pair of ears bent in his direction. 'Why are you doing it?'

'Doing what, dear boy?' She gazed at him steadily, her hands folded over the head of her stick.

'You don't know what I'm talking about?'

'Not when you talk in riddles.'

'On the contrary, Princess, it is you who are the riddle.' He straightened up. 'Well riddle me this then: what is small and white and goes hop hop hop?'

'A rabbit?'

'And blows up in your face when least expected.' Like a conjurer he suddenly produced a golf ball from his pocket and bounced it on the floor in front of her, deftly catching it on the rebound. All movement in the room stopped dead. Thornton turned and tossed the ball towards the iron-pumping young ladies of the Spitskaya School of Modelling. No one moved, except Mira, who visibly flinched.

'Good afternoon, everybody,' he said, flourishing his hat and turning towards the door where his nose hit Ivan's chest at about the fourth rib. Thornton stepped back and waited. Ivan glanced beyond him towards the princess. She waited a moment and then waved her hand in dismissal. Ivan stepped aside.

'Thank you,' Thornton said and left. Ivan followed him. The girls turned to look at Princess Spitskaya. Her face was set, grim.

'Mira, you will stay behind after class. You still have a very important lesson to learn.'

****

'Nothing?' Holly put down the tray, seated herself on the couch and started to pour the coffee.

'Nothing. At least nothing to speak of. For some reason best known to her, the Princess Tatiana Spitskaya is playing some kind of cat and mouse game.'

'And you think you're the mouse.'

'I know she is somehow connected with, or even responsible for, seven apparently motiveless killings... thank you...' as Holly passed him his coffee... 'and she knows I know. What's more, she wants me to know. But why?' He started to stir the coffee even though he hadn't as yet added any sugar. Holly passed him the bowl. 'So, if that is definite policy on her part, what is it in aid of? It seems a really weird thing to do, doesn't it? To raise my suspicions? Put me on my guard?'

'She needs you for something?'

Thornton shrugged and dipped his spoon into the sugar bowl.

'And if you carry on the way you're going,' Holly went on, 'she'll lose you before we find out what it is.' Thornton looked puzzled. 'You've already put six spoonfuls of sugar in your coffee and are about to add a seventh. Death by carbohydrate is about to take place.'

'Sorry.' He put down his spoon and looked ruefully at his undrinkable coffee.

'I'll get you a fresh cup.' Holly started to rise but Thornton waved her back.

'Let's take a look at these,' he said, taking the transparencies from an envelope. 'See what we come up with.' He held one up to the light and squinted at it.

'How did you come by those?' Holly asked, resuming her rise and making for a cupboard.

'It's a long story but to cut it really short, they came from Adrian Spangle's mews house.'

Holly, carrying her projector, was making for the dining table when she stopped. 'You broke in there?'

'I was invited in there.'

'You what!'

'Yes, my dear, believe it or not, I got picked up.'

'You don't have to sound so smug about it.'

'And invited back to his place.'

'And you escaped in one piece?'

'I fought like a tiger for my honour, and these...' he waved the envelope in the air, '... were my reward. But, the whole episode nearly came to a premature end when we were ganged up on at

Piccadilly station.' And he went on to tell her of the lager louts and N'tombi's timely intervention.

'She just happened to be there?' Holly had plugged in the projector and switched it on.

'Another coincidence? I don't think so. I think she followed me from the police station. But this whole crazy thing gets more bewildering with each turn of event because she must have seen me pick up Adrian...'

'I thought you said it was you who was picked up.'

'All right, we picked each other up. And, if Adrian is somehow involved in all this, why did she come to our rescue? Surely it would have been wiser to let the louts get on with it and make sure that our brief friendship, Adrian's and mine I mean, was brought to a sticky end then and there? Thank goodness it didn't come to a sticky end later.'

'No guarantee of the louts truly ending it, and maybe she just didn't want you back chatting to Sergeant Venables a third time. Anyway, get the screen and let's hope your slides aren't merely pornographic. What's his house like, Thorn?'

'We are not here to discuss the decor of a queen's residence, Miss Day. There is serious work to be done. I think you might have liked the bathroom though.'

Thornton set up the screen, Holly dimmed the lights, and they studied the first photograph.

'Recognise the girl?' Thornton asked.

'No.'

'I do. I saw her only this afternoon. She was having a weight problem.'

'Are you kidding? Not in a million years, not with that figure. Lucky bitch.'

'I don't think luck has much to do with it. Not from what I saw going on this afternoon. It looked like bloody hard work to me.'

'I don't recognise the dog either. And it certainly doesn't have a weight problem. Lucky bitch.'

'Probably a member of school staff. How do you know it's a bitch anyway?'

'Figure of speech.'

'Let's have the next one.'

Holly replaced the slide with another. All it revealed was a different pose and the dog looking as though it was about to be sick, which maybe it was. They tried a third. A man had entered the frame. He had his back to camera as he mounted the steps.

'Next one! Next one!' Thornton snapped impatiently. Holly obliged. They stared at the picture. The man was now at the top of the steps. He had turned and was smiling as he looked towards the girl.

'Dominici,' Thornton said and this time it wasn't his voice that snapped, it was middle finger and thumb, an action that made Holly all fingers and thumbs so that it was a second or two before they could examine the next slide. It was almost a copy of the previous one with the three figures standing in exactly the same positions.

'Spot the differences and win the prize,' Thornton said.

'The girl has what looks like a cigarette holder in her mouth and the man is scratching his neck,'

'Scratching? Or feeling?' Thornton left his chair and turned up the lights.

'You don't want to see any more?' Holly sounded surprised.

'No. That was the one.'

She removed the transparency and switched off the projector.

'That school,' he said, 'we've got to go over it with a fine tooth comb. Somewhere in there is the answer, one clue, one tiny clue to tell us just what all this is about, what her little game is. I need your help, Holly.'

'Thornton, we shouldn't even be doing this. It has nothing to do with us.'

'After what happened to you? What happened on the golf course? How can you say that?'

'I know the colonel was a friend of yours but why don't we just turn the whole thing over to the police and let them get on with it?'

'Get on with what?'

'An investigation. Do you want your coffee now?'

'What investigation, Holly? They're already taking their own line of enquiry into the killings and we have nothing to offer them except suspicion. I doubt they'd be inclined to believe anything we said anyway as we're not above suspicion ourselves. In fact, as far as Venables is concerned, prime suspects I would think. What are we going to do? Take along a photograph showing a dog, a girl with a cigarette holder, and a man scratching his neck? Even if that man does happen to be the late Dominici. So are you going to help? There's a great Russian bear in that gilded cage, going by the name of Ivan: he will have to be taken care of.'

'That's my job, is it?'

'You had a good workout this morning didn't you?

'I also, at enormous expense, had my hair done, about which you have made no comment, and I don't want it mussed up.'

'So you would desert me in my hour of need for the sake of a hair-do? Which, I might add, really suits you. It's beautiful.'

'Flattery will get you everywhere. Tonight?'

'Not tonight. Tonight is too close to this afternoon and, besides, I need my sleep. Tomorrow night.'

Thornton might have needed his sleep but he wasn't to have it. It seemed his head had no sooner hit the pillow when the telephone rang. He let it ring a few times and then, in case it was Holly, he lifted the receiver and croaked into it.

'Yes?'

He hoped, whoever it was, would realise they had woken him up and would feel guilty as hell. It didn't work.

'Mr King?' It was a woman's voice, vaguely familiar. He sat up. 'Yes?'

'Mr King, I need your help. Can you help me?'

'Who is this?' He switched on the bedside lamp.

'It's N'tombi. I'm in terrible trouble. Please, you must help me! There is no one else I can turn to. I'll wait for you here. Come and get me.'

'Hey? Where are you?'

'King's Cross Station.'

Thornton looked at his bedside clock. It was one o'clock. 'Well I wouldn't hang around there if I were you,' he advised brightly. 'The vice squad will cart you off before you can say "want to do business?"'

'Mr. King, I have no intention of hanging around, that's why I called you. Please come, as quickly as you can. I'll wait for you by the bookstore, the one by the main doors.'

'Look, N'tombi...' Thornton scratched the back of his head, which had suddenly started to itch crazily. 'Can't you just hop in a cab?' There was a silence. Thornton scratched the other side of his head. 'N'tombi? You still there?'

'Mr. King, I hate to remind you of this,' her voice was low and she seemed to emphasis each syllable, 'but you owe me one.'

'You're dead right,' he said, 'I'm on my way.' He put down the phone and lay there for a second scratching his chest to where the itch had transferred itself indicating his nervous system was temporarily shot to hell. Then he lifted the receiver again and dialled Holly's number. The ringing at the other end went on for a long time; so long in fact that he was on the point of putting down the phone when she answered.

'Yes?'

That one word was enough to tell him she was not pleased. 'Holly...'

'Shit, Thornton! What now?' She was definitely not pleased. 'Do you know what time it is?'

'I've just had a call from N'tombi.'

'Oh, yes? What about?'

'She seems to be in some sort of trouble, or so she says. Wants me to go and collect her.'

'Where?'

'King's Cross Station.'

'In the left baggage? What are you telling me for?'

'I thought you might be interested.'

'You want me to come with you?'

'I think not. If I'm going to shine in white armour and rescue a damsel in distress I can hardly take another damsel along with me can I?'

'Fine. You go and slay the dragon like a good boy. I'll go back to sleep. Just make sure you don't get your whatsits singed.' And the phone went dead.

Thornton sat up in bed holding the receiver and slapping it gently a few times against the palm of his other hand before replacing it. How, as he was ex-directory, did N'tombi get his number?

Holly lay staring at the ceiling. There was no way she was going to get back to sleep now. She threw off the bedclothes, slipped into a robe and furry mules that she wouldn't have been seen dead in had anybody been around, and padded off to the kitchen for that English panacea, a cup of tea. Then she settled down in front of the telly. If anything were likely to make her drop off it would be looking at a test card. She couldn't have been more wrong. She was wide-awake and it seemed she would stay that way.

She wasn't by the bookstore. In fact there was no sign of her. Railway terminals when crowded and bustling were never the most salubrious of places Thornton thought as he looked around, but in the early hours when they were frequented mainly by those derelicts of society nice people don't make it a habit of thinking about, they were truly depressing. The traffic outside the station, both motorised and pedestrian, was still pretty heavy with no doubt a good deal of business of one sort or another being transacted but of N'tombi there was no sign. Had it been a hoax? Or had something happened to her? If it were the former he didn't appreciate the joke as he shivered in a biting wind and hotfooted it back to the concourse for a last look around. Whatever the reason for the girl's non-appearance there was nothing he could do about it and he decided to leave. He had just reached the doors again when she appeared at his side. N'tombi seemed to have the knack of materialising out of thin air. At the touch of her hand on his arm Thornton nearly had a laundry problem, not his usual reaction to a woman's touch. 'Where on earth did you spring from?' He asked, still quivering. 'You should hire yourself out as a conjurer's assistant.'

Wrapped in a sheepskin coat, multicoloured woollen scarf and woolly hat, a sling bag over her shoulder, her hands encased in woollen gloves, 'Where's your car?' Was all she said as she hurried him out, keeping her head down, looking neither to right or left. But Thornton kept a wary eye open as, arm in arm, they moved as quickly as they could towards York Way. Thornton was anxious to get back to the car anyway. All he needed now was for it, or parts of it, to be nicked or vandalised and he was well and truly in the doghouse with Harold. But, apart from having to sidestep one or two lurching drunks, one of whom fell flat on his face and remained where he had fallen ignored by all. Apart from being accosted a couple of times for change, they were mugged by nothing more aggressive than some really bad halitosis and Thornton heaved a sigh of relief to see the car all in one piece. He held the door open for her and she slipped into the passenger seat. Feeling intensely vulnerable standing in the badly lit side street his hackles rose. Like a child, fearful of the dark and not daring to look behind him just in case there happened to be something there, he made his way around the car and only, as he opened his own door, did he look around. There was nothing. He climbed in and settled himself behind the wheel.

'Thank you for coming,' she said.

Thornton slipped the key into the ignition and started the car but made no attempt to put it into gear. Instead he placed both hands on the wheel and stared out of the windscreen. She turned to look at him.

'What are we waiting for?' She asked.

Thornton drummed his fingers on the wheel. N'tombi regarded him for a moment, waiting for an answer, and then she looked anxiously around.

'Mr. King, please! Take me somewhere. Somewhere safe.' There was no denying the tension in her voice but still Thornton did not move. She looked around again; growing even more agitated, and then turned back to him. 'Don't you want to help me? Do you think I'm lying to you?'

It was his turn to look at her. He could make out her features in the light cast by a street lamp. She was an extremely beautiful woman but the strain was telling. The face was drawn and she ran her tongue over dry lips.

'Mr. King, I am in terrible danger. Please! We can't just sit here!'

Thornton never took his eyes from her face. She looked back through the rear window as though fully expecting someone to materialise. Thornton nodded.

'My place?'

'Anywhere, anywhere! But quickly!' In her agitation she dropped her gloves and bent forward to look for them. Thornton immediately leaned across, his left shoulder over her back and, as she groped for her gloves, he deftly opened the shoulder bag she had placed on the seat and groped inside that. His fingers curled around a small pistol and he withdrew it just as N'tombi straightened up and he did likewise.

'Got them? Good.' He had transferred the gun from his left to his right hand and slipped it into his jacket pocket. Putting the car into gear, he checked his rear-view mirror and they pulled away, nosed down passed the station, turned left, and the car climbed the hill that is the Pentonville Road, down the other side, crossed The Angel, and it wasn't until they had traversed The City Road and turned into Broad Street heading for Shoreditch that Thornton broke the silence. 'Have we been followed do you think?' He asked, positive that they hadn't.

'I don't think so.'

'Do you want to tell me what all this is about?' He gave her a momentary sideways glance, just long enough to see her shake her head before turning his attention back to the road, which was just as well as a taxi driver in a hurry to get home nearly carved him up and he had to swerve violently in order to keep Harold's precious machine intact. 'Phew!' He gave a nervous laugh. 'That was a near thing.' He gave her another glance, looking for sympathetic agreement, but she was staring straight ahead. There was obviously no point in pressing her.

Maybe she would loosen up once they were inside the flat. But, as he opened the front door to usher her in she seemed, if anything, even more nervous which for someone who, single-footed, had been prepared to take on a bunch of hooligans of very little brain but a lot of collective kicking power seemed decidedly odd. Whatever she found so frightening it had to be something dramatic. She had stuffed her gloves and woolly hat in the pockets of her coat which he now took from her and, together with her scarf, tossed casually over the back of a chair as he motioned her to another. She seated herself demurely on the edge, hands clasped in front of her knees, bag by her side. Thornton smiled to himself as he noted this. She was dressed in a chunky sweater as multicoloured as her scarf and what looked like tracksuit bottoms. N'tombi was a girl who obviously felt the cold. She slipped off her shoes to reveal thick black socks. It wasn't the sexiest outfit in the world but it could reasonably be described as cuddly and for some people cuddly is a big turn-on.

'Would you like a drink?' He picked up a decanter and held it out towards her. 'Brandy perhaps. Calm you down.'

She shook her head. He shrugged and started to pour one for himself as she silently watched his back. 'If it would be all right...' she said and Thornton, decanter poised, looked over his shoulder. '... I would like some tea.'

'Tea? You have been anglicised.' He laughed and, having poured his tot, stoppered the decanter. She smiled for the first time, not much of a smile, more of a hint. Or was it the hint of a sneer?

'You Imperialists never really change do you?'

Thornton, who had put his glass down on the coffee table in front of her, looked up in surprise. 'Imperialists? What a quaint old-fashioned word.'

'Old habits and old-fashioned ways of thinking die hard.'

'And I didn't realise you were a political animal,' he said, turning away and making for the kitchen.

'You mean models are meant to think only of contracts and clothes, hair-do's and make-up? Sometimes sex?'

'What did she mean by that?' Thornton thought, raising his eyes from the china teapot in his hand. He still had his back to her.

'Anglicised! Humph! You think it's only the English who drink tea?

'Whoever, whatever,' he said, trying to mollify her. Maybe it was her nerves but her mood seemed to have turned ugly. 'Tea it shall be.' He swilled out the teapot and tipped it over the sink to empty it of old leaves. 'I'll put on the kettle.'

Suddenly she laughed. Thornton stopped in surprise and looked at her inquiringly. 'What's so amusing?' He asked, smiling in response.

'I was just imagining how funny you would look wearing a kettle,' she said.

'Oh, we've recovered our sense of humour have we? Things are looking up.' He turned away to fill the kettle, placed it on the stove but before he could turn on the gas she was behind him and her arms encircled his waist. He looked down at her hands, slender brown fingers entwined, as she lowered her head and rubbed her cheek against his back. He took her wrists and, gently pulling her hands apart, turned to face her. The arms went around again and he could hardly prise her fingers apart behind his back, not without practically dislocating his elbows. Now the cheek was rubbed against his chest. Thornton wasn't at all sure whether he should play along with this sudden display of affection or put a stop to it right then and there. Could it be gratitude? Could it be that she genuinely fancied him? Or, considering recent events, was there an ulterior and sinister motive? Perhaps she sensed his indecision and decided to make up his mind for him because the fingers were now running lightly up and down his back and she was worrying a shirt button with her tiny white teeth.

She stopped this activity to look up at him with those enormous brown eyes and the hands now changed position to glide smoothly up and down his thighs, firstly on the outside, then moving inwards. She smiled a smile so engaging all doubt, all resistance, was coming to an end with ever increasing speed. Thornton's knees trembled ever so slightly as he bent to kiss her. It was a long, lingering kiss. She parted her lips just ever so slightly, just enough to say, we can take this as far as you want, if you want. And Thornton wanted. Oh, how he wanted! If she wanted inside his pants he most certainly wanted inside hers and suddenly that's where a hand found itself, seemingly of its own volition. His other hand she held to her mouth as she licked his palm, as her tongue slid in and out between his fingers, as she sucked his thumb. His own adroit fingers slipped inside that soft sweetness and now caution was for cowards. He was dribbling like there was no tomorrow and maybe there would be no tomorrow but where his fingers were was where his tongue should be, where his tongue should be another part of him would surely follow. He removed his hands and lifted her off her feet, prepared to carry her to the bedroom like a bride across the threshold. She was extraordinarily light for someone equipped with so lethal a kick. She suddenly said quite softly, 'Thornton?' which made him pause in full stride, a fatal mistake. He looked at her, eyebrows raised. 'Could I have that cup of tea first?'

Was he hearing right? What gives with this woman?

Here they were about to experience two of the most historical orgasms of all time even if his happened to be his last and she wanted a cup of tea!

'Tea', he said.

She nodded, smiling happily. He gently lowered her legs to the floor, retrieved his arms and went to put on the kettle. Then he dropped a couple of Earl Grey tea bags into the teapot before returning to his guest who, it appeared, had moved back to her seat. He collected his brandy and dropped into the couch opposite her. 'Cheers!' He said, raising his glass. But he didn't drink, merely lowered the glass again and set it down on the table between them. N'tombi didn't stir. Only her eyes followed the movement of his hand. 'So what is all this about?' He asked, now all suspicious again as she kept her eyes on the brandy and then, lowering her head further, buried her face in her hands. Thornton waited patiently until the sobbing died away and she raised her face to see him regarding her steadily. She sniffed and made to open her bag. 'Here!' Thornton said quickly, a couple of decibels louder than he had intended. He presented her with a clean hankie, which she took.

'Oh, Mr. King...' She sniffed.

'Please, call me Thornton.' Was there a hint of acid in his voice?

'Thornton. I've got myself into such a mess. Could I stay here? With you? For a while?'

This was totally unexpected. The girl was certainly full of surprises. A picture of his one and only bed now definitely occupied by two clicked into his imagination and nestled comfortably there for a while before he replied.

'What a charming notion,' he said as she returned his gaze quite steadily now, the large brown eyes appealing for sympathy. Could it be the girl was genuine after all? After all she had given him a taster. Maybe where she came from, wherever that was, tea drinking was all part of the mating ritual. 'But tell me all about it,' he continued. 'When I've decided just how much of a mess you've supposedly got yourself into I'll decide where would be the safest place to put you.'

'I feel very safe here with you.' This was the "you are my big strong daddy, I am your little girl" approach.

'Very flattering,' said big strong daddy, 'but, to be quite blunt, my dear, all of a sudden I feel far from safe here with you.'

She looked hurt. 'But why?' She cried.

'Because sooner or later your absence, if it hasn't been already, is going to be noticed, and bloodhound Ivan, nostrils flaring, will be picking up the scent and following the trail, and I have no desire to find him sniffing around my front door thank you very much. Not even with you here to protect me.'

'Oh, is that all?' Was her calmer response. 'For a minute I thought you distrusted me.' Thornton didn't bother to confirm that this was also in his mind. She shrugged off the idea of Ivan the Terrible following them. 'No one knows I'm here,' she said.

'Maybe not, but they could hazard a good guess, especially after my little visit to the school this afternoon. Yesterday afternoon. So, by the time they do get around to figuring out where you might be, it certainly won't be here.'

'You mean you're not going to help me?'

He parried the question with one of his own. 'Where are you from, N'tombi? I take it you're from Africa. What part?'

'What's that got to do with anything? Are you a racist?'

'Not that you'd notice. I never do. And I'm not a misogynist either I hasten to add before you start throwing that at me.'

'But you won't help me.'

'I didn't say that. You still haven't told me anything.'

'You're not drinking your brandy, Mr. King.' A little frown crinkled her forehead.

Thornton felt rather than heard the change in her voice and it wasn't just because she had gone back to Mr King rather than Thornton. 'It isn't the right temperature yet.' He lifted the balloon in his cupped hand and circled it gently before sniffing the bouquet. 'Aaah... One of the most appetizing scents in the world,' he sighed, and put the glass down again. N'tombi's frown deepened. Thornton smiled. 'Well?'

'Well what?'

'Come, come, my dear, don't pout. Though I must confess it is extremely becoming. Just start at the beginning and tell me what all this is about.' He looked pointedly at his watch. She took the hint.

'It's the school.'

'Ye-es?'

'You think it's a school of modelling. But it's not. The modelling is just a cover.'

'How you do surprise me. So what exactly is it then? This school of modelling that isn't a school of modelling.'

'It is a school for assassins.'

For a long while they could have been dummies in a window display. It was as if time had stopped. No sound came in from outside, as though a great silence had descended on the city. As Thornton didn't seem inclined to break it. It was N'tombi who continued.

'The students undergo an intensive training course in methods of killing but, more important, methods of getting close without suspicion and in a position to kill.'

Thornton finally found his voice. 'And exactly who are you being trained to kill?'

'There are people in many countries, my own country for instance, who want to... who need to... dispose of certain other people...'

'You're trying to put this in as nice a way as possible aren't you? But euphemisms won't disguise the fact...'

She impatiently waved him to silence. 'They are rich and powerful, but not all powerful, and they would like to be.'

'You mean, for example, there's an opposition party?'

'Or, perhaps, they are in danger and they wish to avert that danger. Or perhaps the powers that be stand in the way of other ambitions. Or perhaps it is the organisation of another country that wishes to change the status quo. Whoever they are, Mr. King, and whatever the reasons, the quickest way to achieve the desired end is by assassination and in my country I have been the one chosen to do it. Please believe me when I say it is not just for material gain that I am prepared to do this. In my case it is patriotism. It is idealism.'

'Good words to hide behind.'

'But, apart from knowing that I will be doing my country a great service, I will be paid well for what I do. I will never have to worry about where the next penny is coming from.'

'No, you will never have to worry about that because, having done the deed, you will probably end up an unidentified corpse in the jungle.'

'We don't have jungle, Mr. King, we have bush. And thanks for the warning. I'll remember it.'

'So that is what she's up to,' Thornton murmured, more to himself than to his guest, but she took it up anyway.

'Princess Spitskaya works on the theory that the person able to get closest to a man is, of course, a woman.'

'Of course,' Thornton agreed, remembering their most re-cent moments together, 'perfectly natural, the majority of men anyway. And, believe it or not, we had already figured that out for ourselves.'

'We? Oh! You mean Miss Day.'

'Do I? Well tell me this, Holly could hardly be mistaken for a man even if she were to emulate my namesake.'

'I beg your pardon?'

'Oh, forgive me, a part of our British heritage that would be unfamiliar to you, a famous music hall star by the name of Hettie King used to perform her numbers dressed as a man.'

'Why?'

'The English tend to like that sort of thing. Anyway, as I said, Holly is no Hettie King so how come she was on the hit list?'

'The princess thought it would be best to get rid of her. It didn't go unnoticed that she followed Anya out of the restaurant the day Mr. Shoggi was... was...'

'I think murdered is the word you're searching for,' Thornton said. N'tombi shrugged. 'And the princess would have had to be totally blotto not to know what Holly was up to.'

N'tombi gave another little shrug. 'Anyway,' she continued, 'as the world is ruled mainly by men, it is women who have been chosen to... put an end to them. All the girls have been sent to the school by people in their own countries. Of course it is not always politicians who are involved.'

'So Tatty takes the girls, trains them, and sends them back to where they came from to do the dirty deed, while she coins another small fortune. After all, think what it costs to train a racehorse. How much is a thoroughbred assassin worth? But why is she doing it? She doesn't need the money.'

'Maybe she longs for the good old days.'

'Good old days?'

'Just how much do you know about her, Mr King?'

'I guess she was always a dangerous woman to get involved with.' It wasn't much of an answer and, to tell the truth, he suddenly realised that in fact he really did not know much about the Princess Tatiana. 'Couldn't she have got it all off her chest by writing an autobiography?'

'Telling it like it really was? The truth, the whole truth, and nothing but the truth?' N'tombi laughed. 'Oh, no, some things are better left unspoken and unknown, Mr. King. Like Laski, for example, found on the line with multiple injuries, fell from the Orient Express. Verdict suicide. Who was his travelling companion? The mysterious woman who disappeared and of whom no trace was ever found. What about Berlin? Wolfgang Bauer. Found dead in a brothel after indulging evidently in the most bizarre perversions. Belgrade, Trebescu, savaged by Doberman Pinschers. Joubert, Switzerland, skiing tragedy. How do you think, Mr. King, she found the capital with which to start her business? But the world of commerce, of manufacture, of buy and sell, wheeling and dealing, what excitement does that hold for a woman who has always lived on the edge of physical danger? I'm sure she had some satisfaction from beating rivals, destroying them even, gobbling them up, but it was not enough. So now, as an old woman who can do no more herself, she relives it all through us. I don't know if that is the reason. I only know we have the greatest teacher of them all.' N'tombi's eyes were alight, her voice filled with admiration. She looked radiant, not a pupil, but a disciple. 'The greatest teacher of them all.' For a while she was lost in recollection.

In the long room she saw the Princess Olga Tatiana Katarina Spitskaya sitting upright in her chair against the wall, her arms outstretched, her gnarled, liver-spotted hands curled over each other and the head of her heavy stick. Her girls, except for five of their number, stand in a line against a side wall, four of them are against the far wall opposite her and a few feet in front of her, in the middle of the room, stands N'tombi. Suddenly, like sprinters responding to the starter's pistol, or through some subconscious signal they all simultaneously sense, the four girls race towards their target, each girl weaving a slightly different course so as to reach N'tombi at fractionally different moments. Within seconds each girl has been sent flying as, in a flurry of movement and yells, N'tombi counters the attacks. The princess raps the floor with her stick.

"Very good, N'tombi, very good. Relax. Right now, let's see..." She surveys the line of girls obviously with the intention of picking out the next team. N'tombi relaxes, turns her back on the princess and moves towards her place against the wall. Immediately the princess raises her hand. The door opposite opens to reveal Amelia armed with a baton about three feet long, capped with a steel spike at one end and a hook at the other. She races silently across the room, the baton above her head. None of the girls give any indication as to what is happening as Amelia brings the spike down hard and fast, aiming for the nape. Seemingly at the very last second N'tombi sidesteps and, as the spike flashes by, back-chops Amelia in the solar plexus. Amelia gasps and doubles up, the baton is twisted from her hands and, as she sprawls on her back whooping painfully, trying desperately to get some breath into her lungs, N'tombi stands over her, the spike an inch from her nose. The girls break into a spontaneous round of applause and shrieks of approval as a grinning N'tombi, moving the baton out of harm's way, offers her hand to the prostrate Amelia who, having recovered slightly, takes the proffered hand and pulls, at the same time placing her foot on N'tombi's stomach and throwing her viciously over her head to skid across the floor almost to the princess's feet. This time it is N'tombi who lies staring up at a weapon for the stick's ferrule has been removed to reveal a wicked looking blade. Tatty smiles grimly down at the discomforted girl.

"Now you know," she says, "why Amelia has past her test with flying colours. How many times do I have to tell you? Never underestimate your opponent. Never relax, not for a second, that second might prove to be your last." She raises the stick. "Get up."

N'tombi scrambles to her feet and turns away. With an agility that belies her age, the princess lunges at N'tombi's back but the girl turns, catches the stick and, swinging it away from her body, keeps a firm grip on it. Tough as the old bag is, serious damage could have been done had N'tombi wrenched the stick from her grasp. For a moment the pair face each other, motionless, then the princess smiles.

"Better, much better. You see, it is not merely a matter of developing quick reactions, it is also a matter of awareness." Although ostensibly addressing her star pupil her words are meant for the whole class. "Our awareness must be such that we know what is coming well in advance. Preparedness and intuition are basic weapons in our armoury. We wear them like an invisible skin to protect us. Discard for a fleeting moment that skin and all the good work I have done is discarded too. Remember, trust no one, trust no thing. That single moment when you feel all is safe is the moment of greatest danger. Be ever vigilant. I will not tolerate failure."

'Why are you telling me all this?' Thornton's voice broke into the girl's thoughts.

'Because I have decided I don't want to go through with it.'

This time it was Thornton who broke into laughter. 'You really expect me to believe that?'

'Yes.'

'Tell me about it.'

'All these killings...' She looked away. There was a long silence. He waited. Finally she turned back to him. 'They are a sort of... a final test.'

'Before graduation, you mean. Do you get a diploma? How does it read? Bachelor of Assassination? M.M.? Master of Murder? D.D.? Doctor of Death?' There was no mistaking the disgust in his voice. 'The whole idea is preposterous, revolting. People are slaughtered in cold blood, innocent people like the colonel, so that... so that...' It was Thornton who was now lost for words. He gestured helplessly. And then another thought struck him. 'But all the girls are still at the school!'

'Term doesn't end for another two days.'

'Oh, all very proper. Is that to ensure you get, your sponsors, get their money's worth? You have a graduation ceremony? Everyone applauding politely as you receive your diplomas? Aren't you among the graduates?'

'No. I haven't passed my final test yet. But I'm supposed to.

Soon.'

'How soon?'

'Very soon.'

'And the chosen victim?'

'You, Mr. King.'

For a moment Thornton stared at her as if she had suddenly sprouted a second head. It was not that the thought hadn't occurred to him. It was just that when it was pronounced so coolly from that young, fresh mouth, from that face that should by rights be adorning the cover of every fashionable magazine, it came as a total shock. He heard himself laughing, hardly the reaction he would have expected, hardly the laugh he knew. It sounded hysterical. He realised the pistol was out of his pocket and in his hand and he was pointing it at her. 'You mean with this?' he heard himself say.

'No, Mr. King... with this.' In her hand was an automatic with silencer attached. He remembered a time when he had undergone some minor surgery, how he lay looking up at the ceiling, the anaesthetist rubbing the back of his hand and then his voice, "We're going to put you to sleep now, Mr. King." The prick of the needle and then, for a split second, the ceiling, every ripple, every indentation, every tiny mark, jumped with a click into sharp focus before he heard himself sigh and knew no more. It was like that now. He had a clarity of vision where every object in the room seemed almost to leap out at him and then, but for the too loud beating of his heart, all was normal again: if a girl in your living room threatening to blaze away at you with a wicked looking automatic could be called normal. 'Stalemate, Miss N'tombi, I believe.' He was not as cool as he thought he sounded. 'Who shoots first?'

'I do, Mr. King. That one is not loaded.'

Chapter Eleven

Holly had finally got bored with the test card but there was still no thought of sleep. She decided to call Thornton's number. There was no answer. On a sudden whim, and with nothing to occupy herself, she decided to paint her toenails, something she had never done. If she wouldn't be seen dead in mules she certainly didn't want to be seen dead with painted toenails. Feet were seldom pretty appendages which was why Goethe said that, whenever they were, they were a gift of nature, so why bring attention to them with embellishment? But a recent guest had left a bottle of varnish in the bathroom and it was something to pass the time.

She left the television on just in case things started moving, trotted off to the bathroom for the bottle and returned to slip off her mules and get started. Instead of this pointless self-indulgence she might have knitted something useful, had she ever learnt to knit, but Holly was not a knitting kind of girl. She'd always had a sort of ambition to try her hand at writing but, when she sat down to start, it always seemed too much like hard work and so it remained sort of an ambition that surfaced every now and again.

Maybe one day, if she ever reached that one day, she would take up painting like Grandma Moses. She had a vision of her work being shown at a prestigious gallery with little red dots appearing on all the frames. Then, of course, Hallmark would buy them for greeting cards and they would be hot favourites for calendars and various other forms of merchandise and she would be rich beyond her wildest dreams. But was it necessary to be stinking rich at ninety? She could become a great philanthropist and give it all away to good causes. On the other hand, the way the world was going, there might not be any causes left. So, for the moment, she would be content to paint her toenails. It would help her relax and concentrate her mind at the same time. She let out a low growl. Either she relaxed or she concentrated.

What the hell was she thinking about? She started on a big toe and was absorbed enough for a minute to forget everything else until the ghost of Ninette suddenly entered the room followed by the smiling figure of the Princess Olga, followed by the memory of Shoggi's face hitting the plate. This thing had got to be sorted out once and for all. She capped the bottle of varnish and frowned at her one scarlet toenail. She didn't like the colour; it was too much like blood. She got up, switched off the television, and padded barefoot into the bedroom where she selected a black turtleneck sweater, black trousers, boots, black balaclava and soft leather gloves. She opened the drawer of her bedside cabinet and took out her gun in its shoulder holster. Having checked the gun, she slipped on the holster and completed the ensemble with a black leather jacket. Then she returned to the living room and tried once more to call Thornton.

****

Thornton remembered the dropped gloves and his lifting the pistol from N'tombi's bag. He had lowered it now so that his hand was resting on his knee and he looked down at the useless weapon. It might just as well be a novelty cigarette lighter or one that produced a little flag embellished with the word BANG for all the use it was. The cunning little vixen had outfoxed him from the start. She stood smiling down at him... a steady mocking smile, and she ignored the phone as it started to ring. Thornton glanced towards it but made no other move. There was nothing he could do. They waited till the ringing stopped then N'tombi waved her gun towards Thornton's glass.

'Drink your brandy, Mr. King.'

'Ah,' he sighed, 'the condemned man's last little luxury?'

'No luxury. What is in the brandy will be a lot harder to detect than a bullet hole in the head.'

Thornton nodded. 'I see.' He eyed the glass. 'Another mistake, huh? Turning my back on you. So I am to be like a latter day Socrates but without even an accusation, true or false, to condemn me, merely a target, an exercise.'

'It's no good, Mr. King, you can't keep putting it off.' She waved the gun again, indicating the glass.

'All right, all right,' Thornton raised a placating hand. 'Just tell me one thing. Why me?'

'Because you are the best. And I am the best.' She said this with obvious pride.

'Really? The best, huh? Well, well... according to who? No, don't answer that. I really cannot fathom for the life of me, and it looks as though it's going to be the life of me, where Tatty got this ridiculous idea. If the truth were known, I am a complete nincompoop. I have to admit it, in all humility, and Tatty is even more of a nincompoop not to realise it.'

'Drink, Mr. King. I know you like your brandy and I assure you the taste has not been affected. That's why it should have been so simple. Why didn't you just drink it straight off?'

'Aha! That would have been my fourth mistake. And three mistakes in one evening are enough for anybody, even a nincompoop as big as me... I.'

'Drink!' She was obviously not in the mood for wasting any more words. The smile had disappeared and her mouth hardened into a tight little line.

'What if I refuse?'

'Then it will have to be a bullet.' The voice had lost its edge. The words came out as more of a whisper.

'Then a bullet it will have to be.'

He was amazed at how quiet and calm his voice was considering he felt an urgent need to urinate. He hoped it wouldn't happen, it would be too embarrassing. N'tombi's finger tightened on the trigger. Thornton felt his stomach contract. He wanted to raise his hands, ward it off with his arms as if they could shield him, and brace himself against the impact. His heart was thudding against his ribs. Suddenly and seemingly out of nowhere there came the sound of a high-pitched wail, so unexpected it was enough to distract N'tombi for a split second. As her head turned towards the sound Thornton shoved against the floor as hard as he could with both legs, at the same time pushing his body back against the couch. It toppled over backwards and Thornton, hugging the carpet, winced as a bullet thudded into the base.

N'tombi, despite her earlier boast, now seemed uncertain as to what to do next. Perhaps if Princess Olga had not instilled in her with such persistence the idea that Thornton was the best she might have pressed home her attack and finished him off then and there. But there was now an element of doubt in her mind and she tentatively approached the fallen couch not knowing what she would find behind it. She was still somewhat unnerved by the continuing banshee wail and Thornton's lightning disappearing act and her hesitation gave him time. He rolled on his back and, holding the useless pistol by the barrel and taking aim at a large vase lamp on an occasional table, let fly.

The vase was a hideous piece of Victorian chinoiserie he had always loathed but which, having been left to him in her will by a favourite aunt, he never could find in his heart to get rid of and, by having it converted to a lamp, he felt it at least had some practical purpose. His aim was a little high but the pistol hit the top of the shade with enough force to send the lamp crashing to the floor. As it shattered, N'tombi turned and fired and Thornton, like a sprinter from the starting block, leapt to his feet and dived for the wall. His hand hit the light switch and he swivelled away just as a third bullet ploughed into the wall. He felt the sting of chipping plaster as it peppered his neck and he dived to shelter behind a well-upholstered chair. Another flash, another bullet. Now, in the dark, all was still except for that insistent wail. N'tombi, gun held out in both hands before her, cocked her head, listening if she could for the slightest sound elsewhere, squinting hard, trying to penetrate the darkness. She felt more secure, even a sense of anticipation, sure that she could wait till her eyes became accustomed to the darkness. Sooner or later Thornton would have to make a move. He was attempting to do just that. He felt in his pocket, found his keys, and gripping them tightly so as to prevent them rattling, pulled them out. Then he tossed them across the room. They hit the skirting board but, despite the clatter, N'tombi wasn't going to be taken in a second time. She stayed motionless. Her next shot, she decided, had to be the coup-de-grace. Thornton pulled a wry face and wondered what the hell he was going to do next.

The telephone rang. He knew she would ignore that too but, with the noise of the phone added to the wailing from the kitchen, he decided to risk a move and, leaving the comparative safety of the chair, he silently circled his way back towards the couch. He knew there was nothing to impede his progress and was fortunate that N'tombi, her eyes fixed on the position of the chair, slowly advanced towards that. She was unsure as to exactly where Thornton might be or what might be in her way. It would be disastrous to trip over an obstacle, especially if the obstacle were a prostrate Thornton. He, meanwhile, had made it to the far end of the couch.

Carefully he stretched out his hand until he felt the edge of the table, which fortunately did not seem to have been knocked, so he slid his hand along the top until his middle finger touched the foot of the brandy glass. He curled his fingers around the stem and pulled the glass towards him until he could take a hold of it and safely lift it from the table. Then he retreated to the cover of the couch, more or less, remaining in a crouching position and suddenly yelled.

'Here!'

N'tombi turned and fired at chest height. From his crouched position Thornton flung the balloon, aiming slightly above the flash of the gun. There was a scream as the brandy streamed out of the glass and N'tombi's hands flew to her eyes.

Thornton darted forward and grabbed her with both hands. Then, realising she must have dropped the gun, he lugged her to the wall, holding her there with one hand and the weight of his body as he groped for the light switch. He flicked on the light and went cold as he saw the bullet hole not six inches from it. It must have missed him by the width of a short and curly. Slowly he shook his head, whether over his ruined decor or his narrow escape it would have been hard to tell, probably both. Then he took the half-blinded N'tombi by the arm and led her to the chair that had so recently been his lunette. The telephone had stopped ringing.

'Three out of ten, Miss N'tombi and go to the bottom of the class. No gold star for you, my girl.' He sat her in the chair, retrieved the automatic from where it had fallen, slipped on the safety catch and shoved the gun down behind the waistband of his trousers, changed his mind and removed it. To accidentally shoot himself now in his most vulnerable parts would not only be the height of idiocy but, he imagined, pretty painful, and would certainly prove his point about being a complete nincompoop. He eyed the subdued girl slumped in the chair. 'I shudder to think where my reputation will stand with the princess after this,' he said jovially though jovial wasn't exactly how he was feeling, 'I can only hope she never gets the chance to start a new term.' Holding the gun in one hand he up-righted the couch and mentally apologised to Aunt Ethel for the state of her Victorian vase that was undoubtedly beyond repair. Then he turned back to N'tombi wondering just what he was going to do with his unwanted guest. She sat shivering, her hands over her eyes.

'Still stinging? Well we'd better do something about it then. But, is that a kettle I hear boiling? I'm surprised it hasn't boiled away. You know, I never realised before just how piercing that whistle is.' He was almost at the kitchen when he stopped and turned back. 'But you haven't had your tea. Would you like it now?'

There was no response.

****

Holly parked the car some distance from the house for no other reason than that was the only parking place she could find, and even that with some difficulty. How was it, she wondered, that in television series there was always a parking place available exactly where a character wanted it? Another few years and the freedom of the open road would be a thing of the past. There'll be more cars than actual road space.

Sandra hadn't been exactly ecstatic about being woken up in the early hours to be asked for the loan of her car. She had stared sleepily at Holly, frowned at Holly, blinked at Holly, yawned mightily at Holly, leaned against the doorjamb, scratched her collarbone, adjusted her negligee, and croaked. "Neighbours are supposed to borrow cups of sugar at a respectable hour not motorcars at ungodly hours. What the hell do you want it for anyway? At this hour of the morning!"

Holly started in on a long rambling tale about Thornton breaking down in the middle of nowhere and needing rescue. She wasn't sure Sandra would swallow it but, at the mention of Thornton's name, she raised her eyes heavenwards and flapped a weary hand to shut Holly up. "I might have known," she said. "That man's a real dickhead, Holly. I honestly don't know why you have anything to do with him; anyway, doesn't he belong to the AA or the RAC or something? Oh, never mind." She turned and schlepped away to fetch the keys. Returning with them, she said, "I don't need the car tomorrow so don't come banging on my door at another ungodly hour." She slapped the keys down on Holly's palm. "That's the doors, that's the ignition. Good luck and good night," and she shut the door.

Holly stepped out of the car onto a deserted and windswept pavement. She turned up the collar of her jacket, locked the car, and set off for *The Spitskaya School of Modelling*.

****

N'tombi lay on the couch as Thornton gently finished bathing her eyes. A bowl of warm water stood on the table together with a towel and a roll of cotton wool. Thornton leaned back and dropped the cotton wool he was using into the bowl. 'There, that should do it.' He handed N'tombi the towel to wipe her face. She took it and he watched as she gently wiped the towel across her cheek. She really was a pretty little thing. But then, when you come to think of it, some of nature's most beautiful creations are also the most deadly. She looked up at him with those large brown eyes. The whites weren't too attractive, rather bloodshot in fact, but Thornton steeled himself against any feeling of sympathy. She had, after all, just tried to close his for good. He looked passed her at the hole in the wall and shuddered.

'What are you going to do with me?' She asked plaintively.

'Do you know,' he lied, still refusing to succumb to sentiment and even though he hadn't as yet come to any conclusion, 'I really hadn't thought about it.'

She turned her head away. 'I failed,' she said with what sounded like a sob, although it could have been a hiccup.

'Oh, I wouldn't let it upset you,' Thornton said reassuringly, patting her thigh. 'Failing exams is one of life's little hazards. You were probably just a little bit nervous. Most people are before they sit an exam. I remember I always was. My mind used to go a complete blank. No matter how much I crammed, the questions always took me by surprise. Seemed to be about things I'd never even heard of let alone studied. I'd sit there for what seemed like hours, gazing out of the window chewing the end of my pen. Practicals were just as bad, worse in fact. I was all fingers and thumbs. Some people take them in their stride, lucky devils. But then some people just seem to go through life wearing a charm bracelet. No, exams are definitely one of life's little horror stories. I still have nightmares about them. And I read somewhere that Japanese students commit suicide like lemmings because of the stress. Mind you, yours wasn't a bad effort tonight I must admit. You did your best. No one could ask for more than that. Pity in a way that Tatty makes it so difficult for you. You could have put a bullet in me the minute we stepped through the front door and got clean away with it. Feeling better now?'

N'tombi nodded. He thought she did seem a tidge brighter; amazing what a little tender care, a string of platitudes, and some counselling could do. He sat there for a while pondering the situation. What was to be done with her?

'If I were to let you go,' he said, after a lengthy silence, 'and you went back to the school, what would happen?'

'I'd be sent home.'

'And then?'

She shrugged and looked away again. Thornton wanted to take her hand or put his arm around her. He resisted the temptation.

'Do you have a family?' He asked.

She nodded.

'Only child?'

She turned back to look at him and shook her head. 'I have five brothers and three sisters. As a matter of fact I am one of twins. I doubt I will be missed.'

'Hey! Don't talk like that.' Thornton sounded genuinely concerned. There was another silence before he went on. 'Nine kids, huh?' Another silence as he thought about this. He had an image of a badly thatched mud hut, parched fields, leafless trees, emaciated cattle, and a family desperately scratching at the arid soil trying to keep body and soul together. No wonder the girl was prepared to do anything to escape the cycle of poverty and despair. An overwhelming desire for fatherhood had never been a part of Thornton's nature. He was not a slave to his genes' desire for immortality and he could never really understand what all the fuss was about. Go forth and multiply might apply to most of the human race; it didn't apply to him. But, right at this moment, he felt an almost paternal sympathy for N'tombi. 'What does your father do?' He asked. He meant for a living, not what he did by way of going forth and multiplying nine fold.

'He spends most of his time sitting under a tree, drinking and talking with his friends, playing awari sometimes. He doesn't really have to do anything. Shouts a few orders now and then, slaps a few people around. He owns a nightclub you see.'

'A nightclub!' The paternal feelings vanished in an instant.

N'tombi, despite her situation, couldn't help smiling at the look on Thornton's face. Gone were the thatched hut, the drought-stunted crops, and the skeletal cattle. In their place he saw disco lights, a well-stocked bar, plushy air-conditioned surroundings, and a seething mass of swaying, sweating, rocking, ravers.

'Oh, it's probably not what you're thinking,' N'tombi interrupted his imaginings. 'The club is in our village, in our house in fact, about fifty miles from the capital. It's not a big village and it's not really a club I suppose. But even people in a village need something to do at night so my father decided to turn two rooms of our house into a place where people could drink and dance. They come from miles around. As children we all got used to it. We could sleep through all the noise that goes on till four, five in the morning. In a way we are lucky living in the bush. We are not bothered much by the soldiers, or the police. But the closer you get to the city the more dangerous life becomes. The power and the money are in the hands of the president, and his family, and his favourites. Graft is a way of life with us. All the money that comes in in aid goes into pockets. You want something? You want something done? You get it if you can pay for it, if you know the right people, if you can return a favour. Try making a telephone call at the airport; all you will find in the booths are dangling wires, yet the son of the president has a telephone in each of his six cars. So you go to the exchange and ask if you can make a call. You're told all the lines are busy, that is, unless you're prepared to pay five times what the call should cost. The president's son got married to the daughter of the president of... another country. The wedding cost millions. Guests from all over the worlds, heads of state, cavalcades, banquets, bands, parades, planes to fly people in, but millions of our people live on next to nothing. For the happy couple a mansion is built, and close to the mansion is a shopkeeper, a Lebanese man. The president's son sends his thugs around to the shop for wines every time he throws a dinner party. Now the man is nearly bankrupt. He asks for some payment; maybe not the full amount, just something on account. So the thugs are sent around again. This time they beat the man almost senseless. They rape his wife and daughter. They threaten to burn down his store. What does the man do? Does he go to the police? The police are there to protect the bandits who pay them. The man would be thrown into jail or, worse, taken into the bush where he would simply disappear.'

'So you want to get rid of the thugs as you call them. All very commendable in its way, but what guarantee do you have that those who take their place are going to be any better? Unfortunately, my dear N'tombi, the lessons of history do not hold out much hope for optimism, human nature being what it is. Sorry to sound so pessimistic but it's a fact of life. Now, how about that tea? Milk and sugar?'

N'tombi nodded again. Thornton smiled, gave her thigh another fatherly pat, took the towel and, collecting the bowl and cotton wool, got up and headed for the kitchen. N'tombi slid from the chair and padded after him. She raised her arms above his head, hands about two feet apart; there was a gleam of triumph in her eye, but it was premature. A fortuitously placed wall mirror undoubtedly saved Thornton's life. He dropped the bowl and had time only to put up his hands, palms out, to protect his throat before the wire was cutting into them. He writhed and twisted, desperately trying to throw her, but she was a match for him. Her knee was jammed against his coccyx as she pulled back and twisted on the wire.

There was only one thing for it. Thornton swiftly hooked a foot behind her leg, taking her by surprise, and they toppled over backwards with Thornton on top. The back of her head crashed against the edge of the table and she went limp. He got to his knees and threw the wire to one side. His face was contorted with agony as he held his hands like claws in front of him, threw back his head and opened his mouth as if to scream, but there was only a long low almost inaudible moan of anguish. He buried his hands in his armpits and rocked back and forth until the pain gradually subsided. It was some time before he turned his attention to N'tombi.

She would put up no more fight. She had not only flunked. She was defunct. A certain African despot could sleep easy in his bed a while longer. Those large brown eyes stared sightlessly back at Thornton, lacklustre now, their brightness gone. He put out a trembling hand and, with the back of it, gently touched her cheek. Then, using his arms and the table top as an aid, he dragged himself to his feet. He had the shakes and it was bad. He staggered on trembling legs over to the phone and with some difficulty tried dialling Holly's number, succeeding at the fourth attempt. There was, of course, no answer.

****

Holly surveyed the house from the pavement opposite. Except for a night light in the hall the place was in darkness but there was obviously no way she was going to gain access from the front. The area windows, she recalled from her previous visit when she had behaved like a litter lout, were guarded with stout iron bars as was so often the case in these period houses, and if she attempted to break in above street level she ran too much risk of being seen. It might be an old truism that there's never a policeman around when you want one but that was no guarantee there wouldn't be one when you didn't, in fact it was more than likely there would be. She had once, coming home at four in the morning, stopped the car and taken a bottle of milk out of a crate delivered and left in a shop doorway. She had no sooner returned to the car when two cops apparently materialised out of thin air and would have arrested her on the spot had she not left more than adequate payment for the milk. They had quite an amiable and interesting conversation about nothing in particular while the cops minutely inspected her car for a possible alternative booking before they bade her a pleasant good morning and sped her on her way. By the time she got home she had no more interest in the coffee the milk had been meant for. Anyway, the chance of being discovered by the police aside, Holly felt quite sure there must be an alarm system even though none was evident. She would have to try around the back.

The rear of the house was some distance from the narrow back street which was actually more of an alley, and was protected by an eight foot brick wall in which was set a solid wooden door, bolted from the inside of course. Normal sensible households were always locked and barred against breaking and entering. If this pile held secrets the chances of getting in seemed pretty slim, but Holly felt luck was with her. The nearest street lamp was out, probably vandalised, and there was just enough light from those further away for her to see by while, in her blacks and with the balaclava now pulled down over her face, she was no more than a shadow. She took a look at the top of the wall: no barbed wire, no broken glass. It was illegal of course but some very ancient walls still had shards here and there that could do a lot of damage. She stepped back a few paces, measured her distance, and made a run for it, leaping for the top where her gloved fingers curled over, gripping the brick as she hauled herself up, swung one leg over, then the other and, facing the wall, gently lowered herself down the other side. She let go and dropped the last half dozen inches, turning around to find herself in a small paved yard. From the shadow of the wall she took a good look at the house.

On one side a few steps led down to a shallow area surrounded by cast-iron railings with a gate. The window and glass panels of the door were, naturally, barred. On the other side, against the wall, was a long narrow flower bed edged with Victorian rope pattern tiles and devoid of anything remotely botanical other than a magnificent hydrangea petiolaris rising from the centre. It was a vine that, considering the slow rate of growth of the species, must have been truly ancient, its gnarled and twisted main stem a good six inches in diameter and it climbed to well over the second floor. Its thick tangled growth should provide plenty of grip almost to the top where, Holly noticed, she could reach a decent sized window with no difficulty. Getting through the window was another matter.

She was not in the habit of going out at night equipped with glass cutters and putty. Shades of breaking into college after lock-up she thought as she moved swiftly to the base of the creeper and, finding her first hold, started to climb. At least she had had some practice. She moved with chameleon like slowness, testing each hand, each foothold, making absolutely sure of it before moving on again. Half way up she stopped all movement as a car turned into and slowly nosed its way down the alley. "Sod's law," thought Holly as she kept her face to the wall, not daring to look. Was it a squad car? She breathed a sigh of relief as the car moved on and disappeared. Then she resumed her ascent.

Level with the window she cautiously looked around the edge of the wall and, shading her eyes with her hand, squinted into the room. Growing accustomed to the dark interior she eventually made out what appeared to be an office and there was definitely no one around. She wondered for a moment why an office should be on the second floor but it wasn't for her to question the princess's arrangements. Having satisfied herself no sleeper would be rudely awakened, she reached inside her jacket pocket and withdrew a small flashlight with which to examine the window itself. Luck was definitely on her side. Maintenance was obviously not a regular concern of this establishment or someone had been careless, perhaps lazy, and overlooked this particular window. Maybe they thought that, two flights up, it wasn't vulnerable which, considering its proximity to the petiolaris, was downright stupid. Whatever the reason, the old wooden frames were almost bare of paint, weather-beaten and rotten, and she calculated a good hard tug on the upper sash should be enough to loosen the screws of the catch. It would then be a simple matter of lifting the window again, raising the bottom one, and climbing through.

It was as she had suspected; one good pull, the catch was ripped off, and the window was open. She waited for the sound of an alarm. There was nothing. She pushed back the upper sash, slowly as to make no noise, raised the lower one with equal care and started to ease her way into the room. She was halfway through when the lower window suddenly fell across her back and trapped her. A pane of glass, up to that moment held in place only by an inch here and there of ancient crumbling putty, the pins having long since rusted away, fell with a splintering crash on the paving below. Holly couldn't help thinking how loud, in the stillness of the night, the shattering of a small piece of glass could be. She closed her eyes, held her breath and waited, mentally cursing rotten sash windows with rotten or nonexistent sash cords. She should have known. Surely someone must have heard that, but all was still. In the meantime here she was, half in, half out and a heavy window lying across the small of her back and, oh boy, was she going to develop some heavy bruising. Fortunately the leather jacket must have prevented any serious injury, like cracked vertebrae. She wondered if, despite the window's weight, she could twist around so that, lying on her back, she would be able to push it up. But then she realised that, if she were to do so, the weight of her legs could possibly pull her the wrong way and she could slide out and end up like the pane of glass on the flags below. Even if she managed to grab at the walls she didn't fancy trying to pull herself up doing a back bend with no support, and if she grabbed the window there was always the chance it would come crashing down again.

She slipped the flashlight inside her jacket and pressing both hands against the sill tried to arch her back. She managed to raise the window a fraction but there was no way she could keep it up long enough to wriggle through. What she needed was a lever of some kind. She took out the flashlight again and shone it around the room. There was the usual office furniture: desk, chairs, filing cabinets, cupboards and, against the wall a short distance from the window, a small Victorian pedestal table with an oval top. She eyed it for a moment and, surprisingly at a time like this, was reminded of a visit to her dentist when he had shown her an eighteenth century instrument for extracting teeth. He called it a key and, indeed, that is what it looked like except that, at the end and to the side of the bar, it had a metal attachment shaped like the figure 'n'. This was placed over the offending tooth, the practitioner, with his fingers inserted in the handle, gave a hearty twist outwards and away came the tooth, probably with a fair amount of gum and bone as well and leaving the patient with a badly swollen lip to boot. The reason this had sprung to Holly's mind was because she was working out a similar strategy against the window with the table as the key. She stretched out and just managed to grip the edge of the tabletop. Gradually she eased the piece of furniture towards her. The last thing she wanted now was for it to topple over and be out of reach. Having got it to the wall and to one side of her, she put the torch back inside her jacket, inserted the top of the table between window and sill and pulled the pedestal up in front of her, keeping two of the three little feet against the wall beneath her. As the top moved from the horizontal to the vertical so it pushed up the window. It was slow work and not easy and Holly feared that at any moment the top might be snapped off but, eventually, she was in a position to push with one hand against the wall beneath the window, holding on to the pedestal with the other, and almost roll into the room.

She sat on the floor beneath the window for a long while before she could bring herself to move then she got to her feet and, holding up the window, removed the table, gently let down the window, replaced the table and drew the curtains. She took out the torch and with the aid of its narrow beam crossed the room to the door and gently tried the handle. The door was locked. She put her ear close to a panel and listened. There was no sound. Satisfied, she crossed back to the desk, switched on a directional lamp, and turned her attention to a filing cabinet. She placed her gun and the torch in a wire basket on top of the cabinet and gently pulled the handle of the top drawer. It was locked. She tried the next one down before turning her attention to a cupboard. That too was locked. They might have been careless with the window but they certainly weren't careless as far as anything in the room was concerned.

She turned back to the desk. No doubt its drawers were locked as well. She tried them. Locked. But on top of the desk lay a large steel paperknife. Returning with it to the cupboard, she inserted the blade between the doors and forced the lock, not without some damage to the surrounding woodwork.

The doors swung open to reveal a miniature armoury; or maybe it was a display of weaponry for some other purpose for although there were handguns and automatic rifles of various calibres, makes, description, and nationality, no two weapons were the same. Intrigued, she lifted out a Smith and Wesson and examined it. The chambers were empty. She put it back and turned her attention to the drawers below the cupboard. It took a little time to get the first one open and she broke the blade of the paperknife in the process but she finally succeeded in forcing the lock. There was nothing in the drawer but a large bunch of keys. She lifted them out, tied together with grubby string, and stood staring at them in her hand. This was beginning to be more and more of a Chinese puzzle and she was in two minds as to whether it was worth her while trying to match key to lock when her dilemma was solved for her.

A shaft of light streamed into the room as the door was flung open to reveal Princess Olga and, behind her, the lurking hulk of Ivan. Holly had frozen, and it wasn't until Tatty had switched on the light in the room and spoken, that she turned to see the princess standing there, stick in one hand, in the other a Luger. It might have looked like a museum piece but Holly was only too sure it was in working order and, unlike the weapons in the cupboard, fully loaded.

'Well, well, Ivan,' Tatty said, smiling, 'what have we here?' Ivan flashed a gold tooth as he grinned over her shoulder. 'Night visitors,' Tatty continued. 'I didn't realise, my dear, just how eager you were to enrol in my school. And where is Mr. King? Ah, yes, unfortunately indisposed I believe.' She stepped to one side and, with a little jerk of her head, indicated to Ivan that he should do something about the intruder. Still grinning he stepped forward. He might not have been quite the tonnage of a Sumo wrestler but he was without doubt an opponent to be reckoned with. Holly raised the remains of the paperknife. The broken end was still enough to cause considerable damage.

'Don't be foolish, my dear,' Tatty said, sounding quite motherly. 'What good will that do you? The game is up, finished. Let's get it over with as quickly as possible.'

Ivan moved further into the room and crossed Tatty's line

of fire. The moment he did so Holly hurled the bunch of keys at him and dived for the filing cabinet and her gun. But Ivan, swifter on his feet than his bulk would suggest, reached it a split second before she did and lifted her bodily off the floor, leaving her stretching out for the basket and her gun like a child stretching for a toy held teasingly just out of reach. His grin turned into a chuckle as he carried her to the princess and stood holding her there, feet inches off the floor. Tatty had lost her smile.

'Well, my dear, as you insist on playing games, how would you like to meet the other members of the class? Come.' She turned away and Ivan, putting Holly down, thrust her from the room.

****

This, Thornton thought to himself as he headed for the Marylebone Road, was turning out to be a very expensive caper. He still had two minders to settle with, useless though they had been, and now an extra day's payment on Harold's car, and Harold didn't hire out his vehicles for peanuts, especially as he was doing it as a favour. Favours cost. If things carried on like this he would soon be paying interest on the interest of his overdraft. Either that or he would be requested to get his account into balance, which would be like trying to get blood out of a stone and he broke into a cold sweat at the thought. He knew from bitter experience the smug expression on his bank manager's face as he sat behind his desk with pen poised to make a few quick calculations. No matter what lengths he went to rehearsing the interview beforehand, and despite the bollocking the banks had been getting for the devious ways and means they employed in cheating their customers, it always ended up with him feeling two inches tall. Thornton had never been any good with money. Even as a schoolboy his pocket money never seemed to stretch as far as anyone else's. He might have to take Holly up on that loan after all if her dad was still solvent and in generous mood. Though, knowing his luck, her dad would probably turn out to be one of those unfortunate names at Lloyds currently being requested to bail out just a few of the world's more recent calamities. Anyway, after tonight he, Thornton, might no longer be all in one piece and the problem would be solved.

Holly! It would be just like her to go in on her own. Having tried to call him, no one else would call at that hour of the morning, and getting no answer, she might have assumed he was already on the job and decided to join him. He wanted to put his foot down, but even at this hour with very little in the way of traffic about, he didn't dare risk being stopped. More haste, less speed, as the old saying has it or, in this instance, more speed, less haste, especially if the cops found N'tombi's automatic on him. And, sure enough, he spotted a lurking patrol car nestling in a dingy recess just waiting for some idiot to come flashing by. Thornton checked his rear view mirror to see if it had pulled out and was following him just for something to relieve the boredom but the road behind was clear except for a solitary taxi.

He heaved a sigh and risked a slightly higher speed, glancing down at the speedometer to make sure he wasn't overdoing it. He remembered how once in his younger days after a night of revelry and just getting on to four in the morning, approaching Piccadilly from Hyde Park Corner, an amazing sight met his eyes. He could see the length of that famous street right to the Circus without a vehicle or a body in sight and, in a moment of daredevil recklessness, put his foot to the floor. Obligingly, and as though urging him on, every light turned green at his approach and the speedometer actually touched a hundred miles an hour. He could die tonight and, if he did, he would be one of the few men, perhaps the only one, who had ever done a ton down the Dilly.

Holly found herself wishing fervently that she were at home and asleep in bed. At least, if she were dreaming, this would be a nightmare from which she would eventually awake. What on earth possessed her to try and take this on single-handed? She must have been out of her mind. The trio descended the stairs and approached the door she remembered led into the room in which the fashion show had been held. Their progress was slow. Tatty's pace was almost on a par with that of a tortoise, the tip of her stick tap-tapping time with each step she took. Holly wondered if this was how a condemned man felt on his last walk. She cast a quick glance around. She could almost feel Ivan's breath on the back of her neck. Should she try and make a break for it? She already had experience of Ivan's turn of speed and didn't think she'd get very far but it was worth a try. Anything was worth a try. She tried to visualise the geography of the place and, remembering the back door, decided that was where she had to make for. The passage from the hall must lead to a door and a flight of steps down to the basement. They reached the foot of the stairs and Holly decided to make her move. It was probably now or never. She suddenly lunged forward; arms outstretched, grabbed Tatty by the shoulders, swung her around and pushed her against the oncoming Ivan.

Then, without a backward glance, she fled down the passage, at the end of which she found what she was looking for, a swing door leading to a flight of steps. It was dark but steps are steps no matter how uneven and she clattered down them as fast as she dared go. It certainly wouldn't do to take a tumble or twist an ankle at this stage of the game. She found herself in a large kitchen, some light filtering in from outside, illuminating the barred window and the glass panes of the door. She gave herself what would turn out to be another savage bruise as she crashed into the corner of a table, worked her way around it and literally threw herself at the door, praying the key would be in the lock. It was. She turned the key and yanked. The door did not budge. Desperately she felt the top of the door, found the bolt and slammed it back, bent down to do the same for the bottom one, straightened up and opened the door. A rush of cold air swept in but it was the only taste of freedom she would have as Ivan's arms closed around her. Holly screamed. She couldn't believe the sound of terror had come from her. Ivan's great paw went round her mouth as he pulled her, struggling wildly, back from the door and slammed it shut. Then he dragged her back upstairs.

Princess Olga and the girls, standing in a semi-circle, were waiting for them. Ivan thrust Holly through the doors, backed out, and closed the doors behind him. Holly stared at the girls who stared grimly back, as did Tatty who, at her age, did not appreciate being disrespectfully pushed about by a slip of a thing. N'tombi was not in the room Holly noticed. She turned to look at Tatty as the old woman spoke.

'Girls...' She banged her stick on the floor, more out of habit than anything else considering the girls were all silent attention anyway, 'We have a new student who seems most anxious to acquire knowledge I am sure cannot be good for her. Is it not an old saying that a little knowledge is a dangerous thing? Perhaps it might prove a salutary lesson to our Miss Day to show her what we know, hmn? Shall we see how many of her nine lives this curious cat has left? Who would like to be the first volunteer?' She looked along the line. The blonde with the bob-cut stepped forward. 'Ah, Mira... good...' She turned to Holly. 'Perhaps, Miss Day, you would like something with which to defend yourself.' She clicked her fingers. 'Sumachi.'

Sumachi, who could have passed for an Oriental Lolita, un-sheathed a Samurai sword two thirds as long as she was tall, and sent it spinning across the floor towards Holly who had to stop it with her foot, fortunately on the hilt. She bent down, keeping a wary eye on Mira and, taking up the sword, waited for the attack. The sword was beautiful, a work of art, with its engraved razor-sharp blade and the delicate pattern of flowers on the hilt. But Holly didn't have time to admire it or wonder how an instrument of death could be made not just by a superb craftsman but a true artist.

Mira made her approach, taking her time, crouching as she came. Holly waited, the sword held out in front of her with both hands. Somehow it felt familiar, comfortable, as though it belonged there, giving her the feeling that with it she could perform wonders. How could Tatty have given it to her to use against an unarmed elfin creature whose bright blue eyes never left Holly's face? They must be pretty sure of themselves. One caress of that glinting blade could slice to the bone.

Mira gave a little jump, stamping hard with both feet. Holly did not flinch. Mira feinted to one side. The sword flashed down without Holly even realising she was making the movement, but it was too late anyway, Mira had spun out of the way. The sword flashed down again. Mira spun to the other side. Holly tried a horizontal swing. It was what Mira intended and the wrong move. The girl jack-knifed with the suppleness and agility of a cat and, taken by surprise, Holly lost her balance, stumbling forward under the momentum of her own making. The edges of Mira's two hands chopped down either side of Holly's neck. The sword fell from her nerveless fingers as both her arms seemed suddenly paralysed. Mira spun away on one heel and the other back-kicked violently into Holly's midriff sending her reeling back and into the arms of Amelia who grabbed and steadied her with a back hammer. Holly almost cried out as her wrist was forced up to reach her shoulder blade. There was a round of applause.

'Excellent! Excellent! Brava, brava!' Tatty cried out enthusiastically. 'Who's next?'

Sumachi stepped forward and picked up the sword. Amelia shoved Holly back into the centre of the room to face her. There was to be no escape. Holly and the Japanese girl stood regarding each other. The sword looked just as comfortable in Sumachi's small supple hands, even more so as she seemed to hold it with what appeared to be a sense of ancestral pride. No doubt she was descended from a long line of Samurai.

'Do not doubt for one moment, my dear Miss Day, that we are going to kill you,' Tatty said in a tone usually reserved for the boardroom of Chinique when addressing a member who had spoken out of place, or a junior with ideas above her station. 'When your remains are eventually found, if they are ever found, it will be concluded that you suffered a nasty accident involving some kind of machinery. Perhaps...' Tatty's mouth turned down at either end and she waggled a hand in a manner reminiscent of royalty waving from a car as she tried to come up with an example, her knowledge of machinery being extremely limited. 'Perhaps a mincer of some sort,' she concluded. 'But, in the meantime, I am sure you won't begrudge my girls having a little practice. Practice makes perfect, yes? Continue please.'

Ivan sat in the hall; leaning back in his chair set against the wall just to one side of the doors, and gently fondled Boris's ears. The Borzoi gazed up at him in mute adoration. Allowing his imagination to run riot, Ivan was smiling broadly as he conjured up his own version of the action in the room behind him. He had leaned over towards the doors once or twice, cocking an ear for some indication as to what might be happening, but the doors were heavy and solid and only the vaguest of sounds emanated from the room. Princess Olga should have left the girl to him. He would have known what to do with her. He looked down as he felt the dog suddenly stiffen beneath his hand. It rose up from its haunches and took a couple of steps towards the passage where it stood quivering. Ivan noticed the skin ripple down its back. The pink, eczema-lesioned skin that showed through what appeared to be a more than slight case of alopecia would explain why the hackles didn't rise, but the lips were pulled back in a show of pearly little teeth and not so pearly fangs and it took a few tentative steps across the hall. The man leaned forward in his chair and peered down the passage but, seeing nothing untoward, relaxed again and clicked his finger and thumb for the dog to return.

Ivan had long ago concluded that Boris was a stupid animal. Any creature with a cranium that narrow and a nose that long just had to be stupid. But Boris was not stupid. His acute hearing had picked up the sounds to which the human was oblivious and he was not a happy dog. He turned his head to give Ivan a quick look and then, with that strange bowed lope characteristic of the Russian greyhound, trotted off down the passage and disappeared through the swing door that led to the basement steps. Probably wanted a drink, Ivan thought. He could have done with one himself. He sat musing for a while longer, his thoughts directed mainly, with anticipation, towards his next bout with a bottle of vodka, but then he decided he had better follow the hound and investigate, just in case. Reaching the end of the passage he pushed back the door and started down the stairs. He stopped half way down. In the lighted kitchen, a bag of vegetarian dog food on the floor, Boris was enjoying an unexpected late supper, or early breakfast, and sitting at the head of the table was Thornton.

'Good evening,' he said with all the affability and aplomb of an invited guest.

Ivan stood on the steps wondering if he were staring at an apparition. Then, recovering what passed for his wits, he let out a roar and lurched down the remaining steps. He was half way across the kitchen before Thornton raised his hand from beneath the table. Ivan skidded to a halt. Boris carried on noisily with his breakfast, pausing occasionally to wag his tail and raise adoring eyes in Thornton's direction. How cheaply his allegiance had been bought.

****

With the sword raised over her head, the blade behind her, Sumachi leapt into the attack and Holly, in a few seconds of calm lucidity between waves of panic, decided her strategy would be to try and use the bodies of the other girls as a defence. She jumped backwards and turned to commit assault and battery on the nearest body, which happened to be Anya's. Taken by surprise by this unexpected turn of events, Anya's reaction was slow which was unfortunate for her. Thrown directly into the line of that flashing blade her beauty, and consequently her career as potential siren, was marred forever.

With a scream she dropped to her knees, both hands covering her face, the blood oozing out from between the fingers to drip onto the polished wooden floor. Sumachi, lowered sword still in hand, stood staring in horror and disbelief that she had been the cause of this disaster. Princess Olga rose shakily to her feet, her eyes blazing with anger. The other girls, with the exception of Mira who was immediately on her knees beside Anya, seemed paralysed by the turn of events. Desperately Mira tried to take Anya's hands away from her face so she could inspect the damage but a terrified Anya would have none of it. Holly, remembering her own eyes and momentarily forgetting her situation, felt a tinge of sympathy. Sumachi put down the sword and joined Mira in the attempt and between them they eventually succeeded. Anya's face was a scarlet mask. There was no doubt it was a nasty cut that would leave a scar almost from temple to chin. But it was the point of the blade that had caused the damage and, although a goodly number of stitches would be called for, it was hardly a death blow. The scarlet mask was the result of Anya's hands smearing the blood across her face. With soothing reassurances they laid the trembling girl on her back and Mira held the cut together with the fingers of both hands. 'We've got to get her to a hospital,' she said, turning to look at the princess. 'We can probably hold it together with strips of bandaid till then. She turned to one of the other girls. 'Fetch a towel,' she ordered. The elf, it seemed, was taking charge whilst Holly, for the moment, had been forgotten.

'I'll get it,' Sumachi volunteered, getting to her feet. But she had hardly moved towards the doors when they were flung open to reveal the figure of Thornton.

'An inspector calls,' he said.

The night was definitely one of surprises. Holly, the models, Princess Olga, they all stared in disbelief as he stood in the doorway, both hands behind his back, surveying the room. Then, the surprise wearing off, it looked as though there was going to be a concerted rush for the door, but one hand appeared from behind Thornton's back and the movement stopped. In his hand was N'tombi's automatic, silencer still attached. Princess Olga's eyes narrowed.

'Come come, Thornton, dear boy,' she said in a voice hardly above a whisper and waved her stick around the room. 'You are well and truly outnumbered. How long do you think you can defend yourself with that?'

'Not long I suppose.' He lifted and dropped one shoulder in a little shrug. 'But, if your girls are so precious to you, you wouldn't want to lose three or four more, would you?'

'More?' Tatty said, her eye on the automatic.

'Oh, of course, you don't know, do you? I'm sorry to have to tell you, girls, but your colleague, N'tombi, is no longer with us. She has, I'm afraid, gone to join the spirits of her tribal ancestors. And one false move from any of you and you will do likewise. Holly?' He jerked his head, indicating she should make a move for the door but this time Sumachi's reactions did not fail her and she was the quicker off the mark. Sword in hand she leapt to her feet and was almost on him when Thornton's finger tightened on the trigger. The gun spat and Sumachi hit the floor.

'One,' he said.

'I doubt you will manage many more,' Tatty snarled.

'Perhaps not, now that you come to mention it. But look what I found in your toy cupboard.'

The other hand came out from behind his back. Like a sleight of hand magician he held a couple of golf balls between his outstretched fingers. Once again the occupants of the room were frozen into immobility.

'Holly,' Thornton said, 'pick up the sword and bring the princess with us for a little chat. How are the casualties?'

Amelia broke ranks and knelt down to take a look at Sumachi and, having done so, got to her feet again and shook her head.

'Anya needs seeing to urgently,' Mira hissed.

'If you ask me,' Thornton responded, 'you all need seeing to urgently. I am only too aware of the vein of insanity that seems to be running through the world but you lot take the biscuit. I'm afraid she will have to wait a while longer.' He removed the key from the door and waited for Holly to usher Tatty out, then he slipped the golf balls into a pocket and, keeping the gun in hand, backed out himself. 'Good night, ladies,' he said, closing and locking the door and then turning to Holly, 'Right, let's go,' he ordered.

'Go?' Holly said. 'Where to?'

'I hadn't thought of that. Where would you suggest? Some-where from where we can make a telephone call is in order.'

'There's an office on the second floor.'

'Good. Après vous.'

They started up the stairs.

'Where's Ivan?' Holly asked.

'Out.'

'Out? Out where?'

'Out cold.'

Chapter Twelve

Holly went in first and switched on the main light. Then she stood aside as Tatty and Thornton followed. 'Funny,' she said, 'I thought the light had been left on. Ivan must have come back up and switched it off, though I wouldn't have thought he was the type to worry about conservation.'

'Maybe someone else did,' Thornton said. 'Anyway, that's the least of our worries at the moment. He crossed to the desk and picked up the phone. 'I wonder what poor old Venables is going to make of all this.'

'And just who might that be?' Tatty asked.

'Oh, a policeman Holly and I have got to know quite well. You remember him surely. You met him in the restaurant when you had old Shoggi done in.' He smiled as he remembered the look on Venables' face then and the smile broadened as he thought of how it would look now. They really should have put a Chief Inspector onto this; it was way out of Venables' class. He was about to dial emergency when he noticed the look on Holly's face. 'What's the matter?' He asked.

'How did you get into the building?' She countered.

'Oh, someone conveniently left the kitchen door open for me; that is, it was shut but not locked, so I just walked in.'

'Such a common little man,' Tatty said out of the blue.

'What? Who?'

'Your policeman friend. What's his name?'

'Venables?'

'Such a common little man, and not much up here.' Tatty tapped her temple with a forefinger. 'So what do you think he's going to make of all this, Thornton?'

Thornton frowned. He wasn't too sure what the cagey old bird was getting at. 'All what, Tatty?' He smiled sweetly.

'You and Miss Day breaking into my establishment in the early hours of the morning, killing one of my girls, seriously wounding another.'

'You can't be serious!' Holly nearly exploded. 'You don't really intend trying to bluff your way out of this do you? You're living in cloud-cuckoo land, woman.'

'Woman!' It was Tatty's turn to explode and she did it with a lot more style than Holly who, in the meantime, had marched across to the cupboard she had investigated earlier and flung open the doors.

'And just how,' she asked, 'do you hope to explain all this?'

'By the time I get around to calling the police, and by the time they arrive here, all that will have gone,' Tatty replied.

'You call the police?' Thornton didn't explode but there was no mistaking the nervy edge to his voice.

'Well of course, dear boy. I will have to won't I? So I can present them with your bodies, yours and Miss Day's. Then the whole mystery will be cleared up, especially as you being the last on the list for this term, there will be no more killings from this quarter: that is, not until the end of next term when the newer girls will take their finals.'

'She's mad!' Holly squeaked. 'Out of her mind! Stark staring mad!'

'Not at all, my dear.' Tatty turned her attention to Holly. 'You don't think I can let you get away with this do you?'

'Just what do you have in mind, Tatty?' Thornton put down the phone.

'Finishing the job, dear boy, is what I have in mind. It's so untidy to leave things in mid-air as I'm sure you will agree.'

Holly felt the goose bumps rising. The princess's voice was so quiet but so ominous and, above all, she sounded so sure of herself, or was it bluff? She crossed swiftly over to the filing cabinet and then turned to Thornton, a note of desperation in her own voice. 'My gun! It's gone! Someone's taken it.'

'Steady on now, Holly...'

'Thornton, who turned off the lights in this room? Who has taken my gun? Everybody was downstairs and accounted for. Where did you leave Ivan?'

'In the kitchen, trussed up like a chicken, which is just how it should be in a kitchen, no?'

'Don't make light of this, Thornton, there's something decidedly wrong.' There was a slight note of panic in Holly's voice.

The princess stood by smiling. She had them dancing and she knew it. 'Would it be all right,' she asked politely, 'if an old woman were to sit down? My legs aren't what they used to be.'

'You stay right where you are,' Holly barked and ran to the door to take a look outside. All was quiet except for a Borzoi loping up the stairs, no doubt in search of his newfound friend.

'Go away!' Holly ordered. The dog wagged its tail. She stamped her foot and waved the sword. The dog turned tail and fled down half a dozen stairs where it turned back to look at her with reproachful eyes, and then it slowly continued on its way. Satisfied, Holly returned to the room.

'What was all that about?' Thornton asked.

'Just a dog,' Holly said.

'Boris,' Tatty added, identifying the animal. 'You have to treat him gently. He's highly strung.'

'Any higher and his strings will snap,' Thornton said jovially.

Holly almost screamed as she felt her strings about to snap.

'Thornton! Will you stop joking? PLEASE!

'All right, all right.' He moved around the desk and stood facing the open cupboard. With his back to Tatty it seemed he did not consider her an immediate threat or, if he did, that Holly could handle her. It appeared he was correct in his assumption for despite the heavy stick in her hand she watched him but did not move. 'Well just in case and to be on the safe side,' he said, knowing full well that until the law arrived he was going to feel far from safe, 'perhaps we had better arm you as well, Holly. Choose your weapon; quite a selection to choose from.'

'Maybe,' Holly said, 'but none of them are any good thank you very much, they're not loaded.'

'Well there must be ammunition somewhere,' he persisted, opening first the forced drawer and then tugging on the one next to it.

'Oh, yes there is,' Tatty chipped in brightly, 'but not in this room. It's kept separate... in case of accidents,' she added as a seeming afterthought and by way of explanation. 'I do wish you'd let me sit down, my dear, my old legs are killing me.'

'If that's all that's killing you,' Holly sounded quite vicious and gave the sword a little waggle, 'consider yourself lucky.' She turned to Thornton. 'Get on that phone, Thornton, for God's sake! The sooner the police get here the better.'

'Hmn...' Thornton grunted, in obvious agreement as he moved back to the desk.

'So, Thornton...' Tatty paused, waiting for him to look at her. 'I must admit I was most surprised at your appearance.'

'I thought the outfit rather dashing,' Thornton said, looking down at his dishevelled self.

'You're joking again,' Holly growled.

'Sorry.'

'Miss Day I half expected, but certainly not you. So N'tombi failed.'

'I'm afraid so, Princess. But then we can't guarantee a hundred percent success every time, can we?'

'Can we not, Mr. King?'

The last time she stopped calling him Thornton and addressed him as Mr King it was followed by what could euphemistically be called "an incident." His scalp prickled alarmingly and it felt like someone had dumped a bag of ice cubes in the region of his groin. Her voice seemed to come out of nowhere but there was no mistaking it–it was the voice of N'tombi!

Slowly the office door, which had been left open all this time and of which no one had taken any notice, there being no reason why they should, was pushed away from the wall to swing closed and reveal N'tombi who had been standing all this while behind it. Despite the fact that she was holding Holly's gun and it was aimed straight at him, Thornton's instinctive reaction was to raise his own, that is the one N'tombi lost and which he now held. They would face each other again but at least this time both guns were loaded and the odds were even. Rather the odds would have been even had Tatty not anticipated Thornton's move and, with unexpected speed and strength, knocked the gun from his hand with a hard blow of her stick. In a way her action probably saved his life.

Without her intervention, odds or evens, N'tombi would more than likely have finished it then and there. The gun went spinning across the desk and, as Thornton made a dive for it, the unsheathed end of Tatty's stick stopped him in his tracks. Under different circumstances Holly might have burst out laughing at the sight of Thornton with his nose an inch from the desk top, the point of the blade an inch from his nose, and he staring at it totally cross-eyed because of its proximity, as hypnotised as a chicken with its beak to a line in the sand.

'I did ask you to let me sit down, Thornton, from which

position I would not have been able to get you into the position you are in now'.

It had all happened so rapidly that Holly, her attention divided, had not really had time to react and, as Tatty's dagger now forced Thornton back against the cupboard, she turned to N'tombi only to find the gun now menacing her. Had she been a follower of Zen she might have found the moment when the speed of the blade proved faster than the speed of the trigger finger but she was not prepared to risk it. On being ordered to drop the sword she did so without further ado. N'tombi carefully moved it out of harm's way with her foot.

'Well, well, well...' Tatty laughed, and there was no concealing the note of triumph in her voice. 'I did tell you, Thornton.'

'So you told me,' Thornton said, staring at N'tombi and rubbing his aching wrist with the undamaged back of his other hand.

'One of the last lessons I taught N'tombi was never ever to under-estimate your opponent. It is a lesson you should have learnt yourself, dear boy. In fact I'm rather disappointed in you. If you had you would not be in the...'

'Shit?' Thornton suggested helpfully.

'Crude, Thornton, crude.'

'But exact.'

'Tickle I believe is the word I was looking for. You would not be in the tickle in which you find yourself.'

'Pickle, Princess, the word you were looking for is "pickle." And you put it all down to my under-estimating my opponent, is that right? Well tell me this, how do you underestimate someone who's dead? Dead is dead. She was dead! Is dead! Dead as a doornail. Dead as a flaming Dodo. She shouldn't be here! She's a zombie. She should be lying on my carpet making irremovable stains.'

'Nonsense!'

'What do you mean, nonsense?' Bloodstains are supposed to be impossible to remove. Isn't that so?' He sought confirmation from N'tombi.

'It would take more than a little bump on the head to kill me, Mr. King. And if you'd taken the trouble to make sure before you left your flat you would have realised that.'

'I was in agony! Look at my hands! Look at them! You did that!' He added accusingly as though it mattered. What is more I spilled water all down my front and it was decidedly uncomfortable, I was in no mood to go poking around a corpse. You gave every indication of being dead. Your eyes were open, staring at nothing. There was no sign of breathing.'

'Thornton,' Holly said, 'don't you think it's just a teeny bit macabre rebuking someone for not being dead?'

'Keep out of this, Holly. This is between me and her.'

'It's called Yoga, Mr. King.'

'Is that so?' Thornton looked around the room apparently now aghast with admiration at the girl's ingenuity.

'He's playing for time! It's a trick he has.' N'tombi cast a nervous glance in Tatty's direction.

'So?' Was the laconic response from her mentor. N'tombi frowned. 'What is time? We have all the time in the world.'

'No! Let me finish him now.'

'Be quiet!' Tatty turned on her protégé. 'I will have you know, N'tombi, I am not pleased with you. You should have finished him off where you were meant to finish him off. His coming here is an unlooked for complication and I have to think this one out. I warned you you were up against the best.'

Thornton laughed. It was meant to be derisive but it actually sounded as if he were going to throw up. 'The best? The best what? Tatty, I really cannot imagine where you got this ridiculous idea. Look at me: since I got involved in this little caper of yours my anatomy gives every appearance of having been dragged through a hedge backwards, or across a mine field. And now here I am, together with Miss Day of course, well and truly, and I don't care how crude it sounds, in the shit! How can you say I am the best? You obviously know nothing about me.'

'On the contrary, dear boy, I have followed your career with the greatest interest right from the start and you have always brought home the beef.'

'You never cease to amaze me, princess. Where do you get these outlandish expressions? Beef indeed! I think you actually mean bacon unless beef is the Russian equivalent. And do please remove that thing from the proximity of my jugular. It's most unnerving. N'tombi will, after all, keep her little gun at the ready so no one is going to do anything silly.'

Tatty obligingly lowered her stick but she did not replace the ferrule and kept within striking distance.

'Thank you,' Thornton said. 'Have you ever killed anyone with that thing?'

'Don't ask stupid questions,' Tatty snapped. 'If you are hinting that I don't know how, or haven't the strength, to use it, try me.'

Thornton raised two much damaged placating hands.

'Thornton!' Holly exclaimed. 'What did happen to your hands?'

'She happened,' he said, pointing an accusing finger at N'tombi. 'Anyway,' he continued, turning back to the princess, 'if you thought I was the tops why didn't you ever think to offer me a job in your school as a tutor? I could have done with the money. Come to think of it I still do.'

'Let me explain,' Tatty said, lowering the stick a little further. There was a hardly suppressed squeal from N'tombi but the princess ignored her. 'Of all the girls who have been sent to me,' she went on, 'N'tombi is going to have the hardest job of all. Is that not so, my dear?'

N'tombi's head nodded vigorously. All she wanted was to get this over and done with as quickly as possible and she would have happily agreed to the suggestion that an American Republican was an atheist and a dyed in the wool communist to boot and his wife a fellow traveller if it had been put to her at that moment. Thornton cast a quick glance in her direction. The hand that held the gun was rock steady but there was an anxious look in her eye. The longer he could stall, the more unnerved he felt she would become. As long as she didn't panic and start blasting away but somehow, in the presence of the princess, he felt there was very little likelihood of that happening.

'Her mission is the one that will require the utmost skill, courage, and imagination,' Tatty continued, well into her stride and rather in the tone she might use in describing the qualities of a new perfume from Chinique. 'You see, the man she is destined to dispatch...'

'Cut out the euphemisms, Tatty. Just say what you mean. The man she is being paid to kill.'

'Are you interested in this or are you not?' Tatty sounded quite put out. 'Because, if you're not, I can stop right now.'

'Oh, please, go on,' Thornton said as if apologising for his effrontery in interrupting her flow. 'I'm really very interested.' He smiled at N'tombi who remained singularly unimpressed.

'The man she is going to assassinate (assassinate was vocally underlined) started life as a street thug and became an experienced assassin himself with more than one trick up his sleeve I can tell you. Not only that, but he is guarded twenty-four hours a day, frequently changes residence, never sleeps in the same bed two nights running, travels in a bullet and bomb proof car and always varies his routes and times. He is only too aware there are those who want to get rid of him. He trusts no one and he's up to every trick in the survival manual. And that, my dear boy, is why you were selected for N'tombi. You were pinpricked for death from the moment I arranged for you to witness Anya at work in François' dear little restaurant. Wasn't that a superb meal? And, as I told you, he is doing extremely well since that incident and all the resultant publicity. You cannot get a table for love or bribe. People are so ghoulish.'

'And just why did you want me to witness Anya at work in François' dear little restaurant?'

'Because I knew how you would react and I wanted to make N'tombi's task as difficult as possible. It would have been too easy if you hadn't been put on your guard.'

'Taking a risk weren't you? You certainly succeeded in rousing my suspicions, I grant you that.'

'Ah, following up with the fashion show you mean. Yes, Schnief was extremely pleased with my girls you'll be pleased to hear. I was too. I thought they carried the whole thing off beautifully. And the colonel... yes, that was a master stroke, even though I say so myself.'

Thornton could not disguise the way he felt about that. His eyes narrowed almost to slits and he clenched his fists, using the one pain to try and expel the other. Holly folded her arms, took a deep breath, blew out hard, and rolled her eyes ceiling ward.

'I knew you could never resist a challenge, Thornton, and I was right of course.'

'As you always are,' Thornton agreed, pretending to be gracious. N'tombi shifted her weight from one leg to the other. Holly snorted. Tatty turned on her.

'As for you, my dear Miss Day, you were merely an un-looked for complication.'

'Thank you very much,' Holly sneered.

'The question now is,' Tatty returned to Thornton, 'just what do I do with the pair of you?'

'Disposal-wise you mean.'

'Exactly. Of course I could let N'tombi put a bullet through you right now and so pass her finals but I could hardly consider it a first class pass, could I?'

'Oh, definitely not first class. I'd flunk her if I were you,' he suggested. 'Though in my humble opinion... do you want my humble opinion? I've given her such a wealth of experience, invaluable experience I might add, I am sure she could be sent back right now and bring the job off beautifully, easy-peasy, no trouble at all. But, if it's twenty questions we're playing, there is one that I would like to ask, something that still puzzles me.'

'Only one?' Holly sounded really petulant. 'Look, Thornton, quit the small talk and DO something about this situation.'

'Do what?' His aggrieved tone counter-balanced her pet-ulance, the implication being that he didn't see why it should be his responsibility to get them out of this mess. 'Anyway,' he went on, 'it is the sixty four thousand dollar question.'

'Look!' Holly pursed her lips and only loosened them a little to keep on talking. 'There is a whole room full of Valkyries downstairs who right this second are plotting their escape, if they haven't already got out, which shouldn't prove too difficult, and they will be flying up those stairs on their broomsticks to rescue this woman from hell here.'

'What are you talking about?' He appealed with a look to Tatty to back him up. 'We're the ones who are captive, not them.' He flicked his fingers towards the two women. 'And Valkyries do not ride broomsticks. They ride very fine horses.'

'Excuse me, Thornton, I think I am about to burst into tears.'

'Stop bickering, you two,' the princess ordered sternly. 'It's very distracting. You're not bridge partners by any chance are you?'

Thornton's forehead crinkled as he tried to fathom out some kind of logic behind this seeming non sequitur. Real bridge partners don't bicker, they draw blood. Maybe it was just that Tatty was finally showing signs of senility, and about time too, he thought, the old girl must be approaching her century.

'I was just wondering,' she continued, explaining herself, 'if you were giving each other clues, using a code. You know, like when bidding for a contract and you use a convention; Blackwood's for example.'

'This is crazy!' Holly almost exploded. 'This is Alice in Wonderland!'

'Never played bridge in my life,' Thornton lied. He was a bridge fanatic.

'Because you would both be familiar with codes wouldn't you? Considering the nature of your work.'

'You know nothing about my work,' Holly protested.

'Oh, but I do, my dear. I took the trouble of making a few discreet enquiries.'

'From what sources?' Holly still sounded disbelieving.

'Mike Aliff of course.'

'That toad!'

'That mole,' Thornton added. 'I always suspected he was a security risk. He isn't part of your organisation I suppose.'

'Don't be ridiculous; the man's an idiot. Absolutely to be expected in his position. It has always seemed to me a terrible flaw in the British character invariably to select the wrong man for the job, in nearly every walk of life. And then, when they've made a complete smash...'

'Hash... the word you want is hash.'

'Hash of things, it's unbelievable but they're rewarded. They're paid off handsomely, enough to spend the rest of their lives in idle luxury.'

'You're absolutely right,' Thornton said, 'take me for example though I didn't get...'

But Tatty silenced him with a wave of her hand. 'Thornton, I don't want any of your shabby dog stories, thank you.' Her conviction of his prowess was not to be diminished. 'You're the exception that proves the rule, Thornton, as has been proved.'

'Shaggy, Princess, the word is shaggy.'

'What?'

'It's a shaggy dog, not a shabby one.'

'Whatever. I still cannot understand how N'tombi botched it but, no doubt, I will find out later in her report. No, sometimes, more by good luck than good judgment, the right man manages to slip in. But, should he prove too successful, that other British flaw raises its ugly head.'

'Sex?'

'Jealousy. After having been praised to the skies for his wonderful work, his talent, his expertise, whatever, the poor man, or woman as the case may be, is ganged up on, kicked out, and the most unsuitable candidate chosen to take his place. Then everyone is happy again, muddling along just as before. Mike Aliff will go far. It wouldn't surprise me if he ended up head of the department. Also he has, how do the Americans say it? The gift of the gob and that is a precious gift.'

'Gift of the gab, princess, not gob.'

'Whatever. Anyway, dear boy, what was your forty-six thousand dollar question?

'Sixty-four.'

'What?'

'The expression is sixty-four thousand. Not forty-six.'

'Inflation again,' the princess said, chuckling merrily. 'Well, go on! Whatever the price, what is the question?'

'Did you ever meet Rasputin?'

There was a silence before Princess Olga found her voice.

'That… is worth sixty-four thousand dollars?'

'No, it just suddenly popped into my head. Well did you? The reason I ask is because it struck me that, like Richard the Third and poor old King John, he might have been much maligned by history.'

'Why don't you add Attila, Genghis Kahn and Vlad the Impaler to your list of misunderstood delinquents,' Holly suggested sarcastically. 'And, if you don't want to plead mitigating circumstances for them, there are quite a few more I could think of including contemporary ones.'

Tatty seemed to listen to this with some interest. Perhaps she was wondering if she were being included in the list. Then she turned back to Thornton. 'I met him once. But I have no memory of it. Except that for many years after I felt quite ill at the smell of vodka.'

'Vodka has no smell.'

'Maybe it was my imagination then. Anyway I was two years old at the time. And he was murdered shortly after.'

'Well at least you couldn't have had anything to do with that,' Thornton said, 'Not if you were only two.'

'Thornton! The girls!' Holly was all but ringing her hands as she silently willed him to do something.

'Oh, don't worry about then,' he replied jauntily. 'They are troops without a general and totally lost. Even storm troopers can't storm if there's no one to give orders. They're probably all in a huddle trying to decide what to do. No, my real sixty-four thousand dollar question is... why?'

'Why?' It was Tatty's turn to frown. She was genuinely puzzled. 'Why what?'

'The whole business,' Thornton said by way of explanation. 'Why?'

'Are you going to tell him?' Holly asked. She couldn't help feeling the whole situation was growing more and more bizarre.

They were carrying on a conversation as though this were a continuation of the reception after the fashion show with Thornton determined to play the life and sole of the party. She wondered, as it was a school, if she could raise her hand and asked to be excused. She badly needed a wee-wee. And what was Tatty playing at? Why didn't she make a move? She had the upper hand. She had a room full of reinforcements downstairs. Somewhere in the building was Ivan who, even if trussed up, could be released. Could it be that the old girl had finally lost her marbles? It was all very confusing.

'Yes...' Tatty said slowly, 'I think I will tell him. You both deserve some kind of an explanation before you die.'

'Well if it's going to be a long explanation,' Holly said, 'why don't you sit down? I thought your feet were killing you.'

'Not at the moment,' the princess said. 'Getting you two where I want you has given me a new lease on life.'

'May it last long,' Thornton said.

'In that case,' Holly went on, casting a wicked glance at her partner in misfortune, 'do you mind if I sit down?' She stepped towards the desk.

'Stay right where you are!' N'tombi snapped.

'All right all right already! I'll be a wallflower. But my feet are beginning to kill me. So, if you have no objections, I'll just loosen my boot, okay?' She leaned against the wall and raised a foot.

'Not there!' N'tombi ordered and waved the gun to indicate Holly should move away from the door and further into the room. Holly obeyed, ending up next to the filing cabinet.

'This all right? Sorry, Princess, do carry on.' She started to slowly ease off one boot with the toe of the other.

'Let me start with what, as children of the capitalist system, you will easily understand. Firstly, I needed the money.'

'There were plenty of children under the communist system

who needed the money. Or, even if they didn't need it, they wanted it and weren't averse to dipping their greedy snouts in the trough.' Holly leaned back with her arms up on the cabinet. 'Sorry, I'm interrupting again.'

'But you've got Chinique!' Thornton protested.

'Chinique is a lame goose, dear boy.'

'Duck,' he corrected her.

'What?'

'The goose lays the golden eggs. It's the duck that's lame.'

'Whatever you say.' Tatty moved around the desk towards the chair behind it. She went around N'tombi's side so as not to pass in front of Thornton. She was not that senile.

Holly closed her eyes and then opened them again to look at N'tombi. N'tombi raised a shoulder, which gesture was accompanied by the appropriate facial expression, all of this body language adding up to "don't ask me." Tatty eased herself into the chair. Thornton perched an inch or two of buttock on the bottom shelf of the open cupboard, which, fortunately, was just the right height to take an inch or two of buttock.

'If you're going to do that,' N'tombi instructed, 'keep your hands where I can see them.' She felt if she asserted her authority by telling him to stand up straight her authority would be diminished by his ignoring her.

'Certainly,' he said, and folded his arms. Then he looked at Tatty, 'Chinique,' he prompted.

'Ah, yes, Chinique.' There was a pause before she went on. 'Tax is a terrible taskmaster, Thornton.'

'Don't I know it?' He agreed with enthusiasm.

'Corporation tax, income tax, capital gains tax, business rates, on and on and on. And, when a company is not doing too well... too well did I say? On the brink of bankruptcy in fact; when you have put so much of your life into that company and you have to service your debts to the bank which, at to-day's rates of interest is not easy...'

'You're preaching to the converted.' Thornton said, nodding, his expression serious.

'One is tempted to do... things... that could get one into a lot of trouble. Thornton, dear boy, whatever you do in life...'

'You mean in the few minutes or so I have left?'

'... never be tempted, no matter what the circumstances, no matter what the provocation, never be tempted to cross swords with the dreaded taxman. You cannot win. Then, to add to my troubles, we suddenly discovered that like so many brand names, Chinique perfume was being pirated and, of course, being sold at a fraction of the price. Where did it come from? Hong Kong? Bangkok? Who knows? But, as you can imagine, it made a huge hole in our sales.'

'Why didn't you call me in?' Thornton demanded. 'I could have nailed the buggers for you.' He had a sudden vision of luxury hotels, an unlimited (virtually) expense account, a huge fee, and dozens of handmade silk shirts bought for peanuts.

'You were still with the Ministry, dear boy.'

'I could have done a spot of moonlighting. Plenty do. I had a builder come and do some repairs in the flat. Got chatting to him one day. Turned out he worked for the local council and every time he came to me it was because he had a doctor's note. Not only that, but the stuff he was using was actually nicked from the council and he had the nerve to charge me for it. All that tax-free, see? All part of the black economy. Anyway, I'm really surprised you didn't think of it, Tatty.' He sounded most put out. 'Especially in view of the fact that you say you rate my abilities so highly.'

'Well, well...' she said, 'be that as it may, these were not my only problems. As I said, the company owed the banks a great deal of money, the result of optimistic forecasts and too rapid expansion. Shops in Paris, Rome, Vienna, New York, Hollywood, Washington, Georgetown of course. And who could have expected such a recession? And then, one day... I will never forget it... such a shock... on top of everything else...' She laid a hand over her heart and shook her head, 'an audit showed there was something not quite right in the accounts. I will not bore you with the details. Suffice to say we went through the books to discover we had been swindled out of a lot of money; a great deal of money, Thornton. And who was responsible for this? A crooked little accountant, an alcoholic accountant, a miserable little worm I could have strangled with one hand. So altogether, as you can imagine, Chinique was in a very bad way.'

'How much did he steal?' By now even Holly was intrigued by the misfortunes of the princess's empire.

'More than enough: any theft, no matter how small, is more than enough and this amount was not small.' Tatty then dismissed the question with a wave of her hand.

'And what happened to him?' Thornton wanted to know.

'As far as the authorities were concerned he died of his addiction. It was tantamount to suicide of course, but it was that that gave me the idea for the school.'

'Oh? And how was that then?' Thornton, looking somewhat bemused, was falling into the princess's speech patterns. The connection between the death from alcoholism of a crooked accountant and the establishment of a school for prospective female assassins seemed a pretty tenuous one.

'Oh, it was such a simple matter to get rid of him, that little bug of a creature. Brilliant with figures maybe, brilliant at manipulation, but an insignificant little toad.'

'Worm, bug, toad, brilliant at metamorphosis as well.' Thornton unfolded his arms and studied his injured hands.

'There was no way the company was going to recover its losses.

Years of work on the point of being destroyed by one person and, for me, nothing the law could do to him would be bad enough.'

'So you took revenge into your own hands,' Holly said flatly.

'Of course, my dear, if you wish to think of it as revenge. I consider it just puddings.' She turned a condescending smile on her accuser.

'Puddings?' Holly queried.

'Desserts,' Thornton said; 'the saying is "just desserts." Sometimes I do declare you do this on purpose, Tatty, just to be cute.'

'What would you have me do, Miss Day? Let him get away with it?'

'If you had turned him over to the law...'

'The law!' Tatty waved a dismissive hand. 'What law? The law is a donkey.'

'You're doing it again, Princess: the saying is ass, the law is an ass.'

'Whatever. Like the man N'tombi is going after I know only one law and that is the law of survival. That, my dear, is what life is all about. Take the present situation. Which of us is going to survive? If I have anything to do with it it will be me.'

'I, Princess, I will survive.'

'Thornton will you please stop correcting my grammar?'

'Yes, Thornton,' Holly chimed in, 'will you please stop correcting her grammar?'

'I remember how I sat in my office late at night, thinking... thinking...' She sat for a moment as she recalled that night. 'For a long time I seemed to get nowhere. My mind was a whirl. I kept going around in circles. And then I had a flash of inspiration. I came to the conclusion that my old talents would have to be, how should I put it, resurrected? Yes, but how? In the world of international espionage I was now useless, an old woman past her time; but there was something I could do, I could pass my expertise, a lifetime's experience, on to others, and that is how the school was born.'

'Oh, Tatty,' Thornton sighed, 'you could have organised acid-house parties, orgies: you could have started a fanzine for the Romanovs. You could have written a book; two books.'

'I could have lived off my old-age pension,' Tatty countered, 'but living would hardly be the right word for it. I would have become a vegetable. No, the school was the answer and, as I think I once said to you, Miss Day, my fees are hardly small change. So, even with overheads being what they are these days, it has been the goose that lays those golden eggs.' She smiled at Thornton.

'Fab for fabulous, fab for the Fab Four, fab for Fabergé,' Thornton said.

Holly did not appreciate his flippancy. 'At the expense of innocent lives,' she growled.

Tatty shook her head disbelievingly. 'You have as much experience of innocence as you have of the law, Miss Day. None of the targets were what you might call nice people.'

'I beg to differ there,' Thornton butted in with some indignation.

'Ah, you're thinking of your friend, the colonel. He, just like you, was the exception, Thornton.'

'Then you must have some regrets,' Holly ventured.

'I regret nothing.'

'Have you no conscience?'

Tatty's face hardened. 'Innocence, regrets, law, conscience; words, words, words.'

'Quite nice ones,' Thornton said mildly. 'Civilised even.'

'A job worth doing is worth doing well,' Tatty snapped, 'to the bitter end.'

'And the end justifies the means. Doesn't life run beautifully on well-oiled clichés? How about ...?' Thornton thought for a moment and then raised a finger in the air. 'Proverbs: "The lips of a strange woman droppeth honey but her end is wormwood."'

'The girls had to finish their training. Half-trained is as useless as no training at all. You train a soldier to kill but how do you know, how can you be sure, when the time comes, that he is capable of killing? Conscience! I have lived through revolution, famine, wars. I cannot remember a day of my life when there has not been fighting somewhere, when the innocent have not been tortured and slaughtered in their thousands, hundreds of thousands, either deliberately or through neglect and stupidity, greed and ambition, long nurtured grudges, tribal hatreds. Don't talk to me of conscience. Where did you learn about this thing, conscience? Sunday school? If you faced life as a realist, my dear Miss Day, you would realise how useless your Sunday School morality is. You mentioned some very interesting names earlier, if I remember correctly, Vlad the Impaler was one. Did you have to go back that far? Do you think the age of the thuggee and the torturer is over? Do you think that through some miracle mankind has suddenly become rational?' Tatty laughed. It was a harsh, crackling sound. 'I have witnessed man's awful cruelty with my own eyes. I have heard the screams of the tortured with my own ears. You think the Nazi concentration camps, the Gulags, the killing fields, the massacres, are isolated examples of man's bestial behaviour? No! They stand out as monuments of horror only because of their magnitude. To a lesser degree, somewhere in this world, these things are happening all the time.'

'She'll be quoting John Donne at us next,' Thornton said. He wondered if Tatty's outburst was an essay in self-justification but dismissed the idea. 'It invariably gets to the point where either John Donne or Oscar Wilde are quoted.'

'Thornton!' Holly turned on him. She looked really wild. 'You and I are going to have words about this!'

'Words words words,' Tatty drawled. Holly turned back on her.

'You've said enough!' She snapped. 'Nothing you can say can justify what you have done, so let's have no more words. If you've decided to get rid of us, which I am sure you have because, just like your accountant, we are likely to spoil everything for you, then get on with it. You are totally mad and there is no arguing with a psychopath.'

'Good point,' Thornton said.

'Will you shut up?' Holly yelled at him. 'Your opinion is no longer wanted.' She swung back on Tatty. 'Obviously you have as little regard for the sanctity of life...' She broke off and they all stared in amazement at the old woman in the chair. Did she actually whoop? She was certainly chuckling merrily to herself. N'tombi looked totally bemused. For a girl trained to action this was neither the time nor the place for dialectic and she just knew it spelt disaster.

'I said something funny?' Holly enquired icily.

Tatty shook her head. 'The sanctity of life.'

'That is funny?'

'That is merely another of man's ridiculous notions. How can you believe in anything so ridiculous when all around you the evidence points to exactly the opposite? Ask the people bombed in railway stations and airports and supermarkets about the sanctity of life; those innocents killed in the game of dirty politics. Have you never heard of Gladio? Would you like to ask the people in the slums of South America about the sanctity of life? Or maybe the Albanians? The Bangladeshis? The Burmese? The Ethiopians? The refugees from Mozambique? The millions who barely scrape by from day to day? They exist, but do they have a life? You live in a country where a child is born with a heart defect and a million pounds worth of technology is used to keep that child alive. Helicopters are sent to fetch a replacement heart. Surgeons stand by to perform the operation all in the name of life, and at the same time thousands of African children die from starvation, thousands die from illnesses that could have been prevented by a few pence worth of medicine. The sewer children of South America are hunted down, tortured and slaughtered by death squads.' Tatty was no longer laughing. She was fierce. Her eyes blazed. 'The whole thing is a nonsense,' she hissed. 'We carry on breeding like the world is an inexhaustible breadbasket; like it can take all the pollution that overpopulation can throw at it. Yes, my dear, that's what I said, over-population: too many people, too quickly dwindling resources. Then, like overcrowded rats, we kill.'

Thornton was more than a little disconcerted to hear some of his own arguments being voiced by this rabid old woman. 'Too much shit to get rid of,' he murmured, agreeing with what she was saying though he could not agree with what she was doing.

'I do wish you would stop using that word, Thornton.'

'Shit is shit,' he said.

The princess decided to ignore him. 'And, if you are still so worried about the sanctity of life, Miss Day, despite the fact that nature's over-abundance proves it to be expendable to a great degree, then here is an ethical argument for you. In N'tombi's country, a tyrant and his henchmen are committing mass murder. Now, for the price of Mr. King's life...'

'Thank you,' Thornton said.

'... and the life of the tyrant, we save thousands of potential victims: two lives for thousands, it is all relative you see. Am I not doing a great deal of good? Conversely, by stopping me, you are ensuring the unpleasant deaths of those thousands of potential victims. Think about that.'

'She has a point,' Thornton said. 'And there's someone at the door.'

They turned to look and, sure enough, the door was slowly swinging open again. Holly, being in direct line with it, was the first to see who it was: Boris. She looked quickly back at N'tombi who was eyeing the door suspiciously. This was Holly's moment and she took it. She suddenly kicked out violently and her loosened boot flew across the room to hit N'tombi full in the face. A hellcat desperately trying to wrest the gun from N'tombi's hand followed the boot.

The princess swivelled in her chair and raised her stick but Thornton had her by the wrist and smiling bravely through his pain, took it from her, wagging an admonishing finger. Then, with his other hand on her shoulder, he kept her firmly in the chair. Boris scampered across to his new friend but, as the tussle between the two young women grew in ferocity, he decided discretion was the better part and slunk under the desk, tail between his legs.

Holly now had N'tombi backwards over the desktop and was battering her wrist against the edge, desperately trying to force her to release the gun. The would-be assassin was definitely taking punishment as she squirmed under Holly's weight with one forearm pressing down across her throat as her own was being mashed against the desk. She let out a piercing scream as she thought her elbow was about to break and the gun clattered to the floor.

'It's a pity, princess, that you taught your girls only how to deal with men,' Thornton leant down and whispered to her. 'You should have taught them also not to underrate women.' He looked up as a figure suddenly lurched through the door. It was Ivan. He raised his arm, the gun in his hand aimed at Holly's unsuspecting back.'

'Holly!'

Thornton yelled the warning but fortunately there was no need. At that precise moment N'tombi found the strength to give a sudden violent shove and the struggling pair rolled off the desk to hit the floor. At the same time Ivan squeezed the trigger.

The gun didn't seem to make much noise but, as the smoke

drifted away and the smell of cordite filled the room, there was a deathly silence. No one moved for a long time and then Holly, who was still on top, got slowly to her feet. She was looking at something beyond her adversary and N'tombi, sensing there was now a whole new ball game, rolled over and got to her hands and knees. It was as if time out had been called. Everyone was looking at Tatty.

The Princess Olga Tatiana Katarina Spitskaya sat in her chair staring sightlessly at Ivan. Between her eyes was a small black hole. The back of her head consisted of a clump of matted hair, no longer silver but bubbling red.

Ivan dropped the gun and walked slowly over to the chair. He knelt on one knee in front of Tatty and, gently lifting one hand, kissed it tenderly. Then he laid it against his cheek.

Boris slunk out of the room. He had disgraced himself beneath the desk.

Chapter Thirteen

They stood side by side surveying Thornton's living room. From the outside came the faint sounds of London going about its daily business. Thornton heaved a deep sigh, crossed to the windows, and pulled open the heavy drapes that had, in keeping out the light, no doubt been instrumental in helping to save his life. Then, as Holly moved further into the room, he went back to switch off the light, stopping on his way to pick up a few pieces of shattered lamp.

'It's not too bad,' Holly said. 'Could have been worse.'

'Could have been,' he agreed, 'I could be dead.' He put the pieces down on the table and regarded them with some satisfaction. There was a time when he had thought of selling that lamp. He was glad he hadn't. He inspected the bullet hole by the light switch.

'How about a cup of tea?' Holly suggested. 'I don't know about you but I really could do with one.'

'Good idea,' he said. 'You know where everything is.'

Holly trotted into the kitchen and he watched her as she turned the gas on beneath the still full kettle. Then, mainly with the use of his forearms, he set the upended chair back on its feet before turning to inspect the couch. He was still staring at it ruefully when she returned and stood beside him, taking his arm in hers. She cocked her head to one side and he knew what she was thinking.

'It's hardly the classiest piece of furniture in the world,' he said, beating her to it. 'It's not even particularly pretty. But I'm very fond of it.'

'It's not badly damaged. A needle and thread would do that,' she tried to reassure him as she stuck a finger through a hole.

'Don't do that! You'll make it worse. And I hardly think a needle and thread will suffice. No, a complete recovering job is called for I'm afraid.' He glanced around and nodded towards the light switch. 'Might as well have the walls done at the same time.' Then he turned his attention back to the couch. 'Here, give us a hand, will you?' They went to their respective ends and replaced the couch. Then they sat on it. After a while Thornton broke the silence.

'Thank you,' he said simply. She turned to look at him.

'For what?' She took his hand. He winced. 'Sorry!'

She transferred her hand to his arm.

'Don't come over all English on me. You know perfectly well for what.'

There was another silence then, with a little shrug, 'That makes us quits,' she said and, deciding to change the subject, 'I wonder how old Venables is getting on.'

'Never had it so good. Open and shut case. Given it to him on a plate. Everything he needs.'

'We're getting pretty good at making statements.'

'Piece of cookie, as Tatty might have said. Talking of which, I wonder if we have any. I'm really quite hungry.'

'I'm not surprised. It's been one hell of a night. I'll have a look when I make the tea. Where do you keep the cake tins?'

'Top shelf on the left, there should be some Russian cake left.'

'Pu-lease!'

'No I'm serious. It's my favourite.'

She laughed and squeezed his hand. He yelled and pulled it away.

'I'm sorry! I'm sorry! I forgot!' She took his hand again, very gently, opened it and inspected the damaged palm. 'It looks really nasty, Thornton.' He showed her the other one. 'Maybe you should get Adrian to look at them.'

'Which Adrian? The Adrian who seduces me? Or the Adrian who sews me up?' He looked at his hands. They were not a pretty sight. 'It'll keep a while longer,' he said.

'Well don't blame me if they go septic because, if they do, you'll be in real trouble.'

'Real trouble, the girl says. What have I been in these last few days?'

'A tickle,' she said, laughing. 'I'll make the tea.' She pushed herself off the couch and started to go.

'Holly!'

She stopped and turned back to him.

'What on earth possessed you to go in there on your own?'

Holly frowned while she thought about this and gave a little shrug. 'There was nothing on television,' she said.

Thornton lay back on the couch and closed his eyes. He was dog-tired but wide-awake. His nerves were raw and he knew sleep would be impossible for a while. He half expected N'tombi, with a Banzai howl, to come leaping out from somewhere in yet another attack. The fact that he had seen her, with the other girls, being hustled into a police van didn't seem real. He wondered who was looking after Boris, good old Boris.

Maybe he should have offered to take him but that wouldn't have been kind, to keep such a large dog in this flat. And, anyway, he couldn't afford the extra mouth and, with that particular animal, the inevitability of vet's bills, which brought him to his other troubles, he still had to sort out Harry and the minders. Ah, well... he'd worry about that tomorrow. Maybe something, other than demands, would come in the mail. The kettle started to whistle and Thornton, who was in fact on the brink of dozing off, woke with a start, his heart racing. He was rather surprised that sleep had overtaken him so quickly but not in the least surprised that he had come out of it even faster. It was going to take time to get over this one. Maybe a holiday was the answer. But who could afford a holiday? It wasn't even as though he had been hired to do the job and could claim expenses. He wondered if his household insurance would cover the damage. Thornton was never one for reading the small print.

Holly returned carrying a tea tray. She set it down on the table in front of the couch. 'Milk's gone off,' she said as she flopped into the cushions. 'I threw it down the sink.' She poured the tea. 'What will happen to the girls do you think?'

Thornton sat upright to accept his cup of tea. 'Those not charged with murder will be deported I should imagine and dealt with by their own authorities. I hate to think what will happen to N'tombi.'

'Thornton! She tried to kill you!'

'Yes, I know. But there was no personal animosity involved and I got quite fond of her really.'

Holly cast her eyes heavenwards. 'Saints preserve us!' She exclaimed and then, suspiciously, 'Thornton, you didn't... didn't...'

'Maybe their own authorities will make use of their talents,' he said just a little too quickly, 'After all, it was an expensive training, why waste it? Where's my cake?'

'Tin's empty.'

'Really? I could have sworn there was some left. Ah well, never mind. Just have to do without.' He looked around the room. 'What would you say to a Russian motif? Something in double headed eagles. No? Maybe not.' He sipped his tea. He hated it black. His taste was for nursery tea, lashings of full cream milk, none of your health-fad wishy-washy skimmed bit for him. He spooned in some more sugar.

'Thornton...'

'Hmn?'

'Why do you suppose she did it really? Tatty I mean. Did you believe all that guff she gave us? Because I didn't, not for a minute.'

'Which guff? The guff about the money? Or all the other guff? I don't know, Holly. I doubt whether anyone ever will. Maybe she did do it for the money. On the other hand, maybe she tried to vicariously relive the spicy days of her youth, the way old soldiers of a certain kind look back on their army days with nostalgia. She must have had a truly amazing life. Wish she had written that book. Don't know really why she did it. Women are such strange unpredictable creatures.'

'Don't give me that.'

'Of course it might have had something to do with her last husband.'

Holly's eyes opened wide.

'He was much younger than her.'

'She.'

'What?'

'Younger than she was.'

'Really? If you say so. A regular toy-boy I suppose you'd call him. I don't know where she found him; under a rock at the Parthenon I think. But she was devoted to him. As poor old Ivan, it seems, was to her. So it was a little unkind of fate that, when she spent so much of her life in the business of making women more alluring, she should lose him to someone younger and more attractive. What better way to seek revenge against the perfidious male than through beautiful young women? Of course that's only a theory. The truth is more likely to be that she was totally off her rocker. What about a mural of Venus rising from the foam? No? You suggest something then.'

'How about another cup of tea? The pot needs refilling. I don't know why you use such a tiny teapot, Thornton.'

'Nag nag nag. I use a small teapot, my dear, because usually I am the only one I pour tea for and two cups are quite sufficient. I will do the honours.' He rose from the couch and picked up the pot, immediately putting it down again as he sucked in his breath.

'Leave it to me,' she said, 'and another thing, Thornton King, what were you playing at in that office making small talk? We could have taken the offensive almost from the start, instead of which you nearly had me giving birth to kittens.'

'If we had made any kind of move we would more than likely have had our heads blown off, Holly Day, and you know it. The only thing to do was play for time and pray for some kind of divine intervention, and eventually it came, in the shape of a pooch called Boris.'

'You had the golf balls!'

'So I did, so I did. I had completely forgotten about them.' He took one from his pocket and bounced it on the table. Holly flinched.

'Don't do that!' She picked up the teapot.

'Oh, it's all right. Absolutely harmless.' He tossed it in the air and caught it as it fell. 'No one thought to call my bluff,' he chuckled, and lobbed it up the passage towards the front door. There was a shattering explosion. Holly dropped the teapot. It smashed on the tabletop. They stood staring at the smoke as it billowed back into the room.

'You don't happen to know a good interior decorator by any chance, do you?' He croaked.

'Try *Yellow Pages*,' Holly said, and passed out.

Other
Thornton King
Adventures

Just
In
Case

ISBN
978-960-99470-4-6

Dead
On
Target

ISBN
978-960-98418-4-9

The
Cinelli
Vases

ISBN
978-960-99470-3-9

www.DCGMediaGroup.com

Angel

South Africa 1950 –

Angelo, is a teenager growing up in a time of innocence, an innocence about to be shattered by events outside of his cosy world.

Angel chronicles the story of one boy and his family's trials and tribulations over one fateful day. Set against a backdrop of apartheid Angel is a spellbinding tour de force of suspense.

ISBN 978-960-98418-6-3

Granny Probyn and the Great Theatre Royal Drury Lane Mystery

Fluffy Yeomans did not want to go into show business, but when Granny Probyn takes him to London to audition for the Theatre Royal Drury Lane pantomime, he quickly becomes embroiled in a plot to retrieve secret documents vital to the allies in the build up to world war two.

As the body count rises in a chain of murders that eventually leads back to the theatre, can Granny Probyn discover who the murderer is before it is too late and the final curtain falls?

ISBN 978-960-99470-7-7

The Museum Mysteries and other Short Stories

On a visit to the new Acropolis Museum in Athens two visitors were particularly taken with a unique artefact, the purpose of which has not been identified but which caused both of them independently to feel a distinct unease, a sense of something horribly unearthly.

This was what inspired a modern Gothic horror novella The Museum Mysteries.

This collection of seven short stories all have a supernatural theme, of love, hate, and revenge that will get your palms sweating, your pulse racing and send that legendary shiver down your spine.

ISBN 978-960-9610-00-1

The Journeys We Make

Rhoda Romayne accompanied by her two young daughters is making the journey of a life time, escaping post war Britain and the forthcoming Olympic games for the sunshine and splendour of the South African coast.

Determined to catch up with old friends she uses Charlotte, her younger daughter to date Anthony, the son of an old flame, and one that she dreams of rekindling. But, everyone else is on a journey too, Charlotte would like to marry well and this journey for her will decide her future. For Jane the elder daughter, it's a journey of discovery and love. For Anthony it's a journey for the truth about his father's past.

Each with their own reasons for travelling along life's highways all come together at a crossroads where anything can happen. Each with a set of choices, each set on their own course of discovery, but one has to come to a dead end....

ISBN 978-960-98418-3-2

Mr Boy

I had an hermetically sealed youth on a dirt road in Southwest Alabama that cut through a land grant of 40 acres bequeathed by a relative circa 1835. Its horizon was the moon and its mornings were slices of light topping loblolly pines with new days holding adventure.

My parents, Helen and Willard Harris, let me open gates in pastures not plowed or planted. They let me eat whatever landed in my hands as I stretched them to the sky. I write these remembrances, not editing myself. This hodgepogeny of stories is a conversation with myself. It's a pleasure to have you in the room listening.

ISBN 978-960-99470-4-6

The Heaviest of Swells

The life of British Music Hall's first Super Star, George Leybourne [1842-1884], also known as *Champagne Charlie,* has always been shrouded in mystery. This book puts the record straight. Delving deeper than ever before Christopher Beeching takes a 'detective-like' approach and comes up with some surprising results, unlocking family secrets, as well as other revelations.

Drawing from his own theatrical career, contemporary descriptions, song cover illustrations of the 1860's to 1880's, Christopher analyses Leybourne's performance methods, conditions, as well as the deterioration in Leybourne's health as constant touring took their toll culminating in his death at age of 42.

Written with style & humour The Heaviest of Swells shows a glimpse of life from the slums of Gateshead where Leybourne was born, to the drawing rooms of the Victorian middle classes, giving a fascinating account of Leybourne's life as a music hall artiste, his career, and the many problems to be encountered by any music hall performer of the period.

ISBN 978-960-99470-0-8